Tag, We're It

THE LOVE GAME: BOOK SIX

ELIZABETH HAYLEY

WATERHOUSE PRESS

ISBN: 978-1-64263-293-4

For everyone on a journey toward a happily ever after...
we hope you get there

Chapter One

RANSOM

"You're acting like a nesting mother. Seriously. Put the Swiffer down." Taylor's voice somehow sounded both frustrated and fond, so I decided I could ignore her demand.

"I would if *someone* hadn't decided to eat cereal out of the box like some kind of Tasmanian devil and dropped crumbs all over the floor."

She took a deep breath as if she were drawing in strength before she spoke next. "Okay, I'm trying *really* hard to be understanding of the fact that you're nervous, which is making you behave like an unhinged Mary Poppins. But"—she came over and ripped the Swiffer out of my hands—"that's enough. Hudson is nineteen, not ninety-five. She's probably hung out in much worse places than your apartment."

"Great. Now I'm picturing her hanging out in a dingy basement with a bunch of dudes huffing spray paint."

She narrowed her eyes. "Your brain is such a scary place sometimes."

"Tell me about it." I made a grab for the Swiffer, but she

danced away from me. "Gimme it."

"This place is clean!" she yelled with some sort of odd deep voice and her arms spread wide. "Of dust, dirt, bad intentions, evil spirits, everything. It's clean. Now go sit somewhere."

"I can't just . . . sit. There are things that need to be done."

"No, there aren't. You've done *all* the things. Pretty much nonstop since she called."

I shot her an annoyed glare, but I couldn't dispute her words. When Hudson had called, telling me she was in trouble and needed help, I hadn't hesitated to offer to fly her up to stay with me.

What kind of brother would I be if I didn't help her when some asshole knocked her up and then treated her so badly she had to run away? I wasn't going to push, but eventually I'd get a name for whoever this guy was and pay him a visit, distance be damned. Roughing up some dude who thought it was okay to mess with my sister would be worth the trip to Georgia.

There was no question that I'd been stress-cleaning since she'd called. Taylor and I had just gotten our own drama settled—or at least *mostly* settled since we'd realized we weren't murderers—but still had to contend with her crazy ex-boyfriend Brad because now we knew he was out there somewhere.

We weren't necessarily thrilled to now be thrust into someone *else's* drama. But after spending a few hours with my biological family at the reunion, I understood why Hudson felt she couldn't turn to them for help with her pregnancy. They couldn't be trusted to raise a Pomeranian, let alone a human. It was amazing Hudson and I had turned out as well-adjusted as we were.

My sister was counting on me. I wouldn't let her down.

And if the first step in showing her how responsible I was meant scrubbing my apartment from top to bottom, then so be it. I smiled at Taylor, lulling her into a false sense of security before I lunged, grabbing the Swiffer back and hoisting it over my head in victory.

She rolled her eyes and crossed her arms over her chest. "You're incorrigible."

"Listen. You dealt with your stress by forcing us to travel the length of the contiguous United States, hitting some states more than once due to your dodgy reading abilities, and—"

"You promised you wouldn't bring that up anymore. How was I supposed to know there was a Georgia, Vermont? Anyone could've made that mistake."

"Mmm," I hummed doubtfully, honestly unsure that anyone else would buy bus tickets for Vermont when they'd intended to go to Georgia.

"And I didn't *force* you. You willfully agreed to go."

"Well, yeah, because I thought we were being hunted by the fuzz."

She scoffed. "Who says 'fuzz'?"

I shrugged. "It sounded good in the moment."

"You should be thanking me," she said, her lips clearly trying to fight a smile. Which made sense because what she'd just said was ridiculous.

"Thanking you? For what? Leading us to a random house that you swore was a restaurant but was really a family home that could've housed the Manson family?" I should've known better than to think I could resist bringing any of this up again. It was just too damn funny.

"You know that the Mansons weren't a real family, right?"

I ignored her and continued. "Or maybe it was when you

got drunk with Owen's grandmother and tried to cuddle with a chicken."

"Now you're just being mean. His mom and grandmother slipped something into my drink. I'm sure of it."

"Yes, that's . . . actually incredibly likely," I deadpanned.

Hands planted firmly on her hips, she stepped closer in a move she probably thought was menacing. But while she was tall, her blond head barely reached my chin. "Do you think Hudson ever would've called you if we hadn't gone down there for the reunion? And do you think you ever would've gone to the reunion if I hadn't said it was a good idea? Nope. So really, you getting to feed your hero complex is all because of me."

"Should I just forget about all the times you profusely apologized for making me go to that reunion?"

"Yes," she said, her voice emphatic.

We glared at each other for a few seconds before we both erupted in laughter.

"I can't believe you brought up my hero complex. That was a low blow." So I'd offered to house-sit and look after a few dogs, babysit a seven-year-old selective mute, and rescue a wayward sister? That didn't make it a *complex*.

She calmed, but the smile stayed on her face as she wrapped her arms around me. "I love that you love your sister. And I also love that you're so worried about being welcoming and accommodating. But she chose to call you because she knew she could count on you. It's not about the state of your apartment or anything like that. It's because you make people feel protected and cared about."

I leaned down and rested my cheek on top of her head. "Stop saying nice things to me. It weirds me out. And, oddly, turns me on." I pressed my erection against her a bit as evidence.

She spluttered out a laugh. "I'm just speaking the truth, you perv."

"Well, your version of the truth makes me horny." I started running my hands up and down her back.

"What time was Hudson's flight getting in?" she asked, her voice breathy.

"She said she'd call when she landed." Her flight had been delayed, so it had been over twenty-four hours since her frantic call, but I was relieved she was on her way.

"With our luck, she'll call as soon as you start something."

I started kissing down her jaw. "Maybe you should start it, then."

"Mmm, I think you beat me to it."

"I can stop," I said as I pulled away from her a little.

She reached up and pulled my head down to hers until our lips touched. "Don't you dare," she mumbled against me before drawing me into a heated kiss.

As our tongues tangled and we gasped and moaned into each other's mouths, I thought about how life couldn't get much better. Against all odds, Taylor and I had somehow grown closer while enduring enough drama to fuel a soap opera.

I began moving us toward the couch so we could stretch out on top of each other, preferably with less clothes on. As soon as Taylor's back made contact with the fabric and I settled on top of her, we began grinding desperately. This was how I always hoped things were for Taylor and me: incendiary. I wasn't sure anyone could go from zero to sixty like we could.

I reached a hand down between us to pop the button on her jeans and then began gliding the zipper down. I'd just gotten my hand inside to tease along her underwear when there was a knock at my door.

Groaning, I buried my face in her neck. "If that's one of our friends, I'm disowning them."

"Well, they tend to travel in packs, so it's probably more than one. They're also impossible to get rid of. Kind of like the herpes of humanity."

I laughed as another knock came. "Yeah, yeah, I'm coming," I yelled, hoisting myself off Taylor.

She snorted. "Not now, you're not."

Jerk.

When I reached the door, I gave a quick look over my shoulder to make sure Taylor was decent. Seeing that she'd refastened her pants and was sitting up on the couch made a wave of longing rush through me. Was it too much to ask to have spontaneous sex with my girlfriend one last time before my sister moved in?

I was going to kill whoever was on the other side of the door. Though not literally. I'd already avoided one murder rap. No need to tempt fate.

Taking one more deep breath to make sure my body was back under control, I opened the door, ready to give hell to whoever was on the other side.

But as my gaze settled on who was there, I jerked my head back in surprise. "Hudson?"

A frown marred her face. "Yeah. Were you...not expecting me?"

I snapped out of my shock and moved to envelop her in a hug. "I thought you were going to call from the airport."

She shrugged against my embrace. "I didn't want to make you come all the way down there to get me. It was just as easy to Uber."

"I would've been happy to come get you." In fact, I was

a little irritated that she hadn't called. She didn't need to be traipsing all over the place in her condition. She'd been through enough already. But coming down on her for it wouldn't help anything. What was done was done. "How did you know my address?" I asked as I pulled away and gestured for her to come in.

"You texted it to me a while back, and I saved it in my phone."

That made me smile. *I'm important to her.*

"How'd you get in the building?"

"Someone opened the door for me because I was holding my bags. It would've been tough for me to get to my keys."

"Because you don't have any."

"Minor detail," she said with a smile.

"Well, I'm glad to know my apartment's got top-notch security." It was one of the more high-end complexes in the area, which was one of the reasons Taylor had stayed here so many nights when Brad had been lurking around town. Though clearly that hadn't done much to protect her from him.

"Well, in case you haven't noticed, I'm not the most threatening human being. Most people aren't very scared of teenage girls."

"Tell that to my high school self," l said with a laugh.

I held the door so she could enter, and after it closed, I spun and saw Taylor hugging her.

"We're so glad you're here," Taylor said.

Hudson chuckled, the sound a little awkward. "I'm sure you have better things to do without being inconvenienced by me. But I appreciate you letting me come anyway." Hudson turned to look at me. "I promise, I'll get my shit sorted and get out of your hair as quickly as I can."

"Don't be silly," I said. "You're not inconveniencing anyone, and you're welcome to stay as long as you need."

She smiled at me, but I could see hesitation in her eyes. I'd just have to work on convincing her that I wanted her here.

"I'll take your stuff into the bedroom. Do you need anything? I ran to the grocery store and got a bunch of things, but if there's anything you like that's not in there, I could run back out."

Settle the hell down, Ransom.

The words had poured out of me almost frantically. I just wanted her to know I was happy to have her here, but I didn't want to oversell it either. She'd probably interpret it as disingenuous if I were too effusive.

"I'm sure it'll be fine," she said, giving me a sweet smile. "I'm not picky."

Maybe she wasn't yet, but I'd heard cravings were a thing when a woman was pregnant. And hormones. *Should I ask about her hormones?* Damn it, I probably should've spent more time on Google instead of with my hand down Taylor's pants.

"Let me take your coat," I said as I started to pass her.

She pulled it off and handed it to me, and I made a mental note to take her shopping sometime soon. Her coat was sufficient for Georgia, but she'd freeze in the winter here.

She'd probably also need some maternity clothes eventually. Not that I really knew what made something maternity, but I assumed it was . . . stretchier.

"We should go clothes shopping," I blurted.

Hudson looked at the jacket in my arms and then down at herself before focusing back on my face. "Why? Is something wrong with what I'm wearing?"

I tried to ignore the *What the fuck is wrong with you?* look

Taylor was shooting at me as I stammered out a reply that wouldn't put her on the spot to discuss something she maybe wasn't ready to.

"Oh, uh, no, I just...thought...um, new place, new clothes, ya know?"

Hudson looked confused, her reply cautious. "I'm good. For now, at least."

Right. For now, her clothes still fit, so she was fine. Maybe shopping for pregnant lady stuff was too much change all at once.

"Ransom." Taylor's voice shook me from my internal musings.

"Huh?"

"Weren't you putting Hudson's things in the bedroom?" she asked.

Oh. Yeah. Shit. I'd been standing here like a doofus. "Right. Yeah, I'm just gonna...do that."

As I walked away, I heard Hudson whisper, "Is he okay?"

"Sure. He's always super weird and awkward. Don't worry about it."

That wasn't exactly how I'd always dreamed of being described by the love of my life, but at the moment it was stunningly accurate, so I decided to go with it rather than argue.

I had a feeling that would be my approach to a lot of things in the coming months.

TAYLOR

Ransom needed to slow his roll way down. He'd been

hovering over Hudson since she'd arrived an hour ago, and I could tell she was beginning to question if coming up here had been a good idea.

Watching him was cute, honestly. He'd been fluffing pillows, fetching drinks, messing with the thermostat, offering blankets, whatever he could think of to make Hudson comfortable. When—a long, long time from now—I was pregnant, he was going to be amazing. Until I got tired of it and killed him. But it would be a really enjoyable few hours before he made me homicidal.

I was watching some reality show with Hudson when Ransom burst out of the kitchen, clutching his phone. "I read something about feet. Do yours hurt?" The look on his face was so earnest I almost laughed.

"Uh, no," Hudson replied carefully. She looked like she'd just realized he might be a pod person she'd need to escape from.

"Ransom, can you help me with something in the bedroom?" I asked as I stood.

His brow scrunched up, and his lip curled in disgust. "My sister is here."

My eyes narrowed in disbelief. "Are you serious right now?" Did he really think I was suggesting we disappear into the bedroom to have sex while his sister channel surfed on the couch?

"I . . . don't know how to answer that," he replied.

Pointing toward the bedroom, I gritted out, "Go."

Sighing, he made his way across the room toward the small hallway that led to the bedroom. As he passed the couch, he hesitated. "Do you like peppermint tea?" he asked Hudson.

"Oh my God," I yelled.

"What? It can settle the stomach."

I simply pointed again, though more emphatically this time.

"Okay, okay. I'm going."

When he'd disappeared, I turned to Hudson. "He's just really excited you're here, so he's trying too hard."

A small smile played over her lips. "That's . . . really sweet. Totally unnecessary. But definitely sweet."

I gave her a smile in return before following Ransom into the bedroom. When I arrived, he was sitting on the edge of the bed with his head in his hands.

"I'm being annoying, aren't I?"

After closing the door, I leaned back against it. "Like next-level annoying."

He groaned. "I just want her to be comfortable and feel welcome."

I truly felt for him. He'd never gotten to have a real relationship with his sister. And now that opportunity was in front of him, so he wanted to make sure he did everything right. But it was turning him into some kind of leech on speed. He hadn't left Hudson alone for more than three minutes since she'd arrived.

I sat down on the bed and put an arm around him. "I know you do."

"She hasn't mentioned the baby or anything."

"She's had a rough few days. She's probably embarrassed by the way everything went down."

He looked over at me, brow furrowed. "She doesn't have anything to be embarrassed about."

"We know that. But us knowing it and her feeling it are two different things. She'll get there. Just give her time to adjust to the shock of it all."

"That makes sense."

"And please stop treating her like some kind of IED. She's not fragile. You don't have to . . . hover."

"I'm not hovering."

"Baby, you're practically a helicopter."

He snorted a laugh and rocked his body into me gently. "Don't call me baby when my baby sister is having a baby."

I laughed. "Now say it five times fast."

After a few seconds, he sat up straighter. "Okay. I'm ready to stop being a basket case."

"That's what I like to hear."

Leaning in, he pressed a quick kiss to my lips. "Thanks for being here with me."

I smiled. "Nowhere else I'd rather be."

Maybe I should've been worried about how true those words were, especially considering the short amount of time Ransom and I had been together, but I wasn't. I was lucky to have found him when I'd needed him the most and that he'd pushed the issue between us until I'd admitted what I felt for him.

Fighting against something that felt so right seemed ridiculous. And though prone to spurts of ridiculousness, I'd vowed to turn over a new leaf. At least as far as Ransom was concerned.

Everything else was probably still fair game.

Chapter Two

RANSOM

"Because I'm not letting you sleep on the couch. That's why." I continued stripping my bed until all the sheets were piled on the floor.

I heard Hudson huff in frustration. "You act like I'm used to staying in luxury penthouses. I think I can handle the couch. It's even a pull-out, right?"

"Yeah, which is why *I'll* be fine sleeping on it." Lying on the normal couch would've been tough because my legs stretched much farther than the couch did, but when opened up, it turned into a queen-size bed—albeit not the most comfortable one. But it wasn't like I'd grown up with lavish accommodations either. I could handle a springy mattress for a couple of months until we could get Hudson on her feet.

I could also look into switching to a two-bedroom in the same complex, as long as Hudson was able to contribute enough to swing it. Of course, I hadn't shared any of this with her yet. That conversation could wait for another day. She was overwhelmed enough.

"This isn't permanent, and this is *your* apartment."

I obviously knew that, but I wasn't about to let my pregnant little sister crash on a sofa when there was a perfectly good bed in my room. "It's not a debate," I said. "The decision's been made, Blink. You'll take the bedroom so you have some privacy."

She stood in the doorway as I shook out a clean fitted sheet for her.

"Why are you being such a protective big brother about this?"

She sounded almost annoyed, but I also detected a hint of appreciation in her voice. It'd been years since we'd gotten to fill these roles together, and it felt more right than I'd expected. Growing up, we'd been split up at such a young age—Hudson to live with our aunt Renee and me to house-hop through the foster care system. The last time I'd gotten the opportunity to play the part of older brother, I used it to put her in headlocks and frame her for eating all the cookies by crumbling one side of the Oreo on the floor by her favorite spot on the couch.

I finished tucking the top sheet so tightly under the mattress you would've thought I'd gone to military school. Then I turned toward Hudson, hoping my expression would firmly impress upon her the seriousness of my decision.

"Because I *am* your older brother. And you came here to ask for my help, so just shut up and let me help you."

She rolled her eyes dramatically and let out a loud sigh as if my offer had caused her some sort of inconvenience. "Fine," she said before walking over to pick up a pillow that lay on the ground. We put the cases on the pillows and spread the comforter on the bed together in silence.

When we were done, Hudson took a seat on the edge of

the bed. "Thanks, Ran. I mean that."

I took a seat next to her and put my arm around her shoulders so I could pull her toward me, squeezing her tight. "I'm honored to be the person you look to for help. It makes me feel like I get to make up for lost time."

"Me too," she said. "Though considering who my other options were, I don't know that it's as great a compliment as you're making it out to be."

I laughed at that, thinking of our crazy uncle Lester or any of the other lunatics I'd met at the reunion a few weeks ago stepping in to provide Hudson with any type of comfort or protection. There was also the obvious problem of being too close to home and whoever this guy was she was trying to get away from.

Though I chose not to let those thoughts cast a shadow on more positive ones that made me feel like the big brother who had come to his baby sister's rescue when she needed it.

But that feeling was still marred by sadness for my sister because the life of a single mother wouldn't be an easy one, and it wasn't one she would've chosen, especially after watching our own mother struggle with her demons.

When Hudson had shown up, I'd vowed right then that I'd do whatever I could to make this journey easier for her.

I just hoped it didn't include a ton of babysitting.

TAYLOR

Something about the holidays always made the kids at Safe Haven nuttier. In truth, it probably made kids everywhere nuttier, myself included when I was that age.

As Thanksgiving break approached and the weather began to get even colder, the usually chatty, energetic elementary and middle schoolers Ransom and I had come to know at the after-school program where we worked transformed into wild, untamable beasts. Most of them were cute beasts, but beasts nonetheless.

I watched a little boy named Josiah snatch a girl's water bottle and, with a gleam in his eyes, squirt his friend Kyle in the face.

"You think we should take them outside soon? Burn off some of their energy?" I asked.

Ransom had a similar level of fear in his eyes. "Soon as they've done their homework, we're outta here."

They'd spent eight or so hours in school, and some of them had even come to Safe Haven in the morning for the before-school program, which meant that since it was almost four thirty in the afternoon, they'd had about all they could take of organized indoor activities. I couldn't blame them.

Over the next fifteen minutes or so, we got the room cleaned up, belongings in backpacks, and the kids bundled up. A few older ones refused to wear their hats, but I guess we were lucky they'd put on their coats at all, let alone zipped them when we'd asked them to.

Ransom took the walkie-talkie off its stand on the counter and pushed in the button. "We're going out to Playground B for a while."

Playground B was on the other side of the building from where we usually went with the kids, so we needed to let the director, Harry, and his secretary, Edith, know where we were headed so they could tell parents when they arrived to pick up their children.

"Got it" came Harry's reply, followed shortly after by Edith's.

"Don't forget that other girl's supposed to come in for training today," she said.

Ransom grabbed his jacket and counted the heads of the kids in line in front of him.

"What girl?" Ransom asked, but his question was directed at me and not Edith. Once all the kids were accounted for, he pushed open the classroom door and headed down the hall.

"How would I know what girl?" I said. "I'm here less than you are."

He shrugged. "Edith likes you better than me. Figured maybe she talked to you about it."

"She talked to *me* about it." The voice came from Roddie, another guy who'd worked the afternoons at Safe Haven for about a year.

I wasn't surprised Harry had hired someone else. It was true we needed another person, but it took a special kind of mindset to train someone, and I didn't think Ransom was in it right now.

"She came in to interview Friday when I stopped by to get my check," Roddie continued. "Harry asked me to show her around. She's *hot!*" The way he emphasized the last word made him sound both excited and surprised by the observation.

Ransom raised an eyebrow. "*Asked* you or *let* you against his better judgment?"

"Whatever," Roddie said. "Does it matter?"

"I feel like it does, yeah," Ransom said.

"Well, Harry came through big-time on this hire. No offense, Taylor." He looked over at me like he'd realized verbally drooling over a gorgeous girl in front of me might somehow make me feel inferior. "You're hot too, but you're taken, so I don't have a shot."

"I doubt you have much of a shot with this girl either," I deadpanned, causing Ransom to laugh.

Roddie seemed unfazed by my comment as he went on to describe her like commenting on the looks of a new hire in front of small children didn't strike him at all as inappropriate.

"Smooth, dark skin. Tall and..." As Roddie walked alongside Ransom, he seemed to remember that whatever he was about to say was not appropriate for the company we were currently keeping, so he moved his hands up to his chest like he was cupping his own imaginary breasts.

Ransom nodded slowly, seemingly unimpressed by the new girl's looks or Roddie's description of them.

"Do you even know her name?" Ransom asked.

"Of course I know her name," he said, like Ransom's question was not only ridiculous but also insulting. "Inez. I know as much as I could find out about her without seeming like a complete creep. She grew up on the West Coast, is a Pisces, has two younger brothers and an older sister, and her favorite animal is a Siberian cat. I wasn't sure what that was, but it sounded cool, so I looked it up."

"Well, I'm glad you didn't come off as a *complete* creep," I told him.

He ignored my comment and continued walking with us. "I'll take the older kids over to the basketball court once we get outside. Make sure you tell her where I am."

"I'm sure she'll appreciate the warning," Ransom said.

Roddie gave him two thumbs up before disappearing into the closet where we stored the basketballs and some other equipment.

Ransom pulled on his jacket and zipped it up. "He's so strange." When he opened the door to the playground, the kids all filtered through it, taking off in different directions.

I was last to exit. "He is. But better to expose him to some hot stranger than Hudson. I was going to suggest she apply here, but I wasn't sure how you'd feel about it."

"I hadn't really given it much thought. I'm not sure it would've been the best idea to work with family, but I wouldn't have stood in the way of Hudson getting a job, no matter where it was. She obviously needs the money. She said she was gonna look for one today, but I haven't heard from her yet about it. I kinda don't wanna text in case she didn't find anything."

I understood that. "She could always try a few shifts at the Treehouse or even the Yard. I don't know how many hours she'd be able to get, but it's better than nothing if she can't find anything today."

"Yeah, that's true. I'm hoping she's able to find something with predictable hours so she knows how much she'll be able to save, but I have no idea where she's planning to apply."

We made our way out toward the larger of the two jungle gyms and stood about eight feet apart so we had eyes on all the kids but could still talk to each other. Ransom wore a relatively thin jacket while I'd come prepared for all possible winter conditions.

I took my hat out of my pocket and put it on, pulling it down over my ears before removing my gloves and sliding those on too. It was already cold out, and the wind didn't help. If it dropped ten degrees, I'd be ready. If it started hailing, my puffy coat and fuzzy scarf would protect me from the elements. If someone decided to go on an impromptu trek up Mount Everest, all I would need is an oxygen tank.

Ransom watched me bundle myself up, a small smirk stretching over one side of his mouth.

"It's not *that* cold out."

"I like to be ready for anything."

"Like a trip to the North Pole?"

"As long as we get to see Santa," I said with a smile. "That used to be where I said I wanted to go for my tenth birthday, so I'd be stupid to turn it down now."

"Speaking of Santa." Ransom gave a nod toward Roddie, who'd just appeared again, holding a large mesh bag over his shoulder.

"Anyone who wants to play basketball, come with me!" he yelled so everyone could hear him. Then he winked at Ransom. "Remember to tell her where I am."

Ransom looked like he wanted to respond, but our conversation was interrupted by Edith calling to us from the doorway.

"Don't you ever answer your walkie?" Her voice was raspy and filled with the usual feigned annoyance she exhibited toward Ransom any chance she got.

Ransom looked over at the fence, where he'd hung the bag with the first-aid kit. Clipped onto the strap was the walkie-talkie.

"It didn't go off."

"It went off. You just can't hear it from where you're standing. You're supposed to clip it to your belt, not to a bag ten feet away."

"That's no more than five feet. You sure those glasses work?"

She glared at him intensely for a long moment before stepping aside to reveal an unfamiliar girl, who I could only assume was Inez, behind her.

"Well, your new trainee's here," Edith said. Then, before she left to head back to the office, she said to Inez, "Good luck with those two." It was loud enough for us to hear but low enough that she could pretend she didn't want us to.

Inez didn't hesitate to stroll toward us, clearly confident. And why wouldn't she be? She looked to be about five foot nine with a springy ash-brown afro and faded-denim-clad legs that were so long I was a little jealous of them, even though she and I were probably the same height. How difficult was it for her to find pants? She had on a puffy coat too, but hers fit perfectly over her curvy hips and cinched in around her waist. It was a deep wine color that contrasted with her cream scarf. *Is that cashmere?*

She approached us with a broad smile that looked sweeter than I'd expected from someone who looked like she'd come to audition for a Gap catalog instead of provide care for children. She was the type of girl who looked like she used a disposable coffee cup as a fashion accessory.

I wanted to know her instantly.

"Hey, I'm Taylor," I said with a wave.

"I'm Inez. It's spelled *I*-n-e-z," she clarified. "People always want to put an E at the beginning."

Ransom and I both nodded like the explanation was one we needed to hear, even though it wasn't.

He extended his hand toward her. "Well, I'm Ransom. Spelled just like the hostage money."

Inez looked unsure of how to react, but when Ransom laughed a bit himself, Inez did too. She looked around at the playground of children.

"How many kids are out here?" she asked.

"Twenty-three," I said, knowing the exact number for emergency purposes.

"Wow. It feels like"—she raised one of her perfectly shaped eyebrows before she had to practically jump out of the way to avoid getting run over by a few of the second graders racing by her—"a lot more than that."

Ransom chuckled. "Yeah. It's like dog years. Take the number of kids and multiply it by seven."

Inez laughed at that, but she looked a little uneasy. Like she was waiting in line for a haunted house but wasn't sure she wanted to buy a ticket.

"So are you in college or . . ."

"Or," she answered. "I'm kind of in an in-between stage of my life right now, I guess you could say." I wondered what that meant exactly, but I didn't want to ask. "What about you guys?"

"Going for my master's in sports medicine," Ransom answered.

"And I'm graduating in December with a degree in criminal justice and will be heading to law school in the fall."

That was a conversation Ransom and I still needed to have, though I wasn't in a rush to do so. The last thing I wanted to do was limit my educational options just so I could stay closer to a guy. I'd been dreaming of going to an Ivy League law school ever since I'd decided on my path to becoming a lawyer. But even the closest one was still two hours away.

But that guy was Ransom. I knew I couldn't ask him to move just so he could be with me while I attended school, especially since he was finishing up his master's in May and would likely have a job in the field by the time I enrolled in law school in the fall.

"Wow"—Inez looked from Ransom to me, her expression suddenly revealing a shyness that surprised me—"I feel really inadequate."

"Inez," we heard Roddie call from the door. "It's good to see you again."

Inez gave him a small wave, like she was confused about why he might give her such an enthusiastic welcome. I imagined that she frequently received this type of attention from the opposite sex—and maybe the same sex as well—but Inez seemed like she genuinely hadn't been expecting it.

We only had another hour or so before most of the kids left for the night, and Ransom soon left me alone with them so he could show Inez where everything was kept in the classroom and what our daily routine was.

"How'd it go with Inez?" I asked Ransom once all the kids had been picked up and we were alone in his truck on our way home.

"Fine, I guess. It'll be good to have someone else helping out, especially so we don't feel so guilty when one of us needs to take off."

"You planning to go on the lam again?"

Ransom glared at me like the comment would've been amusing if there hadn't been so much truth to it.

"Too soon. Got it."

As he pulled out of the parking lot and onto the street heading for his apartment, he muttered, "It'll probably always be too soon."

Chapter Three

RANSOM

It wasn't long before Hudson started making herself at home. At first, that meant not asking before she grabbed a bottle of water from the fridge, but that quickly morphed into hanging bras from doorknobs and leaving half-full sixteen-ounce bottles of Dr. Pepper on all pieces of furniture that weren't tables.

Are pregnant women even supposed to consume that amount of caffeine?

"Are you setting up for one of those modern art shows where someone takes a bunch of shit no one wants and displays it in a way that makes some sort of social statement?"

"Huh?" Hudson looked up from the notebook she'd been writing God knows what in.

"Your stuff's everywhere, Blink."

"So is yours."

"It's my apartment."

"Yeah. Which is why I don't really have any space to myself. I mean, I know you gave me your room, which is sooo generous and totally unnecessary."

Seeing what my room looked like made me disagree. It was a good thing at least some of her stuff was contained to a room that had a door.

"But," she continued, "I don't have drawers or anything. I don't mean for stuff to accumulate, but I guess it does."

I picked up a pile of CVS receipts from the counter and an open soda bottle and held them up. "You normally put trash in drawers?"

"Okay, so maybe I could—and *should*—clean up a little. But the receipts aren't trash because they have coupons attached to them. There was a lot of stuff I needed, like toiletries and whatnot, when I got here, and I had to make a couple trips to the drugstore. That place wastes so much paper, they should be fined by the EPA or something. I'm gonna use them. I promise."

Tossing the receipts back onto the counter, I sighed and let my gaze roam over the rest of the place, which, now that I'd had a chance to examine it, looked like I was auditioning for *Hoarders*. A few more weeks with Hudson, and I might actually make it on the show.

"We gotta clean some of this shit up," I said. "Come on. I'll help you. We'll do it together. Taylor wants to have some sort of Friendsgiving on Wednesday before some of the gang head home to their families, and I don't wanna get stuck doing all of it tomorrow and Tuesday when I have work and class."

"I'll do it. I swear." Hudson hopped up from the couch and reached her arms above her to stretch into some sort of yoga-type pose. "Right after I get back from work."

My wide eyes beamed with pride. "Seriously? You got a job? Where? Doing what?" I hadn't meant for it to come off as insulting as my shock made it sound, but Hudson had been here over a week, and she hadn't even gotten a call back from any of the places she'd applied to.

With the holidays approaching, I figured many of the stores and restaurants had already found extra help, and I was sure it was even more difficult to find a job when she didn't technically live here.

"That's awesome!" I said.

"Well, I'm glad one of us is excited for it." She laughed. "It's some kind of weird coffee shop slash dog-grooming place. It just opened a few weeks ago, so they need people."

"What's it called?"

"Bark Bar. I don't totally get how it all works, but it can't be that hard, right?"

"Guess it depends whether you're catering to the dogs or the humans."

Hudson paused at the bathroom door and turned around like my comment caused her considerable thought. "Shit," she said before disappearing into the room and shutting the door behind her.

There was no way I believed Hudson would clean up the whole house after she got done with work. At least I didn't think so. So while she showered, I threw out a lot of the stuff I knew was trash and grabbed some of the dishes she'd left in my room. I'd just grabbed the dustbuster when my phone rang in my pocket.

Surprised to see it was Kari, I hesitated before answering. My biological mom wasn't in the habit of calling me, even after we'd reconnected. I hadn't spoken to her since the reunion several weeks ago, and though we'd both promised to make an effort to stay in touch, life—or Hudson—had gotten in the way.

I hadn't even texted Kari, much less called her.

"Hey," I said, holding the phone to my ear with my shoulder. I didn't want to run a vacuum while I was on the phone with her, but I'd at least get the trash out of the can and set it by the door since it was almost full.

"Hey, Ransom. What're ya up to?"

"Just weekend chores and stuff. Nothing exciting. What about you?"

"Pretty much the same. I just got back from the market a little while ago."

We chatted about everyday things for a couple minutes, like the stray cat my mom had been feeding but couldn't bring inside because her landlord would evict her. Then we talked about what each of us was doing for Thanksgiving. Kari was going to my aunt Renee's house.

"That's good," I told her. Renee and I hadn't left the reunion on the best of terms. Not that we ever had been. It's difficult to really like someone who took in your little sister and allowed you to bounce around the foster care system like it was a fucking trampoline park. "She's a good cook, right?"

"Yeah, the rest of us are just bringing some side dishes, but Renee's doing the turkey and stuffing."

It surprised me that Renee and my mom and grandma had made up so soon. They weren't usually the type to back down or apologize, so I wondered how they'd been able to move on from the fight at the reunion.

There was a long pause on the other end of the line before my mom said, "I'm just not sure if Hudson'll make it, though."

And there it was: the real reason for her call. How could I not have thought to ask Hudson if our mom knew where she was or when she'd be home? I needed to figure out how to play this, and Kari's silence told me she was waiting for me to speak before she said anything further.

"Oh. Yeah?" I was already heading toward the bathroom to see if Hudson had shut off the shower yet. My answer came when the door opened and Hudson darted across the hallway to the bedroom in a towel. I hurried toward my bedroom door, which she'd just closed, and knocked a few times, covering the phone in anticipation of Hudson's response.

Too concerned about finding out what Hudson had told our mother about where she was and exactly what she was doing there, I hadn't exactly been paying attention to whatever Kari had said in response to me.

I'd pulled the phone from my ear so I could text Hudson and hope she had her phone in the room with her. Who was I kidding? She always had the phone with her.

"Ransom? You still there?" I heard my mom's voice low in the phone, and I brought it back to my ear.

"Yeah. Yeah, I'm still here."

Suddenly the bedroom door swung open, revealing Hudson in nothing but a bra and underwear, her eyes wide.

The fuck? I mouthed at her, covering my eyes.

"Sorry," she whispered.

Like a child watching a horror movie, I spread my fingers so I could see through the space between them only slightly. Thankfully, Hudson had pushed the door closed enough that I could only see her face peeking around the edge. I put my phone on speaker so Hudson could hear Kari too.

"Is she there?" Kari asked.

My eyes widened at my sister, hoping she could give me some sort of nonverbal help here. Hudson did a little shrug before giving me an open-handed gesture like she had no idea what to tell her. How could she not have anticipated this phone call?

"Um, no. She's not *here*," I answered like the possibility wasn't at all plausible.

"'Kay. Well, whenever she comes back, can you have her call me so I know what she's planning to do about Thanksgiving? I've texted and left messages, but she hasn't given me a straight answer. You know Aunt Renee. She's gotta know all the details about who's coming and when."

"Oh. Yeah. Of course. I'll let her know she should call you when I talk to her next." *That's vague enough.*

Kari thanked me, and I got off the phone as soon as possible.

Once the phone was in my pocket, I glared at my sister. "Really, Blink? You didn't think to tell me that Mom knows you're staying here? I had no idea what to tell her."

"It was an unintentional oversight. I've had a lot on my mind."

Well, damn if that didn't make me feel like a jerk.

"Sorry," I said. "I don't mean to make things harder for you. But that's also why I wish I knew what you told Mom. I got your back."

"Thanks." She gave me a shy smile, like the declaration almost made her feel guilty. "I didn't even think about telling you. I never expected Mom to call you because..." She didn't finish her sentence, but there was more in her silence than she could've said with words.

"I know," I said softly, hoping that the two words would convey more than they probably did. "So what are we telling her if she asks again?"

"What do you mean?" Hudson seemed genuinely confused.

"If Mom calls again because she's looking for you and you don't call her back. I wanna help you out, but I don't wanna get in between you and Mom, ya know? I don't wanna make things more stressful for you. Stress can be bad for..." I stopped myself before I said "the baby" because Blink still hadn't chosen to formally share the news with me, and I didn't want to push her into something she wasn't ready to disclose. "It can be bad for your health," I decided on.

"Yeah, I know." She laughed, but it was empty of any real happiness. Then she shut the door and called to me that she had to get dressed for work. "Stress is kind of unavoidable, though, given my current circumstances," she yelled through the door.

That was obviously true, but I still didn't want to add to that. And though my mom had spent most of our time together lying to me about where she was or why she was sleeping all day or a million other things I was too young at the time to realize were lies, the man in me didn't want to lie to her now. I was better than that. And part of me thought Kari deserved better than that too.

But Hudson was my sister. My only sibling. And I was hers. Our bond began when she was born, but it hadn't ended when we'd gotten split up. I didn't want to sever a connection that had somehow managed to survive so many years and miles.

Hudson continued. "I guess just tell her..." She sighed deeply like she wasn't sure what was the best option. "I guess just tell her I'm staying with you for now, but my whereabouts and who I talk to are none of her business."

That I could do. It was the truth, though I might soften it a bit when I said it to Kari.

It was strange to think that only a few short weeks ago, Hudson and I had little to no relationship, and now here we were trying to figure out the best way to approach our mom's questioning. I wondered how we would've fared as kids attempting to cover up how a vase broke while we were building a fort or why there was a stain on the carpet after a party we'd thrown while our mom was away. We might've made a good team if we'd grown up together like normal siblings.

Either that or we would've killed each other.

TAYLOR

"Can you hold the door, please?" I hurried toward my apartment building, hoping the woman entering would wait for me so I didn't have to dig through my bag to find my keys. Every time I came home, I told myself to have my keys ready, especially in the evening, because my apartment wasn't in the safest of neighborhoods, and I didn't like the idea of standing in front of my building for longer than I needed to be.

During my whole Brad-stalker phase, I'd gotten comfortable staying with Ransom, but now that Hudson was there—which I understood and supported completely—the place would've been cramped with all three of us. Not to mention there was very little privacy there now.

Of course I loved when Ransom stayed here, but it was farther for him to drive to classes, and it was already kind of sketchy that Hudson was staying with him since he hadn't added her to the lease. I knew he didn't want people to realize she was there frequently when he wasn't, even if she was his sister.

"Thanks," I said, grabbing hold of the door and keeping it open so the woman could walk through.

"Sure."

She looked like she couldn't have been much older than me—thirty maybe—and had the eyes of someone who was both tired of life and tired from the day. It was like looking in a fucking mirror.

She turned back around and eyed me up and down like she wasn't sure she should've let me in, but when I got to my mailbox, she seemed to relax a little. Guess I wasn't the only one on edge from living here.

This time I had no choice but to dig through my bag because I didn't want to have to come back down to get my mail, which most likely consisted of bills anyway.

My dad had paid for school until I'd up and moved here with no valid explanation. Of course, he'd assumed it had to do with a guy—and he hadn't been completely *wrong*. I'd just been running *from* one instead of *toward* one.

When I'd moved out of the summer apartment I'd shared with Sophia, I'd decided to get my bills delivered in paper form. I'd had trouble keeping track of what I owed to various stores if the reminder wasn't glaring at me from the counter every day. Paperless was great before I realized that when my debt was out of sight, it was also completely out of mind.

And though I hadn't bought anything that would be considered a luxury, I still had plenty to pay for and didn't want bills to be late simply because I forgot about them. If they were gonna be late, it should be due to a real reason, like I'd blown the money on margaritas and designer jeans.

I grabbed the small stack of envelopes from my mailbox and began flipping through as I headed up the stairs to my apartment. I didn't even want to think about the money I'd spent while Ransom and I were on the run from... Well, *nothing.*

Thankfully, he'd agreed to pay for some things, but I felt bad about that. Especially since I wasn't sure if he still had his second job. It wasn't easy to find a good time to ask the person you were in love with if they still got paid to take their clothes off.

I knew Ransom hadn't taken any jobs recently, but I wasn't sure if he'd technically *quit.* And that distinction was an important one. At least to me.

But then the whole Brad thing happened, or *didn't* happen, and we'd gone to the reunion with Ransom's wacky family. Ransom's other source of income had been the furthest thing from my mind.

I jogged up the last few steps, unlocked my door, and entered my apartment. After tossing my bag on the small table by the door, I headed toward the bathroom, already beginning to undress before I got to the hallway. After pulling off my shirt, I was stopped in my tracks by something red on the floor.

As I looked closer, I saw what looked to be a flower petal, maybe a rose. Then I noticed the ones after it leading to the bedroom.

"Hello?" I spoke cautiously, wondering if I should head back to the door and outside. Or maybe I should go to the kitchen and get a knife. A voice inside me told me I was acting crazy paranoid when there was no need to be.

Except there was.

But how could Brad have gotten in without my noticing? The door had been locked and hadn't looked tampered with. And, taking a quick look around my place, there was no other sign that he'd been here. As far as I could tell, nothing was out of place or messed with.

"Hello," I said again when I heard a rustling from the bedroom but no response. My curiosity got the best of me, and despite my better judgment, I headed for my room unarmed— and also nearly naked—following the small path of rose petals through the doorway slowly like I might be in some sort of fucked-up fairy tale where the breadcrumbs led me to danger instead of safety.

I held my breath as I entered, preparing myself for whatever waited for me inside.

"Shit, what are you doing here?"

Thankfully, it was Ransom's voice, and though he looked frantic, tossing a roll of wrapping paper to the side of the bed and sticking some more tape to the top of the gift that sat on top of my bed. It looked like a six-year-old had wrapped it, but since it was probably for me, I chose not to point that out. Plus, I'd obviously rushed whatever he'd had planned, which made me feel a little bad.

I leaned against the doorframe, now in only my bra and jeans, and gave him an amused smile. "It's my apartment. What are *you* doing?" I covered my mouth to keep from laughing at him as he tried to position himself casually on my bed, wrapped gift in hand.

"Trying to surprise you."

"Well, you did a good job of that. I didn't know what I was walking into back here."

"Who else would've gone into your apartment and put down rose petals?" He finished his question, but the way the words slowed down at the end told me he'd realized the answer before his question had ended.

"Oh my God," he said. "I'm so sorry. Jesus, I wasn't even thinking clearly. We just haven't had much time together on our own lately, and I wanted to do something special, not freak you out. I thought you'd be out until later. I was gonna make dinner."

"You were gonna make dinner?"

"Probably more like make a phone call to *order* dinner, but the intention was there."

"It was," I agreed, taking a few steps toward him. I crawled onto the bed, loving how comfortable it felt underneath me and how nice it was to be lying next to Ransom again. "You didn't have to do this."

Shrugging the best he could while propping himself up on his elbow and resting his head on his hand, he said, "I wanted to. Things have been so crazy. And besides, our one-month anniversary is next week. I couldn't wait." He leaned over and gave me a kiss on my forehead before moving his hand to my back. "Is this what you wore to work?"

Between the stuff with Brad and the reunion and Thanksgiving and Hudson and both of my jobs and school and who knows what else, I hadn't even realized we'd been officially together for almost a month. It simultaneously felt like we'd just met and like we'd been together for years.

"Is it a sign that I'm getting old that I forgot all about it?"

"You really forgot to wear a shirt?" Ransom's eyes were wide with horror.

"No! I mean my birthday. I haven't even thought about it. I wore a shirt, I promise. I don't think I would've been allowed to wait tables if I'd shown up topless."

Ransom laughed. "Their loss, then."

I laughed at that too but couldn't help but let my thoughts

drift back to what I'd wondered about earlier. "Can I ask you a question?"

Ransom pulled back a bit, and his hand stopped moving over the skin on my side. "Yeah. Is everything okay?"

It was amazing how well he knew me—that whatever I was about to ask was something meaningful.

"Yeah, fine," I assured him, thinking that especially compared to what we'd dealt with over the course of our relationship, this was nothing. Not really, anyway. "I was just wondering... Are you still stripping?"

It was difficult to look him in the eye, so I let my gaze drop to the blue paisley swirls of my comforter, allowing my finger to trace over some of the lines.

Before we were in a relationship, Ransom had initially kept his second job from everyone except for Brody, and somehow Brody had managed to keep it a secret. Ransom hadn't known any of us for very long, so I couldn't blame him for wanting to keep that tidbit to himself. It wasn't until Sophia's bachelorette party—when Ransom had coincidentally shown up as the entertainment—that I'd found out.

"No, not anymore."

I let my eyelids lift enough that I could look at him as he spoke.

"Once we got more...serious, I just figured it was in poor taste, ya know? I don't really remember exactly when I made the decision to stop, but it didn't feel right to take off my clothes in front of other women."

I tried to conceal my relief at his answer, but my shoulders fell and the breath I'd been holding slipped past my parted lips.

"I don't want you to feel like you can't make money because of me, though."

He'd have to start paying back his school loans soon, and he lived in a nice apartment—which I guessed had more to do with his second job than Safe Haven.

"I know." He shifted up a bit so he was sitting on the bed instead of lying down, and I could sense that the conversation was turning more serious than I'd meant for it to. "But it doesn't feel right."

"I trust you, you know," I told him.

He stroked his fingers over my hair lightly as I looked up at him. "I know you do," he said. "And that means a lot to me. It does."

"But?"

He let out a sound that sounded like a laugh that didn't quite make it to the surface. "But the idea of having anyone else's eyes—or, God forbid, hands—on my body . . ." He paused like he was choosing his next words carefully.

But he didn't need them. We both knew what he was thinking.

He was mine, and I was his.

"Thank you," I said softly, bringing his hand to my mouth so I could kiss it. "So you're really never stripping again?"

He gazed down at me, his eyes burning into my skin as one of his dimples came to life with his little side smile. "I don't think I ever said those words *exactly*," he said. "I was practicing some badass choreography for the title track to *The Greatest Showman* when I decided I should probably quit."

"The what?"

"It's a musical about P.T. Barnum starting his circus." He climbed over me, hovering above me on his forearms but not touching me. "I'm not sure how historically accurate it is, but it's hella entertaining." His voice was low, husky.

I could feel the vibration of his words against my skin.

"The fact that I'm turned-on imagining elephants and bearded women right now speaks to how disarmingly sexy you are."

He chuckled in my ear as he kissed it, causing a shiver to run down my spine and settle below my waist. "I could show you sometime," he whispered. "I have a red ringmaster costume with a cane and everything."

"A cane? Even hotter," I joked.

"Mm-hmm," he said as he moved his mouth down my neck slowly, paying attention to every bit of skin along the way. "They use one in the movie. We should watch it sometime. Hugh Jackman and Zac Efron star in it."

Well, shit. "Sounds good, but it doesn't sound like it would compare to whatever show you had planned for me." My bra strap fell at Ransom's fingertips. "You didn't bring that red suit with you by any chance, did you?"

"Nope. But I will next time. Besides, as long as I have clothes on, I have clothes to take off."

After removing the rest of mine, Ransom stood, not bothering to close the blinds as he reached down and crossed both arms to fist the hem of his T-shirt. Then, lifting it at a painfully slow speed, he revealed why Hugh Jackman had nothing on Ransom Holt.

Chapter Four

TAYLOR

I wasn't sure what time it was, and I didn't care. Ransom and I had spent most of the night in bed, leaving it only to shower together and then returning to do dirty things again.

Neither of us had to work, so we could spend the rest of the day in bed too if we wanted. The idea increased in its appeal the more I thought about it. Or maybe it was pressing up against a sleeping Ransom that had me thinking I never wanted this to end. Either way, last night had highlighted how badly I'd missed him.

Ransom groaned as he slipped an arm around my waist, his hand settling low on my belly. "You know guys wake up hard anyway, right?"

I laughed a little, but his comment only made me want to tease him more. "Oh, do they?" I said, rubbing over him a little more.

"Mm-hmm."

I thought I heard his breath tremble a little, and I took more pleasure in it than I probably should have.

"If you keep doing that, we're gonna have to take another shower."

"You say that like it's gonna deter me."

This time it was he who laughed, but the sound was soft and deep, like it died in his chest before it had a chance to fully find its way out. After clearing his throat he said, "Oh, I'm definitely not trying to deter you."

I continued moving over him for a little longer until we both grew more frantic. And as if we thought it at the same time, we both moved our clothes out of the way just enough to give ourselves access to each other.

It was filled with a primal energy that I couldn't remember feeling with Ransom before, as if both of us *needed* this. I could tell Ransom was straining to hold back until he couldn't any longer, and his harsh grunts of "Go. God, go," had me following him over the edge.

Probably because I'd follow that man anywhere.

RANSOM

Eventually, after spending a few hours in bed, both of us managed to get ourselves together for the day.

"You wanna get breakfast somewhere?" I asked Taylor as I leaned down and examined the contents of her fridge. There wasn't much to examine, which was the reason for my question.

"I guess we did work up an appetite. Where do you wanna go?"

There weren't many places we could sit for a good meal that were close to Taylor's apartment, so either way, we'd be driving to get there.

"What about that café where Hudson works?"

"The dog place?"

"Yeah." I shrugged, like the idea of going to a café that doubled as a beauty salon for dogs held mass appeal. I'd been wanting to go but hadn't wanted to make it seem like I was checking in on her by popping in alone.

"But we don't have a dog." She said it like she was informing me of some secret she wasn't sure she should reveal to me.

"I don't think you *need* one. I doubt they'll turn down paying customers for something like that. And I think the café's basically next to the dog place. It's just run by the same people and connected. Like Gap and Baby Gap or something. That's how Hudson described it, anyway. And she's been working mostly on the café side I think."

"I still think it's weird to go there without a dog. Aren't people allowed to have their dogs in the café with them? Who would choose to eat with a bunch of dogs if they didn't have one themselves?"

"I feel like we're overthinking this," I told her. "No one there will know we don't have a dog. It could be getting groomed while we eat, for all they know. I'm sure people do that—get a cup of coffee or something while they wait for their dog to get cleaned up or whatever."

Taylor didn't look like she'd been listening, her eyes doing that thing where they stare at me and also *through* me, like I wasn't really there. Somewhere off in the distance, she'd focused on an idea and wrapped her mind around it like a lion preparing to capture its prey. It was pointless to try to tell her otherwise. That gazelle didn't stand a chance.

"What?" I asked, my voice holding a caution I was sure she could hear.

"This'll be fun. I swear."

"The fact that you're swearing before I even know whatever it is you have planned makes me want to do it even less."

"Just hear me out."

"Oh God," I said, but she'd already begun her explanation.

"What if we asked Owen to come with Gimli?"

"No way. We're not inviting Owen."

Owen was Carter's buddy. We'd given him a ride home to Virginia on our way to Georgia for my family reunion. I'd figured Owen would be harmless enough until he'd shown up with edibles and come back from a rest stop with an abandoned dog up his shirt. A dog which he'd taken home to his farm for his visit and then back with him to his college apartment, where, as far as I knew, his landlady didn't want any pets at all, let alone a scruffy dog he'd found on the side of a highway.

If you'd asked me what I thought the chances were that Carter would find a person stranger than himself to befriend, I would've said someone would have a better chance of getting struck by lightning after winning the lottery. It was actually sort of impressive, when I thought about it.

"Okay, we could just borrow Gimli, then."

I pressed my eyebrows together at her curiously. "Isn't showing up with a strange dog weirder than going without one?"

Taylor shrugged and then crossed her arms. "Guess that's for you to decide."

X_0

An hour or so later, we were pulling up to Bark Bar with Owen's white-and-brown dog, Gimli, riding shotgun on

Taylor's lap. Thankfully, he wasn't too dirty now, but he would definitely still benefit from another bath.

When we—and by *we* I mean Taylor—had called Owen to see if we could dognap Gimli for a couple of hours for our reconnaissance mission, he'd been happy to oblige. He didn't even ask if he could come along because he already had plans to go sledding. There hadn't been any snow on the ground since last year, but Taylor hadn't questioned him about it. She probably knew there'd be an explanation she'd regret asking for, so she'd moved on to figuring out when we could pick up Gimli.

However, her whole plan backfired when Owen handed Taylor a wad of cash to get Gimli groomed. Seemed she wouldn't be sitting in a dog café with a dog after all.

As soon as I put my truck in park, the scruffy beast seemed to know he was about to escape the car. He began throwing himself against the window and bouncing back onto Taylor's lap like a kid in a bounce house.

"What the hell, Gimli?" I asked before jumping out of the truck myself and jogging around to the passenger's side to open the door for Taylor. Gimli practically leaped onto me once the door was open wide enough that he could clear it. I managed to catch him, but he didn't seem content in my arms for long.

He squirmed his way out of my grasp until I put him down in the parking lot, taking hold of his leash so he couldn't escape. As soon as all four of his legs touched the concrete, he bolted toward nowhere in particular, running so fast the poor guy flopped backward when the collar and leash stopped him from going any farther.

He seemed momentarily stunned but popped right back up, ready to take off again. Since he'd been heading in the right direction, I followed after him, calling to Taylor that I'd meet her inside. Gimli's tail stood up almost as straight as his ears as he trotted happily toward the row of stores.

Once we made it to the entrance, I looked back to see how far Taylor was behind us, and since she was relatively close, I figured I would wait for her to catch up before I went inside with this... I looked down at Gimli, who was panting heavily, his pink tongue flopping from side to side as he looked around at his surroundings.

A woman walked toward us, pushing a toddler in a stroller. "Uppy," the little kid said, pointing at Gimli. The woman smiled at me and my "uppy," but once she got within range, Gimli jumped on the front of the stroller and snagged some of the cereal the boy had been eating like a seagull snatching his lunch from an unsuspecting beachgoer.

"Gimli," I scolded, pulling him back. "I'm so sorry," I said to the woman whose smile had turned to an angry scowl after her son began crying.

"Control your animal," she said back.

"I'm sorry," I said again. "He's not mine." Of course I knew that didn't matter, but the fact seemed important to share anyway.

"Ugh, you're not one of those guys who uses other people's dogs to try to pick up girls, are you? Pathetic," she said before I could correct her. She threw the remaining cereal away in a nearby trash can, handed the boy some more, and wiped down his tray before continuing on her way, clearly disgusted with both Gimli and me.

Fucking Owen.

Taylor approached us shortly after, both of us aware that I knew she'd taken her time getting to me after witnessing the

Cheerios attack. Gimli jumped on her again when she got to us, and she leaned down to pet the slobbery thing. He licked her face, an action that I silently cataloged in my brain. There were few things that would prevent me from kissing Taylor, but her covered in Gimli's saliva was certainly one of them.

"You're such a good boy, Gimli," Taylor said in a voice that would've been more fitting for the boy in the stroller than the crazy canine she was speaking to. "You ready to get a bath?" She scratched her nails over Gimli's coarse fur before standing up again.

Relieved I'd get to hand this wildebeest over to someone else for a little while, I opened the door so we could go inside.

The two of them seemed equally excited to discover what lay ahead. The lobby consisted of a small waiting area with a few benches and chairs. Next to it was a room that reminded me of a nursery with the glass that went from the middle of the wall almost all the way to the ceiling. Inside, two people stood in front of large steel washbasins that held dogs both bigger than Gimli. They also looked more relaxed than I thought Gimli would be while being shampooed, squirted with water, and eventually dried with machines that sounded louder than a 747 about to depart.

I hoped Hudson wasn't working on this side today, because she'd have her work cut out for her with Owen's dog.

About thirty seconds later, another employee who looked like he might be in middle school came to the barn-style door that led to the dog washing room and opened the top half.

"Hi, welcome to Bark Bar. My name is Ryan. How can I help you?" He said it with about as much enthusiasm as someone might use to order a plain pizza from a place they'd gone to a million times.

"Hi, yeah," I said. "We wanted to get"—I almost said *our* dog, but I couldn't bring myself to follow through with the verbiage—"*this* dog washed."

"Can I have a name and phone number, please?" Ryan grabbed an iPad that was sitting on the small white desk and unlocked it.

"Sure. The name's Ransom. And the number's—"

"Oh, I actually need *your* name here. The place for the pet's name is on the next screen."

I caught a glimpse of Taylor pressing her lips together to keep from laughing.

Rather than correct him and highlight that my name was better suited for a dog, I simply said, "Taylor," and then gave him my phone number. I might've unintentionally renamed Gimli Ransom, but there was no way I would say *my* name was Gimli. Clearly, the one on my birth certificate gave me enough problems. It occurred to me that I could've picked *any* name, but I'd already gone with Taylor, and there was no going back.

Ryan finished typing in all our info, and after Taylor declined the additional spa treatments, which included a mango pedicure and lavender oil rub, we handed over the hound to the seventh grader.

"All right, Taylor," he said to me. "We'll send you a text when this guy is all done. It might be a bit because we're shorthanded today, and there are still some clients ahead of Ransom. Ransom," Ryan said with a laugh, "that's a dope name. You steal him from a fenced yard or something?"

"Take your time" was all I said.

And after the kid shut the door, he scratched Gimli's head and said, "You're such a cute little dude, aren't you, Ransom?"

Taylor immediately burst into hysterics as we made our

way farther inside to look for the café.

The main area of the dog side had a large open space where a few dogs were playing with each other and one of the employees. There were ramps, tunnels, balls, and frisbees around the room, and as we got closer to the half wall that allowed us to get a clearer view of what was happening, I saw a few piles of poop.

"Seems like a strange place to have a café. Who wants to eat this close to a pile of shit?"

"This place is awesome!"

I looked toward the voice, which I recognized immediately.

Carter and Toby were standing in the doorway that led to the café side of the property. They must've gone in the other door but came over to check out the doggy day care side of things.

"What are you guys doing here?" I asked.

With a wide smile, Carter appeared more excited than I would've thought someone might be to visit a place like this. "We came to meet you for breakfast," he said, like the answer should've been obvious and therefore there was no need for a question.

"Who ... How did you—"

Owen.

But unsurprisingly, the story was more complex.

"Xander heard from Aniyah, who I think heard from Sophia because I think you told Brody, who told Drew, who then told Sophia." Toby looked to Carter like he was hoping to get confirmation on the order, not that it actually mattered.

This sounded like some boring version of *Whisper Down the Lane* that somehow managed not to get fucked up by the end of it. I didn't know whether I should be glad I'd found my way into a group of such close-knit friends or if I should look into the restraining order process, just in case.

"Well, I'm glad you guys are here," I told them. "Maybe Hudson won't think I've come just to spy on her with you guys here."

"Or maybe she'll think we're *all* spying," Toby offered with an innocent shrug.

"Let's just get a table."

"Oh, we got one already," Carter said. "We pushed a few together."

I figured they'd found a couple of two-seaters and slid them next to each other, but when we entered the café side, Brody and Aamee were already seated, drinking mimosas. There were only four empty seats, which meant no one else would be joining us. At least I hoped not.

Brody raised his champagne glass like he was about to give a toast. "This was such a good idea. Thanks for inviting us!"

I didn't want to crush his fragile spirit by telling him that I hadn't actually invited anyone other than Taylor. When Brody had texted this morning to ask what we were up to this weekend, I'd mentioned that the only plans we had so far were checking out Bark Bar, but I'd never thought he'd take that as an invitation. Thankfully, Hudson had hung out with our friends a few times, so it wouldn't be *too* weird to have us all show up here.

"Sure," I said, pulling the seat out a bit for Taylor before taking my own seat across from her. "So the rest of the crew couldn't make it, I guess?" I tried my best to sound disappointed, but I wasn't sure it came off as I'd intended for it to.

I did a quick scan of the café for Hudson but hadn't spotted her yet. At least I'd taken a seat with my back to the front window, so I had a good vantage point to see most of the restaurant.

Not surprisingly, everything was canine themed. Large photographs of various breeds of dogs hung on the walls, which were also decorated with small signs that said things like *I love my dog. I tolerate you.* They also sold gourmet dog treats at the counter, which said they were baked in-house. There was even a large flatscreen hanging in one corner with some movie that had a golden retriever in it.

"How was Gimli when you dropped him off on the other side?" Brody asked.

The way he said "the other side" sounded like he was describing some sort of underground animal-trafficking ring.

"Fine, I guess." Since I'd never owned one of my own, I had no idea how a dog usually reacted to entering any type of grooming facility, but Gimli had gone back with Ryan without a problem. "He lives with Owen, so I can't imagine much fazes him."

The group laughed as the server approached our table to ask Taylor and me if we'd like anything to drink. Since there was already a carafe of coffee on the table and a pitcher of water, we both declined anything else.

"Lame," Aamee said with a roll of her eyes as the server walked away.

"What?" Taylor asked. "She seemed totally normal."

"Not the waitress. The two of you. Coffee and water?" She practically spat the names of the two beverages. "Live a little. It's the weekend."

"It's the morning," I countered, pouring some coffee into

Taylor's mug that I'd flipped over before doing the same to my own.

"And?"

"And I'm not opposed to having a mimosa or Bloody Mary or something, but I'm fine without one. I came to see Hudson and get breakfast."

"Well, there's a poodle over there who's been eyeing me up since we sat down. There's no way I can sit in this place sober," Aamee replied.

Carter was sitting next to Taylor, and he turned around to see the dog Aamee'd been referring to. "I don't blame you," he said. "Poodles look like hairy humans with long noses. They always look like they're judging you."

"Exactly!" Aamee said excitedly.

"A *poodle*?" Taylor said. "Is judging you?"

"Yes, a poodle. Their eyes are all big and totally judgy."

Carter nodded along as he and the brown dog stared at each other. "Like they think they're better than you because they have perfectly groomed curls and more brain cells."

Jesus Christ.

Brody chimed in with his assessment of other types of dogs that were stuck up, such as Pomeranians and Chow Chows, before I forced myself to ignore them—though it was definitely difficult—and decide what I wanted to eat.

Thankfully, the server came back a few minutes later, and we all placed our orders.

"Is Hudson around?" I asked before she left.

The girl—who looked to be about Hudson's age—glanced back toward the kitchen. "I think she's supposed to be, but I honestly haven't seen her yet."

I couldn't stop myself from thinking she'd flaked on a job

already. I felt guilty for jumping to this conclusion so quickly, but the fact was, I didn't know Hudson. Not really, anyway. We got along well enough, and we obviously shared a sibling bond, but I didn't know her well enough to know her tendencies when it came to this type of responsibility.

Did she quit jobs as easily as she got them? Did she show up late and get told to go home for the day? Did she . . .

I widened my eyes when I spotted her.

She was being pulled by an enormous dog that looked like a black bear. The dog's blue leash was pulled taut as Hudson clearly tried her best to maintain control of the animal. A slobbery pink tongue flopped out of its mouth happily until it got to the table with the person I assumed was its owner.

Four children who all looked to be about five and under sat at the table with the woman. And the dog, whose face was as tall as the table, immediately rested his nose on it, probably hoping to get some table scraps from the kids.

Hudson appeared relieved to hand the leash to the woman who, despite being surrounded by toddlers, somehow looked way less stressed than Hudson did. After putting a paper in front of the customer, Hudson took her credit card and hurried off.

Would she return? And if she did, should I say hello? I didn't want to make the day any more hectic for her.

But when she returned a few minutes later with the credit card, she caught my eye.

And apparently Aamee's too.

"Hudson!" Aamee called loudly, her mimosa in one hand and a mini blueberry muffin in the other. I wondered where she'd gotten it but didn't care enough to ask. "Hudson! Come chat with us, hon."

I gave Hudson a quick wave as I said, "I don't think she can just come *chat*. She's working."

Aamee's blond hair flipped when she set her attention on me. "Then why are we here?"

"Breakfast and mimosas, remember?" Brody answered. He reached a hand out to rub her back. It was a sweet gesture, like he was trying to comfort her, even though there was no reason to do so.

Hudson put up a finger like she'd be over soon.

It seemed to appease Aamee for the moment because she went back to her muffin and drink.

The six of us talked while we waited. Carter said that Sophia and Drew were supposed to go over to Drew's parents' house for Cody's birthday celebration later on, and since they knew there'd be a ton of food there, they'd opted to skip breakfast.

Aniyah and Xander were . . . Well, no one really seemed to know why they weren't here, but we were all in agreement that they were most likely with each other, even though they'd both adamantly deny it.

Toby shook his head and moved back in his seat so the server could put his food down. "I don't get why they're so secretive about whatever's going on between them. Everyone already knows. They should just embrace it."

"Some people just don't want everyone in their business, I guess," Carter said.

"Well, they better find different friends, then, because this group knows everything about everyone, and that doesn't seem like it's changing anytime soon," Toby replied.

Carter didn't reply, but the way he moved the scrambled eggs around on his plate told me he didn't exactly agree that people shouldn't get to keep anything from the rest of the group.

We spent the next ten minutes or so chatting about the upcoming Christmas party we were throwing at the Yard and filling up on eggs, bacon, toast, and more minimuffins that the server brought out.

Eventually Hudson must have caught a couple of extra minutes, because she made her way over to us. Her hair was pulled up into a messy ponytail, and she appeared to have a shadow of mascara below one eye. I wasn't sure if it had been caused by tears or sweat, but I figured it didn't matter.

"Jesus, what happened to you?" Brody asked, causing Taylor to elbow him in the ribs.

"Be nice," she scolded.

"Yeah," Aamee said, followed by, "Seriously though, whatever they're paying you, it's not enough. You have some hair stuck to the side of your neck that I'm pretty sure isn't your own."

Hudson groaned and swiped at her neck. Then she grabbed a napkin off the table and wiped her neck and hands. "This guy Jason called out today, and we're always busy on Saturdays. He usually does the baths and trims the dogs' nails. I am *not* cut out for this. They gave me the 'easy' ones," she said, using air quotes to show that they were probably the opposite of easy. "The last one I washed licked my face the entire time I put the shampoo on her."

Okay, so the mascara was from the dog slobber.

"I'm sorry," I said, genuinely feeling bad that she had to endure that. My time watching Harry's dogs made me more empathetic than I would've been otherwise. I'd grown to love those animals, but I'd definitely want no part of bathing any of them. Which was probably why this place would make a killing. People could drop their dogs off without actually having to leave and come back. "Are you over there all day?"

"I'm sure." She looked down at her wet, stained clothes, which were luckily only a Bark Bar T-shirt and jeans. "I don't think they'll want me serving anyone looking like this."

It was a valid point.

"How was your breakfast?" she asked.

"A...ma...zing," Aamee said, sliding on a pair of large sunglasses. "I swear these mimosas are pure champagne."

"You're such a lightweight," Toby said.

"Fuck off. I've had like six of them."

Brody rolled his eyes at her but smiled a little. "She's an expensive date."

"Speaking of expensive," I said. "Do you know how much Gimli'll cost?" As I took the rubber band off the wad of money Owen had given us and began to flip through it, I could see it was mostly ones. Even though we'd chosen the most basic grooming option, I had a feeling I'd have to put some of my own money out to cover the cost. I hoped Owen would pay me back the rest, but since that offer might be in the form of indie band tickets and CBD oil, I figured it couldn't hurt to ask what I might be out sooner rather than later.

"Gimli?"

"Yeah, he's Owen's dog. The brown-and-white one with rough, scraggly fur. We dropped him off before we sat down."

Taylor put a hand on my arm. "You told them the dog's name was Ransom."

Ugh.

Hudson and the rest of the group laughed loudly. "Why did you give your own name as his?" she asked through her laughter.

"I didn't," I answered quickly. "Not exactly. I gave my name, and the kid at the desk thought it was the dog's name. I just . . . chose not to correct him."

Still laughing, Hudson pulled out a walkie-talkie and pressed the button. "Hey, can someone tell me when *Ransom's* bath'll be done and how much it'll cost? His owner is asking."

I hate you, I mouthed.

Hudson let go of the button and listened for a response, a smirk on her face.

"You know, you're not really in a place to laugh about someone's name," I joked, but despite the quizzical looks I got from everyone except for Taylor, I didn't elaborate.

A couple of seconds later, the walkie-talkie clicked to life. "Ransom had some fleas on him, so we treated him for those first. It'll take a little longer than usual. The groomer said he'll be done in forty-five minutes or so. Looks like the total will be one twenty-seven."

"One twenty-seven? As in dollars?" I opened my eyes so widely, I worried they might drop out of my head and onto my plate. "I thought it would be like fifty or sixty bucks." By this point I'd counted the money Owen had given us—thirty-eight ones, two fives, and some change rolled up in the middle. "The dog isn't even that big."

"Size doesn't matter," Hudson said in a way that made me cringe internally. "And didn't you hear that you had to be treated for fleas?"

Taylor chuckled beside me but quickly calmed down. "Sorry," she whispered.

"Shouldn't they have asked me first? Isn't it like when you get your oil changed? If they find other things wrong, they always ask if you want them to fix it before they do."

"It's on our statement of procedures at the front that they'll treat the animals for fleas if they find any."

"Oh," I said somberly.

Hudson stayed another minute or so before she was called over the walkie that she was needed elsewhere, and since she wasn't sure she'd get to come back over, she said bye to everyone before hurrying off to attend to whatever the task was.

I poured another cup of coffee while we waited for Gimli to finish his bath, and after everyone was done eating, Toby pulled out his wallet and tossed forty bucks on the table.

"We gotta get going," he said, "but this should cover us with tip, I think, since we had one drink each."

Carter moved for his pocket too, removing some cash and setting it on the table under the saltshaker. "I got it this time," he told Toby. He picked up the money Toby had set down and handed it to him, but Toby declined.

"Put it away," he told Carter.

"You paid the other night."

"So?"

"So your money's no good here," Carter said.

"You know," Aamee chimed in, "I've never understood that saying. Money's good anywhere, especially American money. I mean, I get the *idea* behind the saying, but it's dumb."

Carter's mouth opened like he was going to reply but, after gauging the expressions of the rest of us, realized it wasn't worth it. Instead, he turned his attention to Toby and said, "Let me pay."

"Someone just leave the money," Brody said. "Or split it. Or Venmo. Whatever. I feel like I'm out with my dad and uncle the way you two argue about who's picking up the check."

"Fine," Toby conceded, shoving the money back into his wallet.

"Where are you two headed anyway?" Taylor asked.

The server returned with our check and placed it down in the center of the table before clearing some of the dishes out of the way.

"We're gonna go for a hike near Hidden Bear Creek."

"Yeah." The vibrations from Carter's excitement seemed to pierce the air. "We're gonna hold rocks."

Against my better judgment, I said, "Hold rocks?"

"I was listening to this podcast where some dude—well, he wasn't just any dude, he was like a science dude—"

"So a scientist," Taylor said slowly.

"Right," Carter said. "Some scientist said that when you touch rocks and walk barefoot on the earth, the elements and minerals and shit actually get absorbed through your skin and then give you energy or something like that."

Taylor nodded a little and said, "Okay, you guys go touch your rocks, then."

"Well, when you say it like that, it sounds weird," Carter said.

"It *is* weird."

"Maybe a little. But not for the reason you're implying."

I felt I had to chime in too. "Is it weird because you're planning to hike barefoot in December?"

"We're not *hiking* without shoes on," Toby explained. "We'll probably just take them off at certain points where the mineral content in the soil is especially good."

"I kind of want to know how you plan to find that out," Brody said, "but then I remembered I don't really care."

"Hey," Carter said, sounding excited. "Would you mind

if we brought Gimli with us? I bet he'll be able to sniff out the ground with the highest mineral content. We have to go change, but we can pick him up here in like twenty minutes if you think you'll still be here."

"Be my guest," I said, already thankful I wouldn't have to drive with him in my truck again. On the way here he'd left nose prints on my windows until I'd finally caved and opened one enough for him to stick his head out. At some point he'd climbed onto Taylor's lap in the front, and I'd had to open that one too. "You'll let Owen know?"

"Yeah, I'll text him now. He won't care." He turned to Toby. "Let's go so we can hurry back."

Carter and Toby headed out, and a few minutes after that, Brody and Aamee got going too.

Once they'd all left, I turned to Taylor. "I love all those guys. But sometimes I forget how overwhelming it can be to have a meal with them."

The server came back to pick up the check, and when she was gone, Taylor said, "Yeah, usually Sophia and Drew are there to provide a little bit of a balance to the crazy. Carter's been getting stranger by the day, and Aamee's . . ."

"Drunker?" I offered, causing Taylor to laugh.

"Yeah. I feel like *you and I* should've been the ones day-drinking today."

I raised an eyebrow. "There's still time. Hudson doesn't get off until six or so, and Xander sent me a killer recipe for some spiced cranberry bourbon thing. We could make some of those and binge a new show or something if you want."

Taylor bit at her lower lip before leaning in to give me a kiss so light it had me wishing for more before she'd even pulled away. "I think I'd rather binge on you." A blush slipped up her cheeks after she said it, and she let out a shy laugh. "That definitely sounded hotter in my head before I said it."

That had me laughing too. "It sounded pretty hot to me."

And it turned out I was right.

Chapter Five

TAYLOR

It was easy to complain about the crowds during the holidays. Customers at the Treehouse at other times of the year weren't too demanding, but something happened between Thanksgiving and Christmas that caused even easygoing customers to become a bit blunter and a lot less concerned with the connotation of their requests.

But I'd learned quickly that I could use that to my advantage.

I'd always been able to read people well, and more times than not, that resulted in better tips, especially if I could get those customers in a rush in and out quickly. More people meant more money, and this year especially I wanted to be able to buy my parents and siblings gifts that were both meaningful and ... well, expensive wasn't really an option, but I did hope not to get them gifts that were obviously cheap.

Even though I'd told myself that I didn't care what they thought about my choice to finish my degree online and get several jobs just to pay the bills, the truth was their opinions mattered. They probably always would.

I'd worked hard in my classes, worked hard to do well on my LSATs, and worked hard at the Treehouse and Safe Haven. I wanted to make sure I had something to show for it whenever I saw my family over the holidays.

Though I didn't exactly know when that would be since I wanted to make sure I spent Christmas with Ransom. Even though he'd told me a few times not to stick around for his sake, I couldn't help but feel bad he didn't have family nearby.

He did have Hudson, but I wasn't sure either one of them would be capable of cooking an edible, let alone a tasty Christmas dinner.

I actually wasn't sure I was capable of that either, but I sure as hell had a better chance than those two.

After my shift at the Treehouse, I was juggling my purse, my water bottle with cute sayings to encourage hydration, and the food I took to go for a late dinner with Ransom. When my phone rang, I assumed he must have been wondering what was taking so long.

I fished the phone from my coat pocket, slid my thumb across the bottom to answer, and managed to wedge it between my shoulder and my ear.

"Hello?"

"Hello there," my dad said. "Is this my long-lost daughter who seems to have forgotten my number because she's busy being a grown-up?"

I'd known my dad would ask about Christmas eventually, but I wasn't prepared for this call, and I internally scolded myself for not paying attention to who was calling before I answered it.

"Ha-ha," I said dryly. "Very funny. You're not cute, you know."

"That's not what Rita said earlier."

I had no idea why my stepmom would've told my fifty-four-year-old hard-ass father he was cute, or if his claim was even true, but I didn't want to think about it more than necessary.

Instead, I asked, "Why are you so goofy?" It wasn't normal for my dad to be so . . . well, happy. I couldn't help but ask about it.

"Can't a guy just be in the holiday spirit?"

"Another guy? Yes. You?"

"Well, that's not very nice. I'm just excited for Christmas this year."

"Why?" I said it more curiously than harshly, which was good because I'd been kind of a dick to him so far for no real reason.

"Because," he said. "We're not staying in this miserable town for the holidays."

Please don't say you're coming here.

"Where are you going?" I asked, hoping to sound casual.

"You mean, where are *we* going?"

We? As in me too?

"And the answer to that question is Anna Maria Island."

I'm definitely not *going there.*

"Where?"

"The Gulf Coast of Florida. It was Rita's idea. She thought it'd be fun if we all went away for Christmas this year. Someplace warm, relaxing. She went there years ago and loved it. It's low-key, slow-paced. We rented a house on the beach with a small pool. It'll be great. We can grill Christmas dinner this year."

Had he been sniffing Rita's nail polish remover? "Since

when do you grill?"

"I grill." And after an extended moment of silence, he said, "Just not often. Anyway, I called to talk to you about what day you wanted to come down and how long you might want to stay. I figured you might not want to stay the full week, but you know you're more than welcome to. The place has plenty of room." In his excitement, he'd begun rambling, and I found it almost impossible to find a way in. "But I need to buy your ticket soon, so—"

"Dad." I sighed heavily, hoping to prepare him for the blow that would be my declining of the invitation.

"Don't say it, Tay. You have to come." He sounded almost like a child who'd just been told his birthday party had to be postponed.

"I'd kinda already planned to stay up here for Christmas. It'd be different if you were staying home, but—"

"Would it?"

The question sounded more sad than accusatory, but I recognized it as the accusation I knew it was anyway. I hadn't seen my dad, my stepmom, or my little brother and sister in far too long. When I lived on campus, they were only a car ride away. I could—and did—come home on weekends. Sometimes anyway.

"Yeah," I told him, even though I was certain it wasn't only me who knew that wasn't the truth. "It's been a long semester, and I'm not sure I'm up for flying."

"It's a plane ride."

"Yeah, I know. It's just—"

I had no idea how I was even going to finish my sentence before my dad cut in. "You gonna tell me who he is?"

"Who *who* is?"

"Uh, the guy who's keeping you there for the holidays."

"Why do you always think there's a guy involved?" I tried to act offended, but I knew I hadn't succeeded.

"Tell me I've been wrong, then."

I blew an annoyed sigh into the phone. "Dad."

"Taylor," he said back. And just when I thought we'd arrived at a stalemate, he added, "Bring him."

"What?" *Yup, he's high.*

"Bring him. Your brother and sister miss you. I miss you. Christ, the dog misses you. I mean we're not bringing her, but you know what I'm saying. Whatever gets you down there, I'll agree to."

"You're serious?"

"Yeah," he said. "What's another hot dog on the grill? Now can you tell me you're coming before I come to my senses and take back the offer?"

"Yeah. Okay, yeah. We'll be there," I told him. "Thanks."

"You're welcome," he said in the stern voice that I was much more used to. "And just so there's no discussion when you get down there, there's no way in hell you're sharing a room with him."

I wondered if my dad could tell I was grinning. "Wouldn't dream of it."

Chapter Six

RANSOM

"It was cool of Sean to let us use the deck," I said to Drew as we set up the tent heaters.

"Yeah, with the Yard being a hit last summer, he's been pretty easygoing about giving me what I ask for," Drew replied with a laugh. "I'm getting a little spoiled. I think he's worried I'm going to leave for greener pastures."

"Are you?" I put the heater down on one corner of the deck. Since Sean was letting us use the deck on the back of Rafferty's for free, we'd pooled money together and rented a tent and heaters for a Christmas party we were having later that evening.

Shockingly, the party had been Aamee's idea. Since a lot of us would be spending Christmas Day with our families, we'd thrown out the idea of going out to dinner or something as a group beforehand. But our group had grown pretty large over the past year, so Aamee had suggested asking Sean to use the Yard, since quite a few of them had worked there over the summer and stayed on at Rafferty's once it got too cold to have the deck open.

I turned to watch him shrug. "Eventually. Brody's dad is still open to backing us if we want to open our own place, but I've been thinking…"

When he trailed off, I eyed him carefully. "Thinking what?"

Drew and I weren't overwhelmingly close. It was Brody who'd been the link between us, but when he'd said he needed help setting up, I'd instantly offered. I'd had the time, and Drew was a good dude. It was cool to get to spend one-on-one time with him. Still, his hesitance made me wonder if we weren't close enough that he felt he could share personal stuff with me. I hoped not.

He rubbed a hand over the back of his head. "I haven't talked about this with anyone other than Sophia."

"It's okay, man. If you want to keep it to yourself, I understand."

"No, it's not that. I just … feel kinda silly maybe?"

"I just spent a week trekking up and down the East Coast because I was worried I'd killed a guy, only to show up at his funeral and realize it wasn't him. So I'm kind of an expert on silly."

He barked out a laugh. "True. Though, in your defense, we all thought you'd killed him too."

I narrowed my eyes. "Not sure you all thinking I was a murderer makes me feel better."

We laughed together that time.

"You know what I mean," he said.

"I do." And I did. It wasn't that they all thought I was violent. But the circumstances had all pointed to a logical conclusion that ended up not being the conclusion at all.

Which was something that still haunted me when I allowed myself to dwell on it. What were the odds someone else would end up dead in the same alley on the same night we'd encountered Brad?

Not good. Which meant there was probably another piece of the Brad puzzle we were missing, and that scared the hell out of me. Who knew where that whack job was or what he was doing?

When we'd told our friends about the potential connection between Petey and Brad, Taylor had downplayed it, making that connection seem more tenuous than it probably was. But we hadn't wanted them to worry any more about it. We wanted to move on, even if it felt a little reckless to be so blasé about it.

Drew seemed to be debating something with himself for a few seconds before he blurted out, "I'm thinking of enrolling in some classes at Lazarus. Or somewhere. Maybe a community college would be better. I'd probably just need a few business courses to get me ready for owning my own place. Maybe. Or maybe Brody can just handle that side of things since he's finally finishing his degree."

It was like he was talking himself out of the idea as he spoke about it.

"I think that's great, man."

"Really?" He looked genuinely surprised I thought so.

I couldn't lie—it made me a little giddy that he seemed to care what I thought about his plan. "Yeah. There's nothing wrong with wanting to make sure you're putting yourself in the best place possible to be successful. I mean, you've done a great job with the Yard without any classes, so you could probably knock it out of the park either way, but I think it's good that you want to do everything you can to make it work."

His shoulders dropped like he'd let go of some tension he'd been holding. "Yeah, that's what Sophia keeps saying. I guess after the whole thing with pretending to be Brody blowing up in my face, I kind of pushed the idea of college out of my mind. Or tried to. But I feel like . . . part of me wants to see if I could do it, ya know? I get that I'm maybe a little old to be just starting, but . . ." He shrugged as his words trailed off.

"Dude, Brody's been in school for like ten years. There's clearly no *too old* for college."

He laughed, which made me feel better for being able to lighten the mood a little.

"And from what I heard, you were acing all his classes even though you'd never taken any of the introductory stuff," I added. "So you clearly have the brains for it. There's no harm in taking a few classes. If it ends up not being your thing, then at least you'll know."

He was nodding along with my words and then looked up at me. "You're right. Like I said, Sophia's been telling me all this too. But I think . . . I think I just needed to hear it from someone who has no vested interest in my feelings." At my sputtered laugh, he quickly went on. "Not that I don't think you give a shit about my feelings, but . . . ah, fuck it, you know what I mean, right?"

My smile was wide as I reassured him. "Yeah. I get what you mean."

We got back to work after that, moving tables and organizing the space so that we'd have room to move around easily. After about a half hour, my phone rang. Looking down at it, I saw it was from Hudson, which was a little weird because she always preferred to text rather than call, insisting on more than one occasion that she didn't use her phone for that.

Worry made me a little tense as I answered. "Hello?"

"Ransom, hi. You okay?" she asked.

I guessed I needed to do a better job at concealing my emotions when I spoke. "Yeah, fine. Just helping Drew set up for the party. What's up? Are *you* okay?"

She giggled. "You're going to give yourself an ulcer before you're twenty-six with all the worrying you do."

"I am who I am."

She laughed again. "And I'm thankful for it. Anyway, I wanted to call and ask..."

Her hesitation made my anxiety ratchet back up again.

"If it's okay if I bring someone to the party tonight?"

"Oh. Sure. A friend from work?" I asked, happy she was settling in and meeting some girls her own age.

"Um."

Okay, that wasn't a good response. "Hudson?"

"It's actually a guy I met a couple of weeks ago. We've been texting on and off, and I thought it would be fun to bring him. Since, you know, you'll all know each other. This way I won't feel like a third wheel. Or a twenty-first wheel. Whatever. You have a lot of friends."

Dread coiled in my stomach. "Do you think it's a good idea to be...dating right now?"

"Well, I wouldn't say we were dating. Just...talking. With a step toward hanging out if I can bring him tonight."

"Where did you meet him?" If she said Tinder or Bumble or what the fuck ever, I was going to lose it.

"He came into the shop and struck up a conversation. He's nice."

"Does he...*know*? About everything?" Because I had to say, dating a girl who was pregnant with another man's baby was a lot to ask of a guy.

"Yeah. He's been really supportive." When I didn't say anything, she went on. "Listen, I get that this is a friends thing tonight. So if you don't want a stranger coming, I totally get it. But if that's the case, then I may skip it too. Your friends are nice, but it's not really that fun to be on the fringe at something like that. Maybe he and I can go do something else."

That was *not* what I wanted. God only knew what could happen to her with a virtual stranger in an unfamiliar city. At least at the party I could keep an eye on this guy.

"No, it's fine. He can totally come. And I'm sorry if you've felt out of place with all of us. I'd never intentionally make you feel that way."

"No, I know. It's no one's fault. I just need to get to know everyone better. But it'll be nice having my own person there while I do that, so thank you. For letting him come."

"Absolutely. I want you to be happy here."

"That's why you're the best big brother ever."

I paused for a beat. "I'm not sure how to respond to praise like that."

She laughed. "You're so funny." When she sobered, she added, "I love you, Ransom. I don't know what I would do without you."

"I love you too."

"Okay, my break's almost over. I picked up a few extra hours, so I probably won't be home before you've already left for the party, but we'll be there as soon as we can, okay?"

"Yeah, sure. Just don't work too hard." I was proud she'd managed to find a job so quickly, but I also wanted to make sure she took care of herself.

"I won't. See you later. And thanks again!"

"You bet."

After she hung up, I stared at the phone for a second. She'd sounded the most upbeat since she'd come to stay with me, which was good. I just wished I shared in her enthusiasm.

TAYLOR

Sidling up to Ransom, I snuggled into his side. "You look like you're surveying the landscape for mines."

"Just thought she'd be here by now."

He wasn't admitting it, but he was *shook* by the thought of Hudson having a boyfriend. Whether it was because she was pregnant or he was protective in general, I wasn't sure, but he needed to lighten up. She wasn't a child, and he was missing out on a good night with friends by working himself up into a frenzy.

"She said she'd be here by nine. It's not even eight thirty."

He nodded but didn't otherwise respond.

Brody appeared on Ransom's other side and followed our gazes. "Why are we looking at the entrance?" he asked after a few seconds.

"We're waiting for Hudson and her date," I replied.

Ransom's body jerked. "It's not a date. She's just bringing a...person."

Brody nodded sagely. "I'm glad she found a *person* to bring."

Ransom turned what I could only imagine was a glare on Brody since I couldn't see his face. "Shut up."

"I barely said anything," Brody argued.

Ransom drew in a breath, likely to respond, but

movement by the stairs leading up from the parking lot stole his attention.

"Hey, dudes. And dudettes," Owen greeted, giving me a small nod as he entered the tent.

"No way. It can't be," Ransom whispered.

"Relax," I hissed. "I invited him. He's not here with Hudson."

His entire body sagged in relief. "Oh, thank God."

I smacked him lightly. "Be nice. I like Owen."

"I like him too. As long as he isn't trying to date my sister."

Owen reached us just as Ransom finished speaking. "Is this the kind of party where we're all supposed to whisper?" he asked, his voice low.

"No," Ransom replied, his voice loud and tone short.

"Whew. Because doing that would really hurt my throat after a while."

"How've you been, Owen?" I asked as I leaned in for a quick hug, which he returned.

"Pretty good. My landlady still doesn't know about Gimli. She must be deafer than I thought, because he howls like a werewolf."

I laughed. "That's good."

"O-Dog!"

I whipped around to see Carter approaching. He pulled Owen into a headlock when he was close enough.

"Oh, wow, we're still doing this toxic display of masculinity when we see each other. Okay," Owen said, his voice shockingly casual, despite the heavy implication of his words. He didn't even fight to free himself.

Carter let Owen up after a few seconds and smiled at him. "How ya been, man? It feels like I haven't seen you in forever."

"So...like a week ago when you took Gimli on your rock hunt," I said.

They both ignored me as they talked about...I wasn't even sure what. Something about Pokémon Go and traffic hazards.

"Oh, hey, you remember Toby, right? He took Gimli on the hike with me, but he stayed in the car when I dropped him off," Carter said, tugging Toby closer by his shirt sleeve.

"Yeah, we met at that weird horror movie premiere," Owen said.

Toby and Carter exchanged confused looks. "You mean the Halloween party?" Carter asked.

"Is *that* what that was? I was wondering why I never saw any trailers for it."

Carter laughed raucously as he put an arm around Owen and pulled him farther into the party with Toby and Brody following. "This is why I like hanging out with you, man. Such a trip."

"What are you tripping on? Can I have some?" I heard Owen ask before they were too far away to hear any more.

Ransom watched them go before focusing on me. "That is one warped dude."

"Stop. I like Carter."

"I wasn't—" He stopped himself when he saw my smile. "Brat."

"Come on," I urged, pulling on his arm—to no avail because the guy was built like an armored car. "Let's go mingle." My body was at a near-forty-five-degree angle as I tried to pull him away from where he'd been standing all night. When I glanced up at him, I could see how amused he was but didn't notice any strain on his face, damn him.

As I struggled, Sophia appeared by my side. "What are we doing?" she asked.

"Trying to pry him away from the stairs."

Sophia nodded once before going to Ransom's other arm and beginning to tug.

We struggled for about a minute before I noticed we were drawing an audience.

"Is this some weird kinky shit?" I heard Aamee ask. "Like wrestling in pudding but with less skill and intrigue?"

"Have either of you *ever* lifted a weight?" Drew asked. "Because this is just sad."

"Let's take bets on how far they move him," Brody said. "I got twenty that says nowhere."

"Only an idiot would take that bet," Xander argued.

"So you're in, then?"

"Funny, Summer School."

"Hey, lots of smart people end up in summer school," Brody argued.

"Can we focus on what's important here?" Aniyah mediated. "One of those girls is going to pop a blood vessel, and my money's on Sophia."

"Hey!" Sophia yelled.

"Don't argue, just pull," I gritted out.

Suddenly, momentum shifted and I was yanked forward, where I collided with Ransom's body. Somehow, Sophia and I both ended up trapped by his arms as he held us against him tightly enough that we couldn't move.

"Let go of me, you Shrek motherfucker," Sophia said as she squirmed in Ransom's hold.

"Drew, come collect your foul-mouthed fiancée."

When Drew stepped closer, Ransom released her so

quickly, she fell forward, practically toppling into Drew. He simply shook his head at her. "I expected more from you."

"Shut up."

"Remember that time you told me your kickboxing instructor said you could take down a grown man after a class with him?" Drew continued, despite Sophia's glare. "You should get your money back."

Sophia crouched into a fighting stance. "Yeah? You wanna try me?"

Drew let out a sharp exhale, as if trying to expel his disappointment through his nose. Then he dipped so fast, Sophia didn't see it coming. He hoisted her up and over his shoulder.

"You were saying?"

"I hate everyone here," Sophia grumbled.

"Hey," I whined.

She pointed at me, which looked comical as she was still upside down. "Especially you. You're the reason I'm in this mess."

"Let's get a drink, Tyson," Drew said as he smacked her ass and carried her toward the bar.

Ransom still had his arm around me, but I'd relaxed into him rather than struggle futilely.

Brody stepped in front of us. "That was quite a show."

"Glad we could entertain you," I said.

"It makes me glad too," he replied. He darted his gaze to the side, and then he turned. "Oh, hey, Hudson."

"Is this a bad time?" she asked, laughter clear in her voice.

But I didn't actually see her laughing because as I turned toward her, my gaze snagged on her date and lingered there.

"Brad?" I whispered.

Chapter Seven

RANSOM

As soon as I heard Taylor whisper Brad's name, I was moving before I even registered it. I had Brad by the throat and against a nearby wall within seconds. Vaguely, I could hear yelling and the scraping of furniture against the floor.

Despite his precarious situation, Brad smiled at me. "Nice to see you, big brother."

And then... I snapped. My arm was cocked and my fist flying toward his face as if it had a mind of its own.

Brad fell to the floor, but before I could follow him down so I could continue to pummel him, I was grabbed from behind by strong arms.

"We got an audience," Carter whispered in my ear. His words caused me to look to the side, where I saw Sean, who ran Rafferty's, and some of the other staff from inside. They must've heard the commotion and come running. Drew was there speaking to them.

I relaxed as my senses returned to me. I probably should've been horrified that I'd reacted the same way as I had in the alley a couple of months prior—after which I'd spent weeks thinking I'd killed the asshole. But all I felt was relief that Carter had only stopped me because there were witnesses.

I wouldn't have killed him. At least I hoped not. But seeing him next to my sister... Well, let's just say I probably would've done some damage.

As I returned my gaze to Brad, I saw Hudson kneeling next to him, fussing over him.

"Get away from him," I growled.

She swung her head around and fixed furious eyes on me. "What is wrong with you?"

I struggled against Carter, but Brody had appeared to help him hold me, preventing me from getting free.

"Get away from that fucker."

Sophia approached Hudson carefully, as if she were afraid to get too close to Brad, which made me feel like shit. He was our problem, and I hated that we were dragging everyone into our shit again.

"Hudson, we'll explain. But you need to get away from him," Sophia said calmly.

Hudson looked around confused, and I felt a pang in my chest. My sister was already dealing with one douchebag ex, and now she'd somehow been caught up in Brad's bullshit.

Despite my best attempts, I was proving to be a really shitty brother. But as she took us all in, she must've seen something on our faces that made her wary, because she moved away from Brad.

Brad swiped a hand over his lip, which was bleeding, and then he stood, a smirk on his face. He took a moment to straighten his clothes and said, "Well, that was quite a welcome."

I tried to lunge for him again, but Drew got to him first. "You must have one helluva death wish," Drew said, his voice threatening.

"If I do, I've come to the right place, right, Ransom?" he said with a wink in my direction.

"He didn't kill anyone. Unfortunately," Taylor said. "The same can't be said for you though, can it, Brad?"

I looked over at her, angry at myself that I hadn't thought to look for her until now. I was batting a thousand in my response to this nightmare. But as I took her in, I noticed that she hadn't moved from where we'd been when we first saw Brad.

Her arms were wrapped around her middle, but she stood tall and her chin jutted out in defiance. My girl was scared, but she wasn't going to cower. Sophia and Aniyah were also flanking her, like that badass scene in the last *Avengers* movie where all the female superheroes banded together to kick some ass.

At her words, his face darkened. "I'd be careful throwing around accusations you can't prove. Two can play that game."

"What's going on?" Hudson asked, her voice meek and sounding like she was on the verge of tears.

Brad forced his hands into his pockets in an obvious attempt to look casual. "Just a meeting of old friends." He looked at Taylor, and his smirk grew. "And in some cases, more than friends, right, babe?"

This time when I lunged, I broke free. Or Brody and Carter let go. Whatever. All that mattered was that I was up in Brad's face, looming over him in the most intimidating way I could. Satisfaction rippled through me when he tried to shrink away, but his back was against a wall, leaving him nowhere to go.

"You touch me again, and I'll press charges. Not sure you can keep a job working with children with an assault charge on your record." He was clearly trying to sound unfazed, but his voice broke in the middle, betraying his nerves.

I lowered my head so I could look into his eyes. "It'll be worth it." And in that moment, it would've been. Because this asshole was clearly still following us, learning things about our lives. There was no way he'd met Hudson by coincidence. And the fact that he knew where we worked and probably a host of other things about us made me want to send a message he wouldn't forget.

His eyes widened in fear, and I almost pounced on him, but a warm hand wrapping around my arm stopped me. I looked around to see Taylor.

She didn't say anything but shook her head, and I knew what she was trying to convey. Ultimately, it *wasn't* worth it. *He* wasn't worth it. We'd already been down this road, and we didn't need to endure it again.

While I wanted to inflict pain on Brad, I had no desire to do that to Taylor. So as I turned back toward Brad, I kept my hands firmly by my sides, though I kept my posture imposing.

"What are you doing here, Brad?" Taylor asked.

Brad looked over at Taylor, and I moved to break his line of sight. His lips curled in a small smile again. "Your sister is in a bit of a mess, huh? You should probably tell her to be more careful about who she spills all her drama to."

I was irate that Brad knew anything about my sister, let alone her pregnancy, but there was nothing I could do about that now. Not wanting to give him any satisfaction, I did my best to refrain from reacting.

"It would be a shame if the men she'd run from found

out where to find her."

"Oh my God," I heard Hudson mutter behind me.

Men? Had there been more than one? Was she unsure who the father was? Jesus, this was turning into an episode of *Maury*. But I couldn't focus on that yet. "Are you threatening my sister?"

He held his hands up in front of him. "Would I do something like that? I'm merely providing you some advice."

Brody stepped up beside me. "Cut the shit. Just tell us why you're here."

Brad looked contemplative. "Mmm, nah, I don't think I'm ready to do that yet. But don't worry." He sidestepped and moved closer to the exit. "You'll be hearing from me. Soon."

Brad looked very pleased with himself as he turned and hurried toward the stairs that would lead him to the parking lot. But before he got there, Xander stepped into his path, forcing Brad to stop suddenly.

Xander's face somehow looked both friendly and feral. It was . . . unnerving. "Your father is Thomas Lacey, isn't he?"

Brad looked Xander up and down as if assessing him. "I'm assuming you already know the answer to that."

Xander nodded, smiling softly. "My dad is Alexander Alston. I think they travel in . . . similar circles."

Brad's shoulders tensed at the name, and I wondered what the connection was. Xander had never mentioned knowing Brad's dad before.

"How wonderful for you," Brad said through a sneer.

"It has its perks."

Brad stood there for a moment longer before throwing the rest of us a look over his shoulder and then taking off down the stairs.

TAYLOR

I stared after the space Brad had vacated for what felt like an eternity before Ransom filled my vision, his hands gentle on my face.

"Are you okay?" he asked softly.

A riot of emotions zinged around my body as if they were lightning bolts, but *okay* was not among them. I had existed on the outer fringe of okay for the past several months, but I felt even further adrift from that line than I had in quite a while—like I was an astronaut slowly floating away from a docking station.

Brad had infiltrated our weird little family. He was no longer somewhere out there but up close and personal. He was Dracula, set about destroying us all after being invited inside by one of our own.

I was maybe getting a tad hysterical.

"Taylor," Ransom said, giving me a little shake.

I grabbed his wrists in my hands and focused on him. "I'm fine." When he didn't look like he believed me, I gazed more intently at him. "Really."

He sighed, releasing some of the tension he'd been holding, and his stare drifted until it settled beside me. When I followed his eyes, I saw Hudson wide-eyed and shaking.

"Go," I said.

Ransom, with a heart that should've been too big for his chest, looked conflicted.

I smiled. "I'll be okay. Go."

He searched my face for a moment before leaning in and giving me a soft kiss. Then he moved toward Hudson.

After looking at her for a second, he turned to Drew. "Is there somewhere I can take her to talk?"

"Uh, yeah, sure. There's a stock room right inside you can use." Drew led the way as Ransom guided Hudson with a large hand on her back.

She went almost dully, as if she were in shock.

When they disappeared inside, the rest of us all looked awkwardly at each other.

"So, who's your dad?" Aamee asked Xander, breaking the silence.

"Huh? Oh, uh, he owns a cybersecurity firm. Among other things."

"And that's scary to Brad because . . . ?"

Xander shrugged. "A lot of wealthy people have financial skeletons they prefer to keep hidden. I just took a gamble that his dad was one of them. He also might worry I'll get my dad involved, which would get *his* dad involved. Good thing he doesn't know that the only time my dad gets involved with me is when I'm being accused of arson."

I'd only heard the highlights about Xander's burning down the school library, and I knew nothing about his father, but if the connection scared Brad away, I was all for it.

We stood around for another minute before Brody spoke up. "Are we just going to stand here, or . . . ?"

"Or what?" Sophia asked.

"Or are we going to go eavesdrop?" he finished.

I scoffed. "We can't do that." But as I eyed everyone else, I could tell none of us were too sure of our position on it.

We darted our gazes around, waiting for one of us to move.

"It's a private discussion between a brother and sister. It would be wrong to listen in," I added, because damn it, I was, for once, going to be the mature one.

Carter bit the inside of his cheek before speaking. "Isn't he going to tell us everything later anyway?"

"Maybe," I hedged.

"Then aren't we doing him a favor by listening? We're saving him from having to repeat everything."

"That is sound logic," Brody agreed.

"I'd like to go on the record as saying any plan Brody approves of is automatically a bad one," Sophia argued.

"Hey, guys," Owen said, but we ignored him as we argued with each other.

"Doesn't being a catty snob ever get old?" Aamee asked Sophia.

"I don't know. Does it?"

The girls glared at each other as Drew stepped in. "Can we not do this? If another fight breaks out tonight, Sean's going to be pissed."

"Guys," Owen said again.

"I'm so glad I didn't go home early," Aniyah said. "This wouldn't have been nearly as exciting in the retelling."

"So glad we could entertain you," I said blandly.

But she was unfazed. "You know what I mean."

And I did. Aniyah and I weren't very close. She was more Sophia's friend, but she'd been there for the Brad drama, and she hadn't hesitated to stand beside me earlier in case I'd needed her. She wasn't being malicious. We were all just more curious than sane.

"Are we just gonna let that Brad guy go?" Toby asked.

"What do you suggest we do?" Sophia asked.

Toby shrugged. "Follow him?"

"Are you saying we should stalk the stalker?" Aniyah

asked, a wry smile on her lips.

"I'm not sure we're equipped to pull off a stealth mission," Xander added.

"Then maybe we should've, I dunno, kidnapped him or something," Toby said.

Carter smiled like a proud father. "You go to really dark places sometimes."

Toby shrugged, looking a bit insecure while also preening under Carter's praising tone.

"Guys!" Owen yelled, causing all of us to turn and stare at him.

"What?" Aamee asked, her voice irritated.

"That window over there must lead to wherever Ransom is, because when you're all not arguing with each other, I can hear them talking."

All of our gazes seemed to somehow connect with each other's before we moved toward the window.

"Why didn't you say something sooner?" Aamee hissed.

Poor Owen shrugged helplessly.

"Shh," Sophia said as she squatted down to get closer to the window. "Owen's right. I can hear them, but the curtain is muffling them."

"Guys, maybe we shouldn't—" I started.

"Hudson just said she met Brad at work," Sophia said. "Oh God. She called him sweet and charming."

"Okay, that's it," I said, moving toward the window and pushing Sophia out of the way. "If anyone gets a front-row seat to hearing this, it's me."

Everyone else hovered in as close as they could get around me as we listened.

"He works with you?" Ransom practically yelled.

"No. He came in with his dog the second day I worked at the shop. And we just . . . hit it off."

"Does Brad have a dog?" Sophia asked me.

"How would I know?"

She shot me a look before murmuring "testy" under her breath.

"How many times have you gone out with him?"

"Only twice. We've mostly been texting."

"How can this be as far as their conversation has gotten?" Aamee asked. "What the hell were they talking about while we were arguing?"

"Hudson looked a little stunned," Aniyah said. "Maybe it took a bit to get her talking. And he probably had to fill her in on who Brad was."

"Not everyone has your interrogation skills, Aamee," Sophia muttered.

"Thanks."

"It wasn't a compliment."

"It was to me."

"Quiet," I whispered harshly.

"I just . . . I don't . . ." Ransom seemed to be struggling to find words. "Why would you get involved with *anyone* while in your . . . situation?"

"People make mistakes, Ransom," she argued.

"Yes, but people typically learn from them instead of making more."

"How was I supposed to know about Brad? You never told me anything about him."

"I know," Ransom said, sounding frustrated. "But still, I didn't think I'd have to tell you to watch out for guys with ulterior motives. I thought that was something you'd be on the lookout for."

Hudson was quiet for a second. "How did you even find out? I didn't tell anyone other than Brad."

"Well, it was pretty obvious. I know you weren't ready to talk about it, so I respected that, but you definitely hinted at what was going on."

"I was going to tell you, I just...didn't want you to look at me differently."

"I'd never do that. One mistake doesn't define who you are. I'll always be there for you. And for the record, I think you'll make a great mother."

There was a long pause, followed by Hudson saying, "What?"

"I know we didn't have the best example of motherhood growing up, but I really do think you're going to be fantastic at it. And I'll help you however I can."

"Ransom—"

"And Taylor is on board too. We talked, and she's more than willing to help however you need her to."

"Ransom—"

"We'll get through this. It's not optimal that Brad knows, but it's not a huge deal. What does he know? Who the father is?"

"Jesus Christ, Ransom. I'm not pregnant!"

"What?"

"I'm not pregnant. Why did you even think that?"

"Because...you...I... You said... I don't... You're really not pregnant?"

"No."

"Then what the hell is the trouble you're in?"

"I owe some money. To some people. And I can't pay them back."

"How much money?"

She didn't answer, so Ransom repeated his question, a bit sterner.

She mumbled a response at first, and Ransom asked her to repeat herself.

"Two hundred grand!" she yelled.

My eyes grew wide as I processed her words.

And then I blurted out "Holy shit!" at the top of my lungs, and the jig was up.

Chapter Eight

RANSOM

I flung the curtain back, revealing everyone huddled around the small window I hadn't realized was open. The room was already fairly chilly, and my adrenaline was so high that I hadn't even noticed a slight draft coming from behind the curtain.

"Are you serious?"

They all had the decency to look at least marginally ashamed.

"It's Owen's fault," Brody accused. "He told us about the window."

"Did he also make you sprint to it like Usain Bolt?" Carter asked, adding "snitch" onto the end for good measure.

The window was small, but everyone parted like the Red Sea, revealing Owen, who merely shrugged. "I accept my role in this impudent adventure."

Fucking Owen. One second he acted like a kindergartner on speed, and the next he sounded like a walking thesaurus.

I tracked over the guilty faces until I landed on Taylor.

Pointing at her, I said, "I expected better from you."

Taylor looked chastened, but Sophia simply snorted and said, "Really?"

Turning around, I saw Hudson almost curled in on herself. These people truly were assholes.

"We may as well go out there. They heard everything anyway."

Hudson looked up and quickly made eye contact before averting her gaze back to the floor. "Yeah. Okay."

I opened the door and gestured for Hudson to go first, but as soon as she went through, she hung back and let me take the lead. She probably wanted to hide behind me when we came face-to-face with everyone.

When we arrived back on the deck, everyone was standing in a semicircle, waiting for us.

Aamee was the first to speak. "I think I speak for all of us—"

"You don't speak for me," Sophia interrupted.

"When I say," Aamee gritted out as she glared at Sophia, "that we're ultimately good people with poor decision-making skills and subpar impulse control. So, you know, don't judge too harshly or whatever."

"Like listening to a sonnet read by Shakespeare himself," Sophia muttered.

"Okay, you know what? I take back the good people shit. Sophia's a bitch."

"Hey!" Taylor yelled. "Only I can call her names."

"Well, then you need to let about two-thirds of Lazarus University know that."

"Everyone loves me," Sophia argued. "It's you no one can stand."

"I like it that way. You think I'm this abrasive for fun?"

Owen stepped forward. "I hate to intrude, but I feel like this moment isn't about the two of you."

Aamee turned a disgusted look on him. "Who brought the Boy Scout?"

"Oh, no, I was never a Boy Scout. My grandma objected to their exclusion of girls."

"Jimi?" Taylor asked fondly.

Owen smiled. "You know it."

"Jesus Christ, are you guys for real?" I asked, unable to hold back anymore. *Why are all my friends psychotic?* "You totally invaded our privacy."

They all shared a look again, and this time, Xander spoke for the group. "We genuinely apologize for that. We had no right to eavesdrop."

The words were sincere and had caused some of the tension I'd been holding to recede.

"That said," he continued, "it's very likely we'll do it again, and you probably should've anticipated us doing it this time."

"So it's *my* fault?" I asked incredulously.

Xander looked a little nervous, which was wise since I was seconds away from ripping him apart.

"I honestly don't know how to safely answer that," he said.

Probably knowing how little his answer would've quelled my irritation, Taylor took over. She stepped forward and crowded into my space.

"We fucked up. Big-time." She looked around me to where Hudson was standing. "I'm so sorry. We just... We were on edge from Brad and let that turn us into assholes. But there's no excuse for us listening like that. I'm truly, truly sorry."

After a brief pause, Hudson said, "It's okay. I probably

would've eavesdropped too."

Taylor offered her a small smile before turning back to me. "I really am sorry."

I wanted to be irritated, mostly because my emotions were out of control and I wanted to focus them somewhere. But the reality was, I probably would've listened in too. None of us were moral all-stars. We had our vices, but we were also fiercely loyal to each other. I knew that what had been said in that room wouldn't go beyond this deck.

And on top of that, they all had a right to know. Taylor and I had dragged all these people into the shit with Brad. They'd earned the right to know, especially now that he'd rolled up on us at a holiday party. Not to mention, I'd probably need their help dealing with him whenever he came calling next.

"I know," I said simply.

She lifted up and pressed a kiss to my cheek. "I'll make it up to you."

"Ew. Are we all pretending we didn't hear that?" Aniyah said.

"I think that would be best," Toby answered.

I let myself wallow in Taylor's closeness for a second before straightening. "Maybe we should all sit down."

Everyone moved quickly to move chairs so they formed one big circle. It felt like an AA meeting, but our addiction was gossip and bad decisions.

There was no denying that everyone's focus was on Hudson, but they tried to be subtle about it. Though clearly not enough, because Hudson looked on the verge of throwing up.

"If you'd rather go home," I offered.

"No, it's okay. They've heard most of it anyway, and I

know you'll just have to fill them in on the rest," she said.

I was off my chair in a second so I could go to her. Crouching down in front of her, I let my hands rest on her knees. "Not if you don't want me to. I would never do something to betray you. If you want to keep ... whatever else you have to say between the two of us, I will absolutely respect that."

She smiled at me. "I know. I didn't mean it how it came out. I don't know the full story about Brad, but you all obviously have history, so what's going on with him and me affects everybody."

"What *is* going on between you and him?" Taylor asked, and she looked like her stomach hurt.

I moved back to my seat so Hudson could answer.

"Not much. Physically at least. We've only hung out a couple of times. But he was ... a good listener," Hudson said helplessly. "It was so easy to tell him things because I felt like he was outside it all, ya know? It felt ... safe."

For the first time, I was sorry I hadn't killed Brad. Here was my sister, young and in a new city with no friends, and he'd preyed on her. Used her to get to us. The only thing that kept me in my seat instead of tearing the city apart in an attempt to find him was that Hudson needed me to be better than that.

"Brad was really good at that," Taylor said, her voice low and rough. "He's charming as hell, and he's so good at knowing what you need to hear. By the time you find out who he really is, it's too late. You've already given him the keys to every truth he'd ever need to manipulate you with." She leaned forward and rested her arms on her thighs as she looked intently at Hudson. "You did *nothing* wrong. I fell for all the same shit. He should be the one who's ashamed. Not you."

I studied my girlfriend, hoping she truly believed the

words she was saying. She'd come a long way since Brad first reappeared in her life. He still scared her—who wouldn't be scared of a guy like that—but she was more in control of her reactions to him. The fear wasn't paralyzing anymore, even though I wouldn't have blamed her if it were.

But she seemed to have worked through some of her feelings surrounding him and had therefore become better able to see the situation she'd been in with clearer vision. Brad was an abuser and a master manipulator. Nothing that had happened between them had been her fault.

Hudson's eyes glistened, but no tears fell. Instead, she cleared her throat and pressed on. "When I said I was coming to this, he asked if he could come." She laughed humorlessly. "I thought it was sweet that he wanted to meet my brother and friends. Anyway, then we showed up, and . . . well, you were all here for the rest."

"What is it that he knows?" Drew asked gently.

Hudson inhaled sharply, and I could tell she didn't want to share this part. I wanted to scoop her up and take her out of there. And if she'd said the word, I would have. But she was right when she'd said everyone needed to know. Whatever dirt he had on my sister, he obviously intended to use it against us. And we couldn't prepare for what we didn't know.

"I . . . God, this is embarrassing."

"Just take your time," Aamee, of all people, said, her voice warm and supportive. "No one here's a saint, okay? Sophia once pretended to have sex with her brother to fraudulently win a presidency."

"Which circle of hell did you escape from, and how do we send you back?" Sophia asked.

But Aamee's words had the effect she'd clearly intended:

everyone laughed. Even Hudson.

"I'm going to need to hear that story one day."

"Oh, don't you worry. I *love* retelling it," Aamee assured her with a smile.

Hudson smiled back before sobering. "I...honestly I don't even know how it got so out of hand so quickly. One second I was at a friend's party in Atlanta, talking to a hot guy about football, and the next I owed two hundred grand to a loan shark. I know it sounds crazy, but that's seriously how fast it feels like it happened."

"Let's start with the guy at the party," Drew prompted.

"His name was Trevor. A friend of mine invited me to visit her in Atlanta for a weekend. We went to a frat party, and that's where I met him, though he didn't go to school there. We somehow got on the subject of football, and I said my brother used to play." She shot a quick smile in my direction before continuing. "He said I probably knew a lot about it, then, and I said I knew a fair bit. I always followed your games, so I'm not completely clueless. He said he knew a surefire way to make quick money for people who knew the sport. He made it sound easy.

"And it was at first. I gave him twenty dollars and told him who I thought would win a game and by how much. When I won, he called me so we could set up a time for him to give me my winnings. We met at a coffee shop about halfway between my house and Atlanta, and while we sat there, he convinced me to bet some of what I'd won on another game. And then... it just spiraled from there."

As I sat there listening to Hudson and watching her wring her hands in her lap, I couldn't help thinking about how different we were. Even though we'd grown up around the same people, there was an innocence and naïveté about Hudson that I didn't think I'd ever had. And I'd desperately wished I'd been around when this fucking Trevor kid had come into her life so I could've helped her keep it.

"Even when I lost, he said I could just double down to win the money back. He'd text me to get my picks, and I'd just... choose a team. He made it sound fun and casual. It wasn't until two days after the reunion, when three big guys cornered me by my car in a parking lot and demanded their money, that I realized I'd been played. And that I owed almost two hundred grand to some really dangerous people."

Her gaze found mine, and she stared intently as if begging me to understand. "They said since I was new to the scene, they'd give me time to get the money together. Three months. But I panicked. I knew I'd never be able to get that kind of money, especially not at home. I just needed to... get away for a bit. Try to figure out what to do. But then I came here and messed up even worse."

I went back to her then, enveloping her in a hug just as the dam broke on her tears. "You didn't mess anything up. None of this was your fault. We'll fix it. I promise."

As I comforted my baby sister, I wondered if I'd ever stop making promises I wasn't sure I could keep.

Chapter Nine

TAYLOR

We didn't last at the party much longer. After Brody finished rolling around Ransom's truck in case Brad had put a GPS tracker on it and Xander promised to try to monitor Brad's credit cards to see if he could locate him, we hustled Hudson out to the car so we could get her home.

Just as we arrived at the car, we heard a voice say, "Shit, is the party over already?"

We turned to see Cody, Drew's younger brother, walking toward us.

He must've seen something on all our faces because he said, "Seems like it was a great time."

"There was some...drama," Drew explained.

"Isn't there always?" Cody said with a crooked grin. Then, spotting Hudson, he leaned in and extended his hand. "You must be Ransom's sister. I've heard a lot about you. I'm Cody."

Hudson took his hand but looked at us warily.

I couldn't blame her. A stranger who claimed to know a lot about her was probably a frightening prospect.

"He's just saying that," Sophia assured her. "He doesn't talk to us enough to have heard anything."

"Hey! I knew who she was, didn't I? And the phone works both ways in case you didn't know."

Sophia shook her head, and Drew grabbed his brother in a headlock.

"I spent a half hour on my hair. Stop. You're ruining it in front of the pretty girl."

Drew finally released him, and Cody ran a hand through his now-wild hair and smoothed his clothes. "If you ever want a break from these animals, let me know. I'd be happy to show you around the city."

"And on that note, we're leaving," Ransom said, moving between Cody and Hudson and ushering his sister into the car.

As we piled in, I heard Cody ask, "What'd I do?"

The gang all trooped back toward the deck as Ransom started the car, cranked the heat, and began the drive home.

Hudson was quiet on the ride. Not that I could blame her. Brad was like a plague that infected everything he came near, and I felt horrible that Hudson had been exposed because of me.

Though it was knowing me that had brought him into their lives to begin with. Maybe I was my own form of plague. Or something a little less malignant since I didn't *mean* to hurt anyone. Maybe a cold.

"If I was a disease, which one would I be?" I asked.

My question was met with silence for a few seconds, though it felt longer.

Finally, Ransom cleared his throat. "What, and I mean this sincerely, the fuck?"

"It just popped in my head. Sorry for trying to have

a conversation," I replied testily, even though I knew the question was weird.

"You're not a disease. You're a...medicine. Like amoxicillin."

I couldn't refrain from smiling. "I never thought being compared to disgusting pink liquid would be so sweet."

"I'm pretty sure it comes in pill form too," he said.

I patted his thigh. "Let me have my moment."

"Um..." came Hudson's voice from the back seat. "Is this the kind of conversation you guys have all the time?"

"You've spent the past few weeks with us," Ransom said. "What do you think?"

Hudson only hummed in response, which, to me, meant she thought we were insane. But she'd also told a guy she'd known three seconds all about being on the run from some kind of gambling ring, so who was she to judge?

And okay, even I could admit that was a shitty thing to think, but I couldn't help the things my brain came up with.

We drove the rest of the way to Ransom's in silence. I liked how he didn't even ask if I wanted to be dropped off at home. He couldn't have been too mad if he wasn't trying to dump me at my apartment.

Once we'd parked and made our way inside, Hudson said she was going to take a shower and go to bed. Since she'd insisted on moving to the couch after a couple of weeks of being in Ransom's room, despite his vehement insistence she keep the bed, Ransom and I knew that was our cue to hole up in his room so she could have some semblance of privacy.

As I shut the door behind us, Ransom plopped down onto the bed and rubbed at his eyes. I sat next to him and put my hand on his thigh.

"Are other people's lives like this?" he asked.

"I don't think so. I know a lot of normal people with completely boring lives."

"I'm so jealous of them."

That caused me to snort. "Ditto."

He sat up and draped an arm around me, pulling me closer to him. "Are you okay?" he asked.

God, I loved this man. In the seemingly perpetual shitstorm we endured—a lot of it having been caused by me— he was still worried about how I was doing. He was so selfless and protective, I sometimes had a hard time understanding how I deserved any of it. But I wasn't going to look a gift horse in the mouth.

What did that saying even mean anyway? What if the horse was holding the gift in his mouth? Should I still not look?

Jesus, I was really unhinged if that was what I was thinking about when I was pressed against Ransom's hard, muscular body.

"I'm okay," I replied. "Seeing him was just . . . jarring. But it wasn't as scary with all of you there. In some ways, I think facing him was . . . cathartic. Like facing a fear. I just wish Hudson wasn't wrapped up in it."

"I know. That definitely complicated everything. But I'm really proud of the way you stood up to him. I'm sorry if that sounds patronizing or whatever. I don't mean—"

I cut him off by putting a finger against his lips. "It's not patronizing," I whispered as I brought my lips closer to his. "Thank you."

"For what?" he asked softly.

"Everything."

After that, there was no more need for words. I needed to

feel him—on me, around me, in me. Everywhere.

From the moment I'd met him, Ransom had tried to protect me as best he could. But it wasn't the type of protection that made me feel weak but rather gave me strength I hadn't known I was capable of before him.

And as we got lost in each other and the bliss we created together, I vowed to do everything I could to make sure we always had this.

RANSOM

Last night had seemed especially long, not only at the bar but when we should've been sleeping. We'd both lain awake, though neither of us acknowledged the other's inability to sleep with any sort of conversation. Whatever words would've been said could wait until morning because we both needed time to process everything that had happened.

Not only did I have to worry about Hudson's situation—which somehow managed to be more difficult to handle than an unexpected pregnancy—but I also didn't want to let Taylor out of my sight. Brad was not only alive, but he was also in the area, a possibility I'd tried hard to avoid thinking about since we'd gotten back from Georgia.

At some point last night, I'd even considered offing him for good. I'd already had the experience of *thinking* I'd killed him. Did that mean I could handle actually *doing* it?

I'd never voice that to Taylor though, or even myself, for that matter. Thinking it was one thing, but putting the words out into the universe felt like I'd be giving action to an idea that should remain in my mind. Because no matter how much I wished that Brad would just disappear from the earth entirely, I knew I couldn't be the person to make him disappear.

I was still lying in bed, drifting in and out of sleep much like I'd done all night, when my phone rang.

Brody.

"Yeah?" I said, my voice low and deep with exhaustion.

"Yeah what?"

"Huh?" Why did Brody always have to be so hard to understand?

"I didn't ask you a question," Brody said.

"I didn't answer one."

"You said 'yeah.'"

"It's just how I answer the phone."

"Who answers like that?"

Ignoring his question, I asked, "Is there a reason you're calling?"

I heard Aamee's voice faintly in the background before Brody said anything else. "Can you just let us in? It's freezing out here."

"Are you guys outside my apartment building?" I already knew the answer, but for some reason I'd asked the question anyway.

"Yeah," Brody said. "See how I used that word to answer your question?"

"What are you doing here?" I was already climbing out of bed quietly, hoping not to wake Taylor, who'd somehow slept through the phone call. She was probably so tired she'd finally crashed. It made me wonder how Hudson had slept last night.

"Morning yoga," he answered dryly. "Why the fuck do you think we're here? To help you come up with a plan. We can't let this Brad fucker fuck with your fucking lives anymore."

"That's a lot of 'fucks' for a Sunday morning," I told him as I pressed my ear to the phone and pulled on some sweatpants.

"Are you gonna let us in or just leave us out here to freeze our balls off?"

Brody let out an "Ouch," which I assumed was caused by some sort of physical pain inflicted by Aamee, because a second later, I heard her say, "I don't have balls!"

"Hang on," I told them. "I'll buzz you in."

I hung up and opened the app to let them in the main doors. Then I headed out to the living room to unlock the door. Hudson was still sleeping soundly on the couch, and since she slept like the dead, I doubted even Brody and Aamee would wake her.

I was putting a filter in the coffeemaker when the two came inside. Aamee had a coffee in hand, and Brody was holding a carrier with four more, thank God.

"Yes," I said, heading toward the Styrofoam cups. "You read my mind."

"Right. Coffee in the morning," Aamee said dryly. "It doesn't exactly take Charles Xavier to figure that one out."

Brody had been rummaging through the fridge and cabinets for cream and sugar, but he stopped abruptly at her comment, his eyes shifting to an emotion I wasn't sure I'd ever seen in him before.

Aamee must've seen it too because she said, "Why are you looking at me like that?"

"Did you just make an *X-Men* reference?" He swiped a hand under his eye dramatically like he was wiping away a tear.

"Maybe," she answered, folding her arms across her chest. It looked like his question made her uncomfortable.

"I fucking love you," Brody said. Then he grabbed her

face between his hands and kissed her hard, though for once nothing about it seemed sexual. "Marry me."

"I love you too, weirdo, but don't say crazy shit like that. Someone might 302 your ass."

"But I'm not crazy," Brody replied quickly. "Well, I guess I sorta am, but not because I wanna marry you. And I do," he added more firmly this time, "wanna marry you." Brody hesitated before quickly grabbing her hand and pulling it up toward his face.

Aamee's eyes went wide at his words, but for one of the first times I'd seen her like this, she looked momentarily speechless.

"Okay, for once I agree with Aamee." I heard Taylor's voice before I saw her, and when I turned toward her, she was standing in the entrance to the living room, staring at Brody and Aamee like she was watching a magic show and was trying to figure out how the magician had done his trick. "This boy's straight-up nuts."

But Aamee didn't look anywhere but at Brody, who'd dropped down to his knees, still holding her hand. I didn't want to tell him that I was pretty sure you were only supposed to go onto one knee when you proposed because I was worried it would ruin the moment.

"Okay, for reals," Aamee said, turning toward Taylor and me, respectively. "Can one of you see if there's a mental hospital nearby we can call? Let 'em know they're gonna have their hands full soon."

Brody ignored her comment entirely. "I think I've known it for a while now, but I haven't fully let the idea take hold of my reality until now, ya know? It's hard to accept that I'd be choosing to be with one person for the rest of my life."

"If this is a real proposal," Aamee said, "it's a pretty shitty one."

"Sorry," he said. "I'm trying to be romantic, but I clearly suck at it."

"You're serious," Aamee said slowly, seeming to realize what the rest of us already had.

"I am." Brody gave her a nod of affirmation. "Aamee Dorcas Anderson—"

"Dorcas?" Taylor and I both whispered at the same time.

"Shut up," Aamee whispered back without looking at either one of us. "It's a biblical name."

"I've loved you for a long time now," Brody continued. "And I think you love me back just as much. We make a totally amazing couple, and we'd have gorgeous children one day—like the kind that could be in a Gap Kids commercial or something—and I wanna sit on a porch with you when we're old and no one thinks we're hot anymore except each other because I'll always think you're hot, and that's how I know I wanna spend the rest of my life with you. So what do you say?" His words came out practically in one breath, and when he was done, he took a moment to calm down. Taylor and I exchanged glances before Brody said, "Will you marry me?"

Aamee stared silently at him, her breath audibly shaky. I could see her eyes forming tears as Brody had spoken, and eventually she wiped one away.

Brody stayed kneeling on the wood floor but shifted his weight. I guessed the adjustment had to do with his anxiety but also because that floor couldn't feel good on his kneecaps.

Finally, Aamee said through a sniffle, "You'll always be hot to me too."

Brody's mouth broke into a wide smile. "Is that a yes?"

Aamee nodded enthusiastically. "Yes," she said. "It's a hell yes." Then she let out a squeal that I was surprised didn't break the windows.

Brody stood quickly, squeezing Aamee close to him before lifting her off the ground in excitement. "I'll get you a ring soon!" he said. "Promise."

Aamee kept her hands wrapped around Brody's neck, smiling like a little girl who'd just gotten surprised with a chocolate lab puppy for her birthday. The more I thought about it, the more I realized a puppy might actually be less work than agreeing to be with Brody for the rest of her life. They were cuter too.

"You're goddamn right you will," she finally said.

X_O

It had taken a little while for Brody and Aamee to calm down from the excitement that was their spontaneous engagement. I'd half expected them to come to their senses over coffee, but the more time that passed, the more they both seemed to be satisfied with their decision. Taylor and I made a silent pact to allow them to bask in the novelty of their new relationship status, and we both lived up to our promise.

But once Brody suggested asking Owen if Gimli could be the ring bearer, it was time to step in. "Didn't you come here to talk about the Brad problem?"

"Sorry, yes," Brody said. "We definitely did."

"A hundred percent," Aamee agreed. "We're ready." She didn't sound like she was too convinced, so she said, "We should talk about Brad."

"I can't even stand to hear his name." Letting her face plop into her hands, Taylor let out a loud groan.

"Totally get that," Aamee said, sounding as close to sympathetic as her personality would allow for. "We could come up with a code name for him." She offered the idea like the prospect excited her because it made the whole situation more mysterious and therefore worthy of her time. "I'm surprised he's even back here," she added.

I glanced at her before focusing my attention back to my coffee cup. I wondered if Taylor could tell how nervous I was. I always thought I could protect her as long as I was there. It's why I insisted she not walk home alone those times.

And unfortunately, I'd been right about not leaving her by herself. While I thought I'd put an end to Brad once and for all when I mistakenly believed I'd murdered the man in an alley—unintentionally of course—I'd never considered that he might actually show back up. Let alone . . .

"Maybe he never left," I offered quietly, almost afraid to toss out the possibility. Somehow thinking he had the balls to stick around—and now get close to my sister—made him even more menacing.

Taylor shifted so she was facing me, a kind of fear in her eyes I hadn't seen since that night in the alley. And that included last night. The idea that Brad had been around all this time freaked her out too.

"We've gotta do something," she said.

"Like what?" Brody asked. He got up and headed for the cabinet where I kept my snacks. Pulling it open, he said, "Kill him? You tried that once already, and you failed. Remember?"

"We weren't *trying* to kill him," I said, even though everyone obviously knew that. "But I wish I had. Fuck any prison sentence. He goes after my girlfriend, and now he's trying to insert himself into my little sister's life."

Aamee and Brody looked over at Hudson as I said it. "How the hell is she still asleep?"

"She'd sleep through a house fire if you let her."

"That seems dangerous," Brody said, as if my comment hadn't been any bit exaggerated. "You should probably check the smoke detectors to make sure they have batteries." He was already walking toward the one in the kitchen, chair in hand. "Do these double as carbon monoxide detectors?" he asked before hopping up on the chair so he could reach the device.

"No idea."

Brody messed around with some of the buttons until it let out a loud bloop.

"They just replaced the batteries last week," I told him.

"Who did?"

"I don't know. Maintenance, I guess. I wasn't here. I got an email saying they changed the ones on my floor."

Brody was moving through the living room now, heading toward the sliding door that led to the patio. "That doesn't seem weird to you?"

"Maintenance *maintaining* the safety of the complex? No, not really." *What the hell's the matter with this dude? First he rattles off an impromptu proposal, and now he's...* "What are you doing?"

He pointed toward the handle of the glass door. "You go out here lately?"

"I don't... I don't *think* so. It's freezing outside."

"Interesting," Brody mumbled, almost as if he were talking to himself rather than me. "Cause the door's unlocked."

"Guess Hudson went outside at some point."

"Or," Brody said with a dramatic scratch of his chin, "Brad was *inside*."

"You're crazy," I said because I thought he was but also because I didn't want to freak out Taylor any more than she already was. "Brad didn't Spider-Man up the walls and unlock the door from the outside."

Brody headed out to the balcony and looked over the railing. "Maybe not the walls, but I bet someone could scale the balconies if they were strong enough to pull themselves up to the next one."

"Doubt it, Detective Pikachu," I said.

"Brad's sneaky," Taylor said, "but I never knew him to be some kind of parkour expert."

Brody turned back toward us and headed back inside, closing and locking the door behind him. He pointed to Hudson. "Shit, you weren't kidding. She's out cold. You check her pulse?"

Christ. "Well, thank you both for coming over and for all of your concern," I said, "but I think we've got it covered." I put an arm around Brody's shoulder and began leading him toward the front door. "We'll call you if we need anything."

Narrowing his eyes at me as we walked, he said, "You know, if I didn't know better, I'd feel like you're trying to get me to leave."

"That's because I am. I love you, man. I do. But you're not helping minimize our anxiety about any of this by pointing out imaginary security breaches."

He grabbed his jacket, which I took as a sign that he was leaving. "I get it. I was trying to help, but I totally understand if you're worried about staying here now that you know Brad may have climbed up the balcony and gone through your underwear drawers while you were sleeping."

"Goodbye, Brody."

Even Aamee helped push him out the door and mouthed an *I'm sorry* on their way out.

For fuck's sake.

Chapter Ten

TAYLOR

It was almost lunchtime, and with Ransom still at school, I was taking care of some chores around my apartment when my phone rang. I didn't recognize the number, but I had put out calls to some prospective law schools and wasn't about to miss out on hearing back from any.

"Hello?"

"Taylor," Brad's voice said through the line, his tone smarmy and patronizing. "It's so good to hear your voice."

I jolted hard in shock, almost dropping the phone.

I'd been imagining Brad around every corner, but I hadn't been actively trying to think of any solutions to the problems he brought to our lives. Avoidance was likely not the healthiest coping mechanism, but it had been suiting me just fine. Until now.

"Wish I could say the same," I choked out, sadly sounding more afraid than biting.

"Now, now, is that any way to talk to your future brother-in-law?" His tone made it clear he was enjoying himself. "Or is it brother-in-law by marriage? I'm fuzzy on how that works."

"What do you want?"

"So many things."

"Narrow it down."

"I don't take orders from you. Remember?" His voice had lost its easiness and became something steely.

And I *did* remember. Brad had always seemed easygoing until he felt like someone was being disrespectful. He didn't like being bossed around or talked down to. Not that anyone did, but it had seemed to come from a deeper place with Brad. And he lashed out at whoever it was who'd dared come at him in a way he felt was inappropriate. Even if that person was me.

He'd never physically harmed me until that night in the alley. But Brad was an expert manipulator. The scars he left were ones only his victims could feel.

But I wouldn't be bullied by him. Not anymore.

"Suit yourself," I said before hanging up.

Maybe that was stupid, considering what he knew about Hudson, but I couldn't help it. He needed to know that, while he might have the power of information over me, he didn't hold anything else.

As I expected, he called back almost immediately. "Look at you growing a backbone."

"Just tell me what you want, Brad." Impatience laced my words even as unease prickled my skin.

"I want to meet with you and your ... Ransom," he said, seemingly unwilling to call Ransom my boyfriend.

"You can tell me everything you need to over the phone."

"No" was his simple response.

"Why not?"

"I don't need to explain myself to you. The two of you can

either meet me tonight at eight at Gullifty's on Peligro Street, or I can make a quick call down to Georgia and let the bookies know where to find Hudson. The reservation will be under my name."

With that, he hung up. *Dickhead.*

I texted Ransom to give me a call when he had a break in classes and slumped back on my couch. My mind was whirling with things Brad could want, and none of them were good. Deciding I needed to talk to someone, I texted Sophia.

Can you talk?

My phone rang a moment later. "Hey," I said.

"What's up?" Sophia asked.

I sighed heavily. "Brad called."

"That fucking flapdoodle."

That got a smile out of me. "What the hell is a flapdoodle?"

"It's someone who's insignificant."

"How do you even know that word?"

"Are you questioning my vocabulary skills?" she asked, amusement clear in her voice.

"Yes."

"Drew and I have been seeing who can come up with the more interesting insults."

"You guys are so weird."

"Yup," she agreed. "So what did he say?"

"He wants Ransom and me to meet him at a place called Gullifty's tonight. If we don't show, he's going to call the guys Hudson owes and tell them where she is."

"Twatwaffle."

"I've heard of that one. You're going to need to up your game."

"It's still fitting."

"That it is."

She was quiet for a second before asking, "Are you gonna go?"

"I don't know. I guess? I texted Ransom to call me when he could, so I'll see what he says. But since it involves Hudson, I'd assume he'd want to at least hear Brad out."

"Okay. I'll tell the gang to be ready in case the Bat Signal goes up."

"What?"

"The Bat Signal? From Batman?" When I remained quiet, she muttered a curse. "How do you not know what I'm talking about?"

"I'm more confused about what the gang needs to be ready for."

"Oh. To go to Gullifty's." She said it like I'd asked one of the dumbest questions in the world. As if it were a foregone conclusion we'd roll in there squad deep.

"And why would they be ready to do that?"

"You guys can't go *alone*. What if he tries to kidnap you?"

"From a public space with my Thor-like boyfriend in tow?"

"What if Brad waits for you guys outside with a weapon?"

"If his goal was to hurt us, I don't know that he'd go to the trouble of arranging a meeting. He'd just come find us like he did last time."

"That . . . doesn't make me feel better."

I shrugged even though she couldn't see me. I wasn't trying to make her feel any kind of way. I was only trying to be real about it. "We don't have a lot of choices."

"Sure you do. You can sit at a table where the entire

Scooby Gang can watch over you and tackle Brad if the need arises."

"The need arose for that months ago," I replied dryly.

"Well, here's our chance!"

"What if he notices you guys and snitches on Hudson?"

"Don't be silly. We'll be totally inconspicuous."

Since it was important for at least one of us to have some faith, I was glad she couldn't see the doubt on my face.

RANSOM

Gullifty's was crowded, but even despite that, there was no missing the giant crew of people dressed in dark clothing, hats, and sunglasses sitting a table away, though the table Brad had reserved was against a wall and at least six feet from the next nearest one. Despite the distance, the way our friends kept stealing glances at Taylor and me would be a dead giveaway to Brad that they were there.

"I thought you said they'd be inconspicuous," I said.

She looked over at those of our friends who'd been able to show up last-minute as they pretended to look at their menus. "I'm starting to think they don't actually know what that word means."

"That's a real shame."

She hummed in agreement.

"Where the hell is he anyway?" I asked as I looked around the room.

"Who knows. This could all be a power play to make us wait around for him. I wouldn't put anything past him." Including trying to get us to a particular place so he could get to Hudson, which was why we'd asked her to hang at Brody's place with Carter and Toby.

Just as I opened my mouth to unleash a string of expletives, I caught sight of him. Smug smirk firmly in place, he sauntered over to us wearing jeans and a burgundy button-down under a black blazer, his dark hair gelled to perfection atop his stupid head. He looked every inch the trust-fund brat he was.

"He's here. Act natural," Brody blurted in a whisper that was closer to a shout.

Honestly, with friends like these . . .

"So great all your friends could join us," Brad said loudly as he slid onto the chair across from us, looking completely nonplussed. "They look like a bad eighties band named Incognito."

"We'd be a great eighties band," Brody yelled from his table. When he was shushed, he followed with, "Well, we would."

I somehow resisted the urge to bang my head on the table.

"If I'd known this would be a party, I would've reserved one of the back rooms," Brad said, his tone light, but there was something else behind it. Something that let me know he wasn't happy we'd brought everyone with us. But he hadn't, at least according to Taylor, requested we come alone, so he had only himself to blame.

I leaned forward and rested my forearms on the table, hoping to give a sort of looming impression. When his eyes widened slightly, I felt confident I'd achieved my goal.

"You wanted to see us?" I asked.

He smiled and looked at Taylor. "So direct. Is this where you got it from? He may be a bad influence on you."

The urge to rip him across the table and knock all his

teeth down his throat was strong, but I tried to maintain my composure.

When neither of us replied to him, he sighed and shook his head like he was disappointed in us. "So uptight. You guys should work on that," he said before turning a wide smile onto the server who was approaching our table.

"Hi, welcome to Gullifty's. My name is Samantha. Can I start you with something to drink?"

Brad motioned to the waters we'd ordered when she'd already come over to our table when Taylor and I had first arrived. "Either of you want a drink?"

We shook our heads.

He smiled at Samantha again. "So boring. I don't know why I hang out with them. Could I get a Johnny Walker on the rocks?"

"Sure. Can I see some ID?"

Brad nodded before digging into his pocket and extracting his wallet so he could hand his license over. He kept his charming grin on her as she inspected it and then handed it back.

"I'll be right back with your drink."

"Thank you, Samantha." He leered at her as she walked away like the scumbag he was. "So, where were we?"

"You were telling us why we're here," Taylor answered.

"That's right. My memory isn't as good as it used to be. You know how it goes, right, Ransom? Since you seemed to forget you had a little sister when you moved in with the Holts and went on to bigger and better things."

I looked over at Taylor. "We're done here." If this prick thought he was going to get the best of me, he was mistaken. He was clearly trying to provoke me, and I couldn't give into it.

But I also couldn't sit here and listen to him either.

She nodded, and we started to ride.

"Jesus, so touchy. Sit back down, and I'll get to the point."

Taylor and I shared a meaningful look for a second, through which we came to an agreement to hear him out. I didn't want the unknown hanging over us anymore. I wanted him to say what he needed to so we could be done with him.

Samantha brought Brad's drink and asked if we'd like to order an appetizer, which we all declined. I had no interest in eating with this smug prick.

When she left, he focused on us, his gaze appraising as he seemed to chew on his cheek. Finally, he spoke. "My father has something that belongs to me. I want it back."

"How wonderful for you," I said dryly. "But I don't give a shit about what you want."

"Well, you should," he said, his gaze moving from me to Taylor and back again. "Because you're going to get it for me."

A surprised laugh burst out of me. "Oh, are we now?"

But he didn't share in my laugh. His eyes hardened and his jaw tightened. "Yes, you are. Unless you'd like to visit your sister in a hospital while she learns to eat through a straw. Or worse. I'm not really sure how big of a message those guys want to send."

"You can't do this," Taylor said.

That made him laugh. "Sure I can. What are you gonna do? Call the cops?" He leaned forward. "All that would do is piss me off. It wouldn't stop me. *Nothing* can stop me, which you, of all people, should know."

I wanted to look over at Taylor, at our friends. I wanted to know if they'd heard—if one of them could step in and tell me what I should do. I'd never felt more out of my depth, but

I knew I couldn't let Brad know that. I couldn't let him see doubt or insecurity on my face. So I kept my gaze trained on him and my face blank.

"What does he have?" I asked.

"A die-cast car."

"A die-cast car? You're going to have us steal a toy? Are you serious?" What the hell was with this guy?

"As a heart attack."

"Why don't you just take it? Or ask for it back if it's yours anyway?"

"Because my father doesn't want me to have it. My grandfather promised it to me, which my dad resents. So he's hidden it away in his trophy room and has threatened to cut me off if I take it. So I need *you* to take it."

"Wouldn't he still suspect you anyway?" Taylor asked.

"Not if I'm with him when it goes missing."

"Wouldn't it cross his mind that you could be behind a plot to steal it, since you're, you know, behind a plot to steal it?" she said.

Brad took a sip of his drink and sat back in his chair. "Nah, he doesn't usually give me the credit I deserve."

"For being a criminal?" I said.

His eyes narrowed. "For being resourceful and determined."

I rolled my eyes, unable to stop myself and not really wanting to anyway. "How do you even expect us to get to it? You think he's just going to invite a bunch of strangers into his house and let us look around?"

"That's actually exactly what he's doing. Every year, my dad and stepmom throw a huge New Year's Eve party at the house. And while there is security at the door checking invitations, it won't be hard to score a couple extra. Maybe even wrangle a few spots on the waitstaff if your nosy friends want in on the action. Since they seem to have some sort of separation anxiety where you two are concerned."

"Won't your parents notice two people they don't know wandering around their house?" Taylor asked.

"I think you're underestimating the size of this party. So no. They usually don't know half the people there anyway. My dad's assistants send invitations out to anyone they may be interested in courting for business purposes. And they're usually surrounded by ass-kissers the entire night, so they won't even notice you if you make it a point to *not* be noticed."

"Where is this . . . trophy room?" I asked.

"Third floor, in what was originally built to be a servant's quarters. Normally the room is locked in case someone were to break in, but my dad leaves it open on occasions like this because he's constantly dragging people up there to show off all the things he's collected over the years. I guess his hubris trumps security."

Taylor looks baffled. "And he keeps a toy car in this room?"

"It's an heirloom," he answered shortly.

"It's worth a lot of money," I corrected, done with the bullshit about grandfathers and resentments and wanting to get at the *real* reason we were stealing this thing.

"That's none of your concern."

"Oh, I think it is." It sure as shit was my concern if we were looking at a felony that could get us sent to prison for the rest of our lives.

"I don't really care what you think. These are the terms. You either comply, or Hudson gets a visit from some dangerous men. And if you happen to move her somewhere else in the meantime…" He shrugged. "Then I'll just tell them where to find your family. Both the one you were born into and the ones who took you in."

We sat there in silence for a second as his threat simmered between us.

Hudson, Taylor, and I had already discussed the possibility the guys who were after Hudson might go after our family if they couldn't find her. We'd already decided we'd have to tell Kari and the rest of them, but Hudson had begged us to wait until after Christmas. Since the timeline the bookies had given Hudson spanned into February, I was willing to grant that wish. But if Brad contacted them and said Hudson had run, who knew what those guys would do.

"You see," he continued, "there's really nothing I won't do to get what I want. And thankfully for you, I've set my sights on something other than our beautiful Taylor here. You do this, and you'll never hear from me again. I'll be a tiny blip in your past. I'd think that would be an offer that would be impossible to refuse."

"It would be if I trusted anything that came out of your mouth," I countered. "How do we know this isn't a setup to get us caught? Or that you won't rat out Hudson anyway?"

"Ransom, Ransom, Ransom, you of all people should know that there aren't any guarantees in life. But if you think about it, you do have quite a few witnesses over there who will back you if you go to the police and say we met up and conspired. And it probably wouldn't be hard to prove that I got you into the party. So we both have something to lose if this goes wrong. Which is why it's not going to go wrong. You're both going to make sure of that. Because even if we all go down, I can still make phone calls from jail."

When we didn't respond, he added, "Tell you what. I'll even sweeten the deal. You do this, and I'll give you the money Hudson needs to pay off the bookies."

"Oh, come on," Taylor said. "Like we could ever count on you to follow through on that?"

Brad shrugged. "I'm not sure you really have any more to lose."

Taylor and I looked at each other for a long moment before Brad's hand entered my periphery.

"We have a deal?"

I glared at his hand, unwilling to touch him.

He simply smirked and stood, pulling a card from his pocket. "I'll be in touch from this email address. I'll send you details as I get them."

Begrudgingly, I took the card from him.

He then set a twenty on the table to pay for his drink and added, "Pleasure doing business with you. Taylor, always great seeing you." He began to walk away, offering a little wave to our friends as he passed their table.

When he was out of sight, Brody called to us. "Dude, get your asses over here and tell us what just happened."

I looked at Taylor, who shrugged before standing. We carried our chairs and set them down at the head of the table. Hopefully our server wouldn't mind. Drew, Sophia, Brody, and Aamee were all there.

"So. What did he say?" Sophia asked.

I looked around. Where we'd been with Brad had been set off to the side and away from prying ears. But while it was fairly loud in here, the table everyone else was at was a little too close to other people. "We'll fill you in when we're somewhere private."

She nodded in understanding.

Drew took a sip of his drink and then said, "I assume that means we're about to get into something...intense."

I turned my gaze from him to everyone else at the table. "We're not asking any of you to be involved in anything." I didn't mean it petulantly but sincerely. None of them owed it to us to put their own safety at risk, and I'd never ask something like that of any of them.

They seemed to understand what I was saying because they shared a look before Aamee spoke. "You don't have to ask. I was born for shit like this."

Sophia rolled her eyes, but everyone seemed to be on board with the gist of what Aamee was saying.

"I don't know what to say other than...thank you. Thank you so much." My eyes prickled as relief coursed through me. I didn't want to put these people in danger, but I also didn't want Taylor and me to have to do this on our own. Maybe that was selfish, but I couldn't help it. I was scared, but having our friends with us made me braver.

"Maybe save your thanks," Brody said. "We don't tend to make situations better." His words held a clear note of teasing, but he also wasn't wrong.

But that didn't do anything to dampen my desire to have their help. This whole thing was destined to go FUBAR. But somehow, when we worked together, we all tended to come out of things okay.

Hopefully that was a trend that would last.

Chapter Eleven

TAYLOR

Two days later, we decided to meet at Brody's place for our debrief because it felt like safer territory. Hudson was at work, but she'd be going back to Ransom's eventually, and we wanted her as far away from what was going on as she could be. She was in enough trouble, and honestly, we also didn't know her well. Not that we thought she'd turn on us or anything, but we weren't sure how she'd respond to a high-stress situation. It was better for all of us to keep her out of things.

We'd briefly considered meeting at my apartment, but with Brad potentially lurking around every corner, it didn't feel like the best place to meet up. And since Brody's apartment had already been the scene of multiple dramatic episodes, it felt appropriate to plan a large-scale burglary there.

What even are our lives?

In the days since our meeting with Brad, he had only contacted us to send us a Google Earth link so we could see his house and to let us know he'd send pictures of the inside soon.

It all felt very *Ocean's Eleven*, if the director had decided to do away with all the professionals and use crisis-prone college kids instead.

"So let me see if I got this," Xander said after we'd gone through the whole spiel. "He wants us to break into his *own* house to steal a model car from his dad during a party where security will be present? I mean, he has to know we're likely to get caught, right? None of us are in any way equipped to pull off something like that."

"Thank you for repeating everything we just heard and for stating the obvious," Aniyah said dryly.

"And we're not technically breaking in," I added because it seemed an important distinction to me.

Xander stuck his tongue out at Aniyah, ignoring me.

Ransom rubbed his forehead and clearly thought Xander's question was worth addressing. "I initially thought this was all an elaborate plan to get us caught. But the more we talked . . . I dunno. I didn't get the vibe that that was his angle. I think he really wants the car. But we're also expendable to him."

"Are we, though? We know his plan. We could easily turn him in," Aamee said.

"I don't think he has any better options," I explained. "Whatever he needs that car for, it's worth the risk of getting caught, I guess."

"He also may think he can weasel out of culpability after the fact. It'll essentially be our word against his that he planned the robbery," Toby said.

"But he's emailing them," Aniyah argued. "He's basically leaving a paper trail leading back to him."

"I'd also like to note that this isn't a robbery," I interjected. "You rob a person, not a house. This is a burglary, like Xander said before."

They all stared at me, not seeming impressed by my criminal justice lesson.

After a second, Xander shook his head. "I looked into it. He's got a ton of safeguards in place to prevent being traced that way. A gifted computer forensic investigator could maybe connect them, but I don't know. I wasn't able to do it."

"We all saw him at dinner," Sophia pointed out.

"But we couldn't hear him. It would come down to Taylor's and Ransom's word against his. And his is the more believable story—that *they* invited *him* out to fleece him for information so they could break into his parents' house," Xander explained. "After all, what sense does it make for him to ask us to steal something he has easy access to?"

Aamee glared at him. "Your energy is really negative, and I'm feeling smothered by it."

Xander shrugged. "I'm just trying to explain why he may be willing to gamble on it."

"So what do we do?" Drew asked.

I sighed heavily. "I don't know. I feel like there's no way we can pull this off. And I don't *want* to pull it off. Doing Brad's dirty work and *stealing* from someone... I don't want to do any of that. But at the same time, I don't want to risk Hudson's life."

"What about paying her debt?" Drew suggested. "That would get rid of Brad's leverage over us."

"It's two hundred grand," Ransom said. "There's no way I can come up with that. And before anyone says anything, I'm not dragging anyone else's family into this. I know that some of your parents are... well off. But asking for that much money would raise all kinds of red flags."

I was frustrated that he was right. Even my mom, who was

as free-spirited as they came, wouldn't part with that much money without explicit knowledge of where it was going. And while I knew other people in our group had wealthy parents, Hudson's debt wasn't their problem. Though I guess we were kind of making it their problem by asking for their help planning this stupid heist. I just couldn't see a way to pull it off without them.

Our lives were such tangled messes, and I wasn't sure what the right thing to do was anymore. Though I was pretty sure committing a felony wasn't it.

"Brad said he'd have roles open for all of us?" Carter asked.

Ransom shook his head. "I'm not comfortable with that. I just ... can't. We'll take your help preparing, but"—he looked at me, and I nodded—"Taylor and I go in alone."

The room erupted in chaos. Everyone started talking at once. And loudly.

"You can't go in there alone. What if it's a setup?" Brody said.

"Then it's better only two of us get caught," Ransom reasoned.

"But you may need a diversion," added Aamee.

"There should be enough going on to distract everyone," I answered.

Their protests began flying at us faster than we could keep up with.

Finally, Ransom stood and whistled loudly. "Listen, if there were a way for me to do this alone, I would. I already don't like that I have to drag Taylor with me, but I think a young, single guy showing up will be suspicious. I cannot get in there and do what needs to be done if I know what you're all risking. I'll be too distracted."

"You always do this," Brody griped.

"What am I doing?"

"Trying to be an island or whatever," Brody said with a dramatic wave of his hands. "We're your friends, and we're already involved. Just let us help you."

Ransom plopped back down, and I could see the strain in the high-set of his shoulders.

I reached over and laced my fingers with his before turning my attention to the group. "We do want your help. There's no way we can make a solid plan alone. But in terms of executing it . . . that's gotta be just us."

Sophia looked at me, misery clear on her face. "Why?"

"We won't risk you. Even if you're willing to risk yourselves."

Sophia looked unhappy but resigned with that answer. As I gazed around, everyone looked a little dejected. It was as if we'd promised them each an ice cream sundae and didn't follow through.

Suddenly, Xander stood and raked a hand through his hair. "Yeah, that doesn't work for me."

"What doesn't?" Ransom asked.

He'd begun to pace but stopped long enough to point an accusing finger in our direction. "This martyr shit you're pulling. I *need* to be inside the house to help. At least at some point."

"For what?" I asked.

"Surveillance. How can you be sure this model car you're stealing doesn't have some kind of alarm on it? Or if there are cameras around the house you need to avoid? Or where all the exits are? If they have a security system, I can probably hack in and take a look around, but I don't want to raise any red flags or give them a way to connect us to it. It would be easier and safer if I could get inside. There's so much intel you need if you're going to have any chance at this."

"Aw, have you been watching the *Fast and the Furious* movies again?" Aniyah asked.

Xander shot her a glare. "Can you contribute anything helpful?"

She pretended to think for a moment. "No."

"I'm sure Brad will provide those details," I said, my voice sounding weak even to my own ears.

Xander scoffed. "Like we can trust him. No, he needs to get me inside that house before the party so I can look around."

"How do we get him to agree to that?" Ransom asked.

"You tell him that if he wants the car as badly as it seems, then he'll do what it takes to get it. And what it takes is him inviting me for lunch or what the fuck ever at his parents' place within the next week."

We all sat quietly and mulled over what Xander had said. When it didn't seem like anyone was going to say anything else, I picked up my phone. "I'll email Brad and see what he says."

"Wait," Aniyah's voice rang out. "You're actually going to let him do this? What happened to not involving us beyond planning?"

Her accusation made me flush in embarrassment. But before I could take the words back, Xander said, "It's so cute when you worry about me."

She scoffed. "I'm not worried about you."

"Sure sounds like it."

"I just want us all to be on the same page. Besides, weren't you telling us you were worried Brad had something to do with that Petey guy's death? I don't think any of us should be alone with him." She looked at Xander. "Even you."

He put a hand to his chest. "You say the sweetest things."

"She's right," I said. "Who knows what Brad might do?"

Sophia's brow furrowed. "You said you thought the Petey thing was a coincidence."

"It might be," I hedged. I'd entirely downplayed my suspicions about this before because I thought we'd be able to move on. How naïve I was. "But it also might *not* be. We shouldn't take the chance."

"We're taking the chance," Xander declared.

"Since when do we listen to you?" Aniyah asked.

"Since I'm the only one who makes any sense. Which has actually been always, but some of you are slow on the uptake."

"I don't like it," Ransom said.

"Well, no shit. This whole situation sucks," Xander quipped. "But you also know I'm right. And you saw Brad's face when I mentioned my dad. Brad clearly knows who he is, and I doubt he'd risk poking that bear. It'll be fine."

And boy, those famous last words if I'd ever heard them.

RANSOM

Surprisingly, Brad agreed to Xander's demand readily. I wasn't sure if that worried me more or less.

When Taylor sent Brad the email relaying Xander's request, a reply had come back within ten minutes, saying he'd see what he could do and would be in touch. We hadn't heard anything else for a few hours, but when we did, the message was direct.

*Xander and I are expected for lunch Saturday at noon. I'll
pick him up from that dive you all hang out in at ten.*

There was no way I wanted Xander sitting in a car with
Brad for that long. His parents lived over an hour and a
half away. So I told Taylor to ask Brad for an address in his
hometown where we could meet up, and I'd drive Xander out
there myself.

So that was how I found myself idly sitting in the cab of my
truck trying to keep myself from having a nervous breakdown
while I waited for Xander to come back.

They'd been gone for over two hours. How the fuck long
did these people need to eat for? I'd sent Xander a couple texts,
but he hadn't responded to any of them, the prick. If he was
enjoying foie gras over a bed of caviar while I stewed in my
truck, I was going to kill him.

It didn't help that all our friends had been texting me for
updates constantly. Didn't they understand that I was already
anxious enough without their constant check-ins?

After another half hour passed, I resigned to giving them
another thirty minutes before I drove over to Brad's and
knocked the door down to find Xander. I'd be like some kind
of anxiety-riddled Avenger. Maybe Taylor was right about my
superhero complex. My name could be Captain Valium.

The ringing of my phone interrupted that asinine line of
thinking, and in my deteriorated mental state, I answered it
without looking at who was calling and yelled, "Hello?" into it.

"Ransom?" Taylor asked, sounding worried. "Is
everything okay?"

No. No, it wasn't. Because I'd agreed to let someone who
wasn't me walk into a house with a crazy person to help save

my sister from loan sharks.

"Yeah, I'm fine."

"You sure?"

I sighed. "I'm just worried. They've been gone awhile, and I haven't heard from Xander."

"If it helps, I don't think Brad would do anything to him. It definitely wouldn't help him get what he wants."

"What if what he wants is to kill people because he's a homicidal maniac?"

That gave her pause. "Then I guess we gave him exactly what he wanted," she finally replied, her voice sardonic.

I tried to laugh, knowing I was being ridiculous. "I know it's fine. Or at least, I strongly suspect it's fine. But I still feel horrible about making him do this."

"You didn't make him do anything."

"You know what I mean. He wouldn't be in this situation if it weren't for me and my family's drama."

"Eh, I kinda think Xander likes drama. If we didn't keep him supplied, he'd probably make some on his own."

"So we're actually helping him?"

"Yeah, let's go with that." She laughed, and I joined her, though it sounded hollow from us both.

When the mood on the line became somber again, I racked my brain for something to say. Just as I was about to offer some platitude about our situation, I heard the rev of an engine behind me. Looking up, I noticed Brad's Camaro pulling into the lot I'd been sitting in. Even his car was douchey. Though if anyone else had been driving the sleek, red Camaro I would've drooled over it. Brad made everything lose its luster.

"Gotta go," I said to Taylor before hanging up.

I rolled down my window despite the freezing air because

I was desperate to have as many of my senses as possible focused on Xander. He climbed out of the car with a smirk planted firmly on his face, slamming the door without glancing back.

For his part, Brad sped off as soon as the door was closed. *Dickhead.*

When Xander reached the passenger door, I put up my window and turned toward him. He got himself settled and sat placidly in the seat. When I made no move to start driving, he looked at me in a way that said, *What the hell are we waiting for?*

"Well?" I asked.

"Well what?"

My eyes nearly bugged out of my head. *Is he fucking serious?* "What do you mean 'well what'? What the hell happened? You were gone forever."

"We weren't even gone three hours. You're so impatient."

"Dude."

"What?"

"Were you like . . . lobotomized while you were there? Tell me what happened."

He shrugged. "We had a nice lunch. Did you ever have Fourchu lobster? They're found in Canada. It was really good, though I thought it would've been more considerate if they'd asked if I'd had an allergy before serving it. What if I'd gone into anaphylactic shock?"

I just stared at him, which he returned. He managed to hold a straight face for maybe about thirty seconds before his lips started to twitch at the corners.

"Why are you fucking with me?" I asked, exasperated.

"You seemed a little tense."

"So you thought waxing poetic about your fucking lunch would calm me down?"

He shrugged. "Not really. It was just fun for me."

"For Christ's sake," I muttered as I turned the key in the ignition and got us moving. "So?" I asked once we were on the road.

"The place is massive. And they do have a pretty sophisticated security system, but Brad told me a lot of the cameras are disabled for parties like this. Evidently there are some . . . less than wholesome activities that occur at them."

"Like what?"

"From what Brad said, everything from escorts hired to work the room and sneak off to preapproved secluded areas to some shady business dealings. He said this will be especially true in the trophy room because his dad frequently takes guests up there to do business. So if you can avoid getting caught inside the room, it should be smooth sailing."

"Are there cameras that could catch me going up the stairs?"

"Not if you use the back staircase in the kitchen. You'll just have to try to avoid being seen going up or down. But with the way everyone will probably be running around to cater the party, that should be possible."

"What about people working security?"

"They're only stationed at the door. Brad's dad doesn't want them wandering around the party. He thinks it makes the guests uncomfortable."

"What kind of guy is he?"

"Brad's dad? Ha, that rhymed."

I rolled my eyes. "Yeah."

"About as pompous and arrogant as you'd expect. Though

he seems kind of…dismissive of Brad. He was definitely much more interested in talking to me, which makes sense because Brad told him who my dad was. The guy clearly saw opportunity. If only he knew my dad makes him look like Ward Cleaver.

"It was a shame, though. Brad kept trying to engage in the conversation, but his dad completely ignored him. If Brad weren't an epic asshole, I would've felt bad for the guy. And his stepmother spent the meal pushing food around her plate and refilling her wineglass. I got the impression she drinks most of her meals."

We drove in silence for a few minutes before I said, "Do you think we can pull this off?"

When he didn't immediately answer, I glanced over at him. He was staring out the passenger window as the scenery blurred by. Finally, he straightened and said, "It's possible. For a seasoned criminal, this would be an easy job. I'm actually shocked at how lax they seem to be, considering how many valuables they have lying around. My dad guards our house like the *Mona Lisa* is on display. But maybe that's because his work is in security, so he's more paranoid. Who knows."

He paused for a second and then twisted in his seat so he could look at me more fully. "I think your biggest obstacle is going to be the human factor."

I squinted in confusion. "Like the fact that people will be all over the place?"

"No, like the fact that you're human. A good one. And stealing… I'm honestly not sure you guys have it in you."

The grave way he said it made it seem like a put-down, though I knew it was ultimately a compliment. He was disappointed that he thought our morality would get in the way of us getting what we needed to keep Hudson safe, and I could understand that. I had the same concern. But I hadn't hesitated to do what needed to be done when Brad had attacked Taylor in that alley. Even when we'd been racked with guilt at thinking we'd killed him, there had been a tendril of me that had been glad he wasn't around to hurt Taylor anymore.

And I couldn't deny that part of me was upset we'd been mistaken. Without Brad around, none of this would be happening.

So, yes, I agreed with Xander that our sense of right and wrong would be a hindrance, but I was confident it wouldn't stop us.

We could deal with the guilt later.

Chapter Twelve

RANSOM

After listening to Xander talk about how dysfunctional Brad's family was, I was more hesitant than ever to spend a prolonged amount of time with Taylor's family in Florida for a holiday get-together. Not that I thought the Petersons would be anything like the Laceys. But families were . . . messy. And I'd had quite enough mess for a while, thank you.

But I also knew not going with Taylor to see her family for Christmas would send the wrong message. I was a hundred percent in this relationship with Taylor, so I needed to show up even when I wanted to run screaming in the opposite direction. Not to mention, we had bigger things to worry about—namely, carrying out the toy-car heist. We'd ironed out most of the details before we'd left so we didn't have logistics hanging over our heads. Our fear of what was to come was heavy enough.

Thankfully, the flight to Florida went a hell of a lot better than our trip to Georgia. The plane took off without any issue and landed where it was supposed to. We'd even arrived a half hour earlier than expected, and our bags—which we'd been hesitant to even pack heavy enough that we'd have to check them—had been waiting for us on the conveyor belt. Even our rental car had been ready.

It was almost too good to be true. Which meant that this weekend meeting Taylor's family would either be incredibly smooth or horribly disastrous. I couldn't ignore the truth that sometimes a good omen turned into a very bad one. And since I didn't want to jinx things either way, I chose not to vocalize any of that.

"That was so easy," Taylor said with a smile, almost as if she'd infiltrated my mind and pulled the thoughts out of it because I didn't want to.

"Mm-hmm," I said, putting a hand on Taylor's leg and giving it a light squeeze.

She looked over at me. "What's wrong?"

"Nothing." I did my best to sound casual, unaffected, but my response was a lie, and we both knew it.

I was scared shitless. It didn't matter that Taylor's dad had invited me to come along or that I had no reason to think anyone in her family might dislike me. I felt like I was about to walk in front of a firing squad and hope like hell their guns weren't loaded. It made showing up at Brad's dad's place seem about as hospitable as dinner at Martha Stewart's house.

"Just trying to concentrate on the roads," I added.

"It'll be fine," Taylor tried to assure me. She put her hand on mine and gave it a squeeze. "They'll love you just like I do."

That was a lie too. No parents *loved* me. *Tolerated* me maybe. Or at best, *liked*. But I knew from hanging with some of my high school buddies and eating the occasional meal at their houses that no one over the age of forty ever seemed to be too fond of me. Except for Matt and Melissa, of course.

I was the foster kid, the one whose own family would've rather seen him to go strangers than raise him themselves. I was the one with the weird name that sounded vaguely like a crime had been committed. It didn't matter if I'd been a law-abiding citizen my whole life—well, until now. The connotation was there, and it was the reason my friends' mothers made sure to *wear* their valuable jewelry whenever I stayed for dinner, and girls' fathers forbade them from dating me before I even had a chance to introduce myself to them.

But maybe this would be different. Taylor hadn't told her family much about me, so I'd essentially been given a clean slate. They had no preconceived notions about my behavior or background, and while I had no intentions of lying to them about anything, I certainly wouldn't volunteer any information that might cause them to think less of me.

I was college-educated and in school for my master's degree. I had a job working with kids and had even helped Taylor get a job there too. Thankfully, I'd stopped my stripping gig, so I wouldn't have to worry about excluding that from my résumé when her dad asked how I supported myself. Though after the holidays, I would definitely have to commit to finding another job that would help pay for my apartment.

I'd been great at stashing money away when I'd been getting paid to take my clothes off, and I had enough to pay my rent through April. But my job at the after-school program wouldn't cut it long-term. Especially since some of my savings had gone to paying for the unexpected expenses that had accumulated during our journey to Georgia.

I'd been so wrapped up in my anxiety that I hadn't even realized how close we were getting to the house her family had rented until we pulled off the main road of the island, which meant we were only a few blocks away.

"Have you been here before?" Surprisingly, I hadn't thought to ask Taylor that before now.

"Nope. Never. I have no idea why they even picked this spot, but I think my stepmom was the one who actually suggested it."

"It's nice." Definitely different from other beach towns I'd been to, this one seemed to be slower-paced and smaller. I hadn't spotted any rowdy teenagers or random people wandering in the middle of the street like they were cars. "I guess I imagined it'd be packed with college kids or something." Though I had no idea why because it wasn't like it was spring break. Most of them had probably gone home to be with family. It made me feel bad for Hudson, who I'd left back at my apartment.

Even though I'd protested, she'd insisted I go away with Taylor for a few days before Christmas. Taylor had invited her to come along, but she said that was too awkward. Thankfully, Brody and Aamee had offered to stay at my place while we were away so Hudson wouldn't be alone. Though I figured at least part of their offer had been due to the appeal of staying at an apartment that wasn't Brody's. Plus, we would be home in time to celebrate Christmas with her.

Taylor's dad seemed sufficiently satisfied with that because, even though Taylor wouldn't be there on Christmas Day, they would still get time together as a family. He'd understood when Taylor had told him that it was tough to take that many days off from work and she needed the money. It wasn't a lie. But it also wasn't the real reason for our shorter stay in Florida. We needed to get back before Christmas so Hudson wouldn't be alone when the rest of our crew went to be with their own families for the holidays.

I followed the GPS down the last two blocks until it directed us to turn. As we headed down the street lined with homes of all shapes, sizes, and colors, I wondered which one we would be staying in.

The street dead-ended at the entrance to the beach, which we could see just past the narrow path of sand flanked by tall beach grass. To our left was the house the Petersons had rented—a three-story sky-blue home with a two-car garage and double-wide paver driveway, which I pulled into slowly.

The front of the house had two decks with grand white steps leading up to the first that served both a practical purpose as well as an aesthetic one. As we exited the car and took in the entire place, we saw Taylor's family hanging on the top deck like they'd been waiting for our arrival.

Taylor waved up to them as she said, "You ready for this?"

I waved too. "Does it matter if I'm not?"

At least there was a pool out back and a beach a few steps away. How bad could it be?

TAYLOR

This is gonna be horrible.

I'm not sure why I'd agreed to come here, but watching my dad and Rita, followed by my brother and sister, practically run to the deck railing at our arrival like four impatient goldendoodles greeting their owners after they'd been at work all day did nothing to make me feel better. While the beach would be a nice change of pace for the holiday season, having my family interrogate Ransom was not something I was particularly looking forward to.

"Come on up!" Rita yelled down. "You're just in time for lunch."

Ransom grabbed our bags, plastered on a wide grin that surprisingly lacked any type of anxiety, and headed for the steps. And though I hadn't eaten much of anything today, my appetite had suddenly disappeared.

I followed behind Ransom, who practically ran up the stairs. I wondered if he was moving that quickly so he didn't lose his nerve. Or maybe so my family wouldn't notice any apprehension. Kind of like a warrior running into battle toward his enemy.

When we got to the first deck, Ransom dropped the bags by the front door, and then we headed toward the white metal stairs that led to the top deck. Because this staircase was a spiral one, Ransom couldn't ascend it quite as quickly, but he didn't hesitate either. Once we made it to the top, Lila and Sawyer ran toward me and wrapped their arms around me with such force that they practically knocked me over the railing.

I squeezed them back and gave them each a kiss on their heads. Though I'd seen Lila a few months ago, she somehow seemed a foot taller. And Sawyer, only two years younger at eight years old, wasn't far behind. "You're not much shorter than I am, Li. I can't believe you're only in fifth grade."

"That's what Mom says too," Lila replied with a proud smile. I was glad she seemed so happy about it because I'd always been one of the taller ones in my grade too, but I never displayed as much confidence as my younger sister. I don't remember standing up as straight or holding my head up as high as Lila always had.

I remembered well after I should have that Ransom was

probably standing there waiting to be introduced. But when I looked up from Lila and Sawyer, I saw Ransom already over by my dad and Rita. They were about six feet away, standing by the table that was ready with paper plates, plastic silverware, and long rolls.

"I'll talk to you guys in a couple of minutes," I told Lila and Sawyer, and when I managed to pry their bodies from me, I went to join Ransom. It was bad enough I'd left him on his own for any time at all.

I approached my dad like I might a stray animal who might be rabid. Dennis Peterson typically had a stern, no-nonsense demeanor that anyone who encountered him could sense immediately. But when I'd spoken to him about the trip, he'd sounded different. I hoped he hadn't been luring me in with a false sense of security.

"Hi, Dad," I said with a smile that didn't quite leave.

"Hey, Tater Tot."

I cringed every time I heard the name Lila had given me when she was four. Coming from my dad, it always sounded even more ridiculous.

I leaned in to give him a big hug, and he wrapped me up into his large body like I'd done to Lila and Sawyer. I wondered if I'd always feel like this in his arms. Small. Protected. Loved. Because even though my dad could be demanding and a little bit overprotective, even from hundreds of miles away, when it came down to it, I was his little girl and he was my dad. I knew deep down that he only wanted what he felt was best for me. Even if it wasn't always what *I* thought was best.

Once my dad let me go, I gave Rita a hug also. "So you met Ransom, I guess?"

"We did," my dad answered. "We haven't really had a

chance to talk yet, but he came over and introduced himself to us right away, so he passed level one." He turned to Ransom. "Congratulations."

I could tell Ransom wasn't quite sure how to respond because his mouth opened before any words came out of it. "Thank you?" he said, clearly unsure of whether my father had been serious.

"Don't worry about him," Rita told Ransom. "He's harmless."

"Absolutely," my dad said. "They confiscated my shotgun at airport security."

It had been my dad's attempt at humor, but there had also been some truth to it. He owned a few guns—a fact he never hid from any boy I brought to the house. The tradition had begun in middle school. Adam Kirkfield's mom hadn't been too happy to hear that someone had "threatened" her seventh-grade son when he'd come over to work on a science project.

It'd become kind of a family joke after that, but my dad was the only one who considered it funny.

Until Ransom, that is. Because he laughed. Loudly actually. "You shoot?" he asked my dad, who surprisingly let his arms relax from where they'd been crossed over his broad chest.

"I do," he said. "Only ranges, though. Hunting was never really my thing. You?"

"Only if you count water guns. Real ones scare the hell out of me, to be honest."

"Fair enough. What are you interested in, then?" He paused long enough to catch my eye before he added, "Besides my daughter?"

"I'm gonna go get the lunch meat and potato salad from

inside," Rita said, already heading toward the sliding door. She guided the kids inside with her under the guise that she needed their help carrying some of the condiments and drinks.

"Dad, please." My voice was hushed in a way that was both embarrassed for and by him simultaneously. I knew he'd eventually grill Ransom. I just didn't think it would be so soon. "Can we at least wait until we've eaten before you play Twenty Uncomfortable Questions with my boyfriend?"

Ransom laughed at that, but my dad didn't look too pleased. "It's okay," Ransom said. "I have lots of interests." He went on to tell him about how his love of football had led him to pursue a graduate degree in sports medicine and how he enjoyed helping the kids at Safe Haven.

My dad nodded along and gave the occasional generic comment, but he didn't seem overly impressed. And why would he be? When it came down to it, in my dad's mind, Ransom was just a college jock earning little more than minimum wage babysitting kids at an after-school program. I hoped with time, he'd realize what I knew: Ransom Holt was so much more than that.

RANSOM

Somehow I'd managed to survive not only meeting some of Taylor's family for the first time, but I'd gotten through an entire meal with them. Though it had only been a quick lunch of sandwiches and typical sides before we hit the beach, a part of me had been worried that her dad might tell me not to bother unpacking because he'd already purchased my ticket home. Instead, he'd asked me some questions—which were thankfully ones I was comfortable answering—before telling us about their vacation so far.

They'd gotten down here a few days ago and had mostly played it pretty low-key so far because Lila and Sawyer wanted to wait until Taylor and I got her to do the "really fun stuff," as Sawyer had called it, like parasailing and Jet Skiing. I wasn't sure they'd let an eight-year-old Jet Ski, but what did I know? I'd never done either of those things.

But the beach? Those I'd been to. Though I hadn't exactly been to one as beautiful as this one. The sand was softer and whiter than most, and since we were on the Gulf Coast, the water was as warm as it was calm.

But as relaxing as all of it was, I couldn't let *myself* relax. Whether it was my insecurity about Mr. Peterson judging my every move or my promise to commit a federal felony a few days after our return home looming over me, I wasn't sure. But either way, it seemed impossible for me to sit still.

Taylor was sitting next to me on a low beach chair, the back reclined so her face could take in as much sun as possible. She'd been quiet for a while, sunglasses on, not reading a book or talking. From what I could tell, she hadn't even moved in over a half hour.

"Wanna go play catch in the water?" I asked with the enthusiasm of a child begging to go out for ice cream after a tee ball game.

Taylor jolted at the question, and I almost laughed.

"What?" Slow and quiet, her voice sounded almost groggy.

"Were you asleep?"

She let her head tilt to the side so she could stare at me through her sunglasses for a moment before finally pulling them up. "Maybe."

"Really?"

"Yes. Really."

"How can you sleep here?"

"Um...because it's a vacation." She straightened her head again and pulled her sunglasses back down.

That was when I realized I probably hadn't ever fallen asleep outside. I'd never been camping, even in a tent in the backyard, and whenever I'd gone to a pool or beach I'd been with friends, probably doing stupid shit that didn't involve sitting quietly. "So is that a no to having a catch?"

"I'll play!" Sawyer said, already tossing down the shovel he'd been using to dig a big hole.

"Me too!" Lila said. "Taylor's never any fun," she teased.

"I heard that," Taylor said.

"You were supposed to," Lila replied, mimicking her sister's singsongy inflection.

"Jeez," Taylor said, "when did you get so sassy?"

"When hasn't she been?" The comment came from Taylor's father, and it earned a laugh from everyone except Lila herself.

Mr. Peterson had gotten up to adjust the angle of the umbrella so he could get a little more shade for himself and Rita, but he stopped what he was doing so he could reach down to grab the yellow ball the kids had brought. Once he tossed it to Sawyer, I jogged toward the ocean with the kids.

We spent the next twenty minutes or so trying to see who could skip the ball across the water best. I would've liked to have said that I let Lila win, but that would've been a lie that wasn't worth telling. Considering I'd been an athlete all my life and played college ball, losing to a ten-year-old-girl felt a little embarrassing, but I'd had too much fun to care.

It also didn't escape me that I'd decided to spend what could've been a lazy day in the sun by instead playing a game with two elementary-school children. I was sure Taylor would tease me about it later since I'd basically done the same thing at my family reunion. It was almost a shame Hudson wasn't pregnant, because I would've made a damn good uncle.

And despite my best effort to suppress it, I let a thought creep into my brain that felt as unfamiliar as it was true: maybe one day I'd make a pretty good dad.

Chapter Thirteen

RANSOM

"Ouch! Can you be gentler?"

"I *am* being gentle," Taylor said, but every time she touched my skin, it felt like it was going to fall off my body. I hadn't been this burned since . . . well, probably ever. "You should've listened to me when I told you to put on more sunscreen after you got out of the water. The Florida sun is different."

"How can it be different? It's the same sun. And I lived right over the Florida border for years," I reminded her. "It's not like I'm not used to it."

"You weren't baking in the sun for almost two days straight, though, because you didn't live near the beach."

It was true, though I didn't want to admit she'd been right. Taylor's dad had rented Jet Skis in the morning, and we'd taken turns on those before eating a quick lunch and then relaxing on the beach for a few more hours. My skin had been exposed to the sun's rays for way longer than I'd been used to.

"The aloe will help soon. Just let me put it on. It's a few seconds of pain, and then it'll start feeling cool."

"Says who?" I tried not to wince when she hit the spot just above my waistline. Guess I'd missed that spot completely.

"The bottle," she replied.

"I hope you're right. Otherwise the company is gonna get a very angry letter once I can use my hands again."

As much as it stung, I was glad Rita had brought it—though she'd done so in case the kids got burned, not because her stepdaughter's twenty-five-year-old boyfriend was a dumbass. If Rita hadn't brought any, I was sure Taylor would've gone to the store to get some for me. Which would've made me feel like a complete fucking asshole, but the thought of putting a shirt on right now and going to the store was about as appealing as pulling off my fingernails one by one with a rusty pair of long-nose pliers.

"You gonna be good to go out to dinner later?" Taylor asked after finishing my back. She hopped up on the edge of the jacuzzi tub and raised her eyes at me.

"Yeah. Yeah, totally. I'll be fine." I hoped anyway. There was no way I was staying home when Mr. Peterson had invited us to a nice restaurant right on the water for the last night of our visit. "I just need to stay out of the sun for a few hours." At least the sun wouldn't be as strong by the time we went to dinner.

"Okay," Taylor said, not sounding completely convinced. "But honestly, if it's too painful, you can stay home. My dad'll understand."

I didn't have to know Taylor's father well to know he definitely *wouldn't* understand his daughter's boyfriend declining a dinner he was paying for because his skin hurt him. As long as I still had it on my body, I'd be there.

TAYLOR

There was no way Ransom should be going to dinner. He'd spent the last couple of hours hiding out in his room shirtless because even the idea of something touching his skin caused him significant pain.

He'd been worried about what my family would think if he wasn't socializing with them, but I'd assured him that after the beach everyone was doing their own thing anyway. Sawyer was playing video games, Lila was FaceTiming friends, Rita was napping before she had to get ready for the night, and my dad had retreated to a spare room to get some work done.

"You really don't have to go," I told him after watching him wince as he slid on a pink shirt like he was about sixty years older than he was.

"I'm going. I'm fine," he said, probably aware that he didn't sound very convincing. But I appreciated his effort. I watched him button up his shirt and then roll up the sleeves carefully. I wasn't sure if the pink made him look more burned or less, but there was no sense mentioning it. His arms and neck were bright red, and his face mostly matched except for the circles around his eyes from his sunglasses and a few spots on his cheeks that must've gotten a little extra sunscreen.

Even crimson, Ransom was still sexy as hell. Maybe it was the way his blond hair flopped over his eyes until he tamed it or how his chest peeked through the top of his shirt because he'd left the top two buttons open. Or that his fitted charcoal shorts hugged him in all the right places.

His whole life was a perfect contrast—a balance that the universe had blended into a man who was as strong as he was sensitive and as carefree as he was focused.

I didn't know how I got lucky enough to have a man like Ransom love me, but I hoped he wouldn't come to his senses and realize he could probably do a hell of a lot better.

"I love you," I said, looking him deeply in the eyes and wrapping my arms around his solid body.

"I love you too," he replied. "And I never thought I'd say this, but can you hold off on touching me for a while?"

Pulling away from him quickly, I said, "Oh, God, I'm sorry."

"It's fine," Ransom said with a little laugh. And then, "Hey, you okay? You seem . . . off or something."

I shrugged and sat down on the edge of the bed, the weight of everything suddenly settling into every cell of my body.

"I guess so. I just . . . I wish we could just have a normal relationship. You know, one that doesn't involve figuring out how to avoid jail time." I tried to make my voice light, but Ransom knew as well as I did that the majority of the time we'd spent together had been anything but easy.

What should've been a beautiful day had been clouded by thoughts of stalkers, accidental death, and the looming burglary that would hopefully get rid of both Brad and the bookies who were after Hudson once and for all.

"I'm sure eventually we'll live a life without crime," Ransom said. "But for now, at least we know that when our relationship is tested, we'll pass with flying colors. Makes typical worries like meeting your girlfriend's dad seem like nothing." Ransom shot me a casual wink, revealing his insecurity about being here. But I loved that he was putting on a brave face for me.

"Well, you're already past the meeting stage, so you have

nothing to worry about." My dad seemed to like Ransom as much as I'd imagined he might like any guy I brought on a family trip.

"True. But your dad hasn't properly questioned me about what my intentions are and whatever else fathers are supposed to harass their daughter's boyfriend about. And there's no way he's gonna let us leave tomorrow without a thorough interrogation."

"Maybe he's saving that for the first time you go to his house. You know, so he has access to the shotgun he mentioned." It was a joke, but Ransom's expression told me he thought there might be some truth to it. "Seriously, though, we've been here for two days. If he was planning to give you a hard time, he would've done it already."

He seemed to ponder that theory for a moment before his shoulders relaxed a bit and he showed a hint of a smile. "You think so?"

"Totally. Besides, we have enough to worry about without adding my dad's opinion of you to the stress soup we've been cooking."

Ransom stopped putting the gel in his hair and looked at me in the mirror. "I feel like I should probably tell you that your comment wasn't nearly as comforting as you probably wanted it to be."

"Right. Yeah, I realized that immediately after I said it."

RANSOM

Somehow I managed to make myself look and feel somewhat normal, given the circumstances at least. Sure, I resembled a tomato with hair, but other than that, I felt significantly better than I had most of the day. And once I put clothes on, I didn't look quite as red.

It still felt like my skin was being burned with an iron when Taylor touched it, but I tried to look at that as a blessing in disguise. Normally, seeing Taylor in a bikini for the majority of the day would mean I wouldn't be able to keep my hands off her at night.

But the third-degree burns I'd suffered at the hands—or rays—of the Florida sun had been a special kind of cock block. And since Taylor's dad never had any intention of letting us share a room, Taylor had been sleeping in the other twin bed in Lila's room, while I had a room with a queen bed and bathroom to myself. They were the most comfortable accommodations I'd experienced in a while.

"You look like a lobster dipped in ketchup," Taylor's dad said to me when we arrived at the restaurant.

They hadn't seen Taylor or me since earlier that afternoon, and if Taylor's dad's reaction was any indication of how I looked, I didn't look as "normal" as I'd hoped.

"Dad!" Taylor said, obviously embarrassed and annoyed.

"What?" he asked, shrugging like it was no big deal. "Anyone care to disagree?"

Taylor's sister spoke up before anyone else. "I think Ransom looks handsome," she said, blushing almost to my current shade.

Sawyer laughed. "Handsome Ransom," he sang mockingly. "Lila has a crush on Ransom."

"I do not!" Somehow she grew a darker shade of red, though I still had her beat. It made me feel terrible even though I hadn't been at fault.

"Dad," Taylor scolded again. "Look what you started."

I hoped no one knew how awkward I felt, because I'd tried to remain casual, but having my girlfriend's father tease me about my sunburn and her kid sister tell me in front of her whole family that she found me attractive wasn't really the way I'd envisioned beginning the night.

We were standing outside waiting for a table to be ready, and I was happy when Rita looked at her phone and announced that we were ready to be seated. Hopefully we could move on to other topics.

We followed her to the host station to check in, and when the hostess grabbed menus, she led us to our table by the water.

"Which one of you is gonna marry Ransom?" Taylor's brother teased.

"Sawyer," Taylor said. "Stop already."

"Okay, everyone," Rita said. "That's enough. Let's try to have a normal family dinner." She looked sternly at Sawyer, then to Taylor, on to Lila, and even her own husband, who put up his hands in surrender.

I wondered if this was always how things got settled in the Peterson household. From how Taylor described the dynamics, her dad was always the one calling the shots. The overprotective hard-ass no one contradicted. But so far, he hadn't shown that side of himself. At least not to me.

Once bread made it to the table, Sawyer's and Lila's mouths were too busy eating to do anything else with them, which left all the conversation to the rest of us.

I hadn't really sat down with Taylor's dad and stepmom since I'd gotten here. Not like this, anyway. We'd gone to the beach and grilled dinner the previous night at home, but those times had been filled with swimming and playing catch or shuffling in and out of the house while everyone filled their plates and ate wherever they felt comfortable.

Mostly, the kids had taken their dinners to the small game room that housed various video game consoles, and Dennis and Rita had retreated to the lower deck outside their bedroom.

At the time, I'd thought it was nice that everyone kind of did their own thing so we all got the chance to relax on vacation, but I remembered how when we'd stayed with Matt and Melissa and played Parcheesi, Taylor had mentioned that her family never played games like that together. I wondered if the distance last night had been the rule instead of the exception.

"So," Rita said, "what should we discuss?"

Taylor's dad rolled the cuffs of his shirt before grabbing a roll and buttering it. He raised an eyebrow at her as he looked up from his roll with only his eyes. "Why do you always ask that when we go out?" Then he turned to me. "She always asks that, even when it's just the two of us."

"Just making conversation." Rita smiled politely at her husband.

"Actually, you're asking *other* people to make conversation because you can't think of anything to talk about."

I wasn't sure if Dennis was serious when he'd said it, but his smirk and Rita's light elbow to his side told me he was messing with his wife. This dude was a tough read. Even Taylor looked unsure of how to react.

"Fine, smartass," Rita said to him, causing Sawyer's head to jerk up from the focus on his roll and Lila to pause just before her straw hit her lips. "I'll do the talking."

Mr. Peterson took a sip of the malbec he'd ordered for the four of us and let it settle in his mouth for a moment before swallowing. "In my defense, I tried to talk and you silenced me."

"Your comment to Ransom was a little inappropriate, don't you think?"

"No. I do not think," he said simply. "Inappropriate would've been saying..." He swirled his wineglass around as he thought. "He looked like a lobster dipped in *blood.*"

"Oh my God," Rita said. She covered her eyes for a second before putting her hands on the sides of her face and rubbing her temples. "I'm so incredibly sorry."

"It's fine," I told her, almost laughing.

"See," Mr. Peterson said, gesturing toward me without putting down his wine. "The blood image is way more inappropriate. Ketchup is ... almost cute."

"I'd never try lobster," Sawyer announced, "but if I had to, I'd definitely put ketchup on it. Everything's better with ketchup."

I gave him a firm nod. "I totally agree."

"So," Rita said with a sigh that made me think a subject change was coming, "how were final exams, Taylor? Did you even have them with the online classes? How does that all work?"

I wondered if that was still a sore subject because her dad had adamantly objected to her finishing the year so far from campus, but I assumed since Rita clearly wanted to lessen any awkwardness that she wouldn't have brought up something she thought would make Taylor uncomfortable.

I looked at Taylor, taking in her usually smooth features to see if they stiffened at Rita's question, but if it bothered her at all, even I couldn't tell.

"Finals were good, I guess. I passed them all." She smiled

in a way that made me wonder if she was being humble or was just reluctant to elaborate. She'd done more than passed her exams. She'd earned As on all except for one, and that one had been an A minus. "The classes are online, but the tests are all taken at a testing center and proctored."

"Good," Mr. Peterson said firmly. "Long as everything's on the up-and-up, because any law schools you applied to will see that you finished your last semester online."

I wondered if that was even true. From what Taylor had told me, the courses were the same as the ones offered on campus—same content, expectations, and assessments. They were even taught by the same professors. I imagined that since virtual classes had been around for a while, colleges, especially good ones, were able to deliver the instruction seamlessly.

Taylor didn't reply, so her dad continued. "How's all that going? You hear back from any yet?"

Taylor shook her head and then reached for a roll.

Lila spoke up excitedly. "Dad said you got an A on your lawyer test." I could tell she was thinking hard about something, but she didn't spend much time in silence. "That one with all the letters. I forget what it's called."

She looked to her dad, who replied with, "The LSATs."

"Yeah, the LSATs. Was it an A or an A plus that you got on it? Was it hard? It was, wasn't it? When do you get to be a lawyer? Does that mean you get to send people to jail?"

Taylor smiled, her cheeks turning a light pink at Lila's words. Clearly her little sister thought the world of Taylor, and of course I could see why. It warmed me to watch their interactions. Or maybe that was still only my sunburn.

"Which question should I answer first?" Taylor said, leaning in toward Lila, who was seated to the other side of her.

Lila thought for a second again before answering. "Um, how hard was it?"

"Really, really difficult. I worked incredibly hard in high school and then college and then studied my tail off, and it was *still* the hardest test I've ever taken."

The server returned, causing Taylor to stop talking for a moment so the appetizers could be placed down.

"But you got an A still?" Lila grabbed a coconut shrimp from the plate in the center of the table and dipped it into the orange sauce next to it.

Rita handed her a plate and gave her a nonverbal correction that even I picked up on. Lila put a spoonful of the sauce on her plate and stabbed two more shrimp with her fork.

"The LSATs don't really use letter grades like regular school. But I did do pretty well."

"Well enough to have a shot at some of the top schools she's had her eye on." Taylor's dad sounded so proud of his daughter, and though he could definitely be hard on her, I had no doubt he was thrilled about her accomplishments. Even if he didn't have a say in some of them anymore. "You get those in first like I suggested, Tay?" He poured some more wine into Rita's glass before picking up his soup spoon.

I took a bite of the salad I'd ordered, happy to be a spectator in the conversation and not a participant. Taylor hadn't spoken much to me about the specifics of her law school applications, and I hadn't asked her much about them. Not only did I not want my opinion—if I even had one—to influence her choices about her future, but we'd both been a little preoccupied with Brad's almost murder and the recent task of executing a die-cast car heist that even Bonnie and Clyde might have trouble pulling off.

Taylor finished chewing the small bite of bread she'd just broken off. Then she smoothed her napkin on her lap before answering. "Most schools don't have application deadlines until the spring."

"I know that. But why wait? If you get into Stanford, you'll know you won't need to apply anywhere else and you can concentrate on other things."

Like stealing from your stalker's father.

He continued. "You'll have to find an apartment and possibly a roommate. You might even want to get out there early and get a part-time job there so you can get to know the area and meet some people."

"Can I come see your new apartment?" Lila asked excitedly.

I'd been watching Taylor as her father spoke, trying to read her expression but failing. I had no idea what she was thinking, and that realization caused an emotion to creep up inside me that I couldn't recognize either. Anxiety maybe. Sadness. But those were feelings I'd reserved for myself, not for Taylor, so I'd never share them with her. She'd accomplished so much, and I'd be an asshole to stand in the way of her dream school because I was a selfish dick who didn't want his girlfriend to leave him.

"Sure, Li. Of course you can come." Taylor put an arm around her younger sister and squeezed her close. "When I find out where I'll be and everything, we'll make sure we plan something."

"Stanford's a little far to visit, though, Lila," her dad said. "And so is Chicago, which is where your sister will probably go if Stanford doesn't happen. Unless it was on a longer break from school and Mom or I went too, I think you'd have to wait until Taylor comes home to see her. I don't like the idea of you taking a plane across the country alone."

"I'm ten," Lila reminded him proudly. "And I'll be eleven by the time I go."

Mr. Peterson raised his eyebrows at his daughter. "That argument isn't as convincing as you probably think it is."

"It's because I'm a girl, isn't it? If I were your son and not your daughter, I bet I'd be allowed to go."

Sawyer opened his mouth, but Rita silenced him before he could get any words out. "You're not going either." Then she looked at her daughter. "Now isn't the best time to discuss this, but I agree with Dad. I'm definitely not putting you on a plane and letting you fly five hours without adult supervision. Boy or girl, a solo cross-country flight is not happening for either of you."

Both kids looked immediately disappointed by her words—Lila because she wanted to visit her sister, and Sawyer because he probably just thought the idea of going anywhere without his parents sounded cool...especially if his older sister wasn't allowed.

"Hey," Taylor said, turning toward her brother and sister. "You know what? I might not be going too far after all." Her tone sounded hopeful, like the words were meant to cheer up Lila and Sawyer.

"Really?" Lila's eyes opened wide and lit up like Taylor was a puppeteer controlling the lids.

"Really. I might stay closer to where I am now, which isn't *that* far. It's within driving distance easily."

"Taylor," her dad started, but she stopped him before he could say anything else.

"Dad, don't," she said quickly but then drew in a deep

breath and released it slowly. Surprisingly, Mr. Peterson was quiet. He exchanged glances with his wife just as Taylor and I had exchanged glances a moment ago. "I've given this a lot of thought."

"You gave Stanford and Chicago a lot of thought too."

"I'm allowed to change my decisions."

"Not this one because—"

"Let her talk," Rita said, putting a hand on her husband's hand.

I wanted to hear what Taylor had to say too, but a dinner that had barely begun wasn't the ideal place for it. If the conversation got heated, I doubted we would get up and leave like we'd done after my family reunion.

This restaurant was definitely nicer than that one had been, and I also figured my family handled conflict differently than Taylor's. I hoped I hadn't entered the tenth ring of hell by agreeing to a formal family dinner with the Petersons, because I had little chance of escaping anytime soon. We'd ordered our entrees, which hadn't been cheap, and they hadn't even arrived yet.

Taylor had been quiet, most likely contemplating the best way to explain why her plans had changed.

She may as well just point to me.

"I know what you're thinking," Taylor began. "It's because of a boy."

That was when she looked at me, and I wasn't sure whether to smile or apologize. I decided to do neither.

"But I love that boy," she continued.

At that, I felt the need to at least mouth *I love you too.* Though I'm sure her family had seen it, it had felt wrong to say it out loud. Like I'd be taking up space in the air that was reserved for Taylor's words.

When I looked back at her dad and stepmom, I could've sworn I saw the end of her father's eye roll. "So you're just… what? Going to throw away a dream you've had for years because of something that's only existed for a couple of months?"

"Some*one*." Taylor grabbed my hand from where I'd had it on my lap and brought it up to rest on the table between our plates—a nonverbal display of our feelings for each other to complement our words. "But Ransom isn't the only reason I'm rethinking going far away. So much has happened in the last couple of months, I can't even explain it all."

"Try," her dad said. Then he looked at me. "If my daughter tells me she's pregnant, I'm not even giving you a head start to the parking lot."

Whatever Taylor was going to reveal, it had to be easier for Mr. Peterson to hear than learning that his bright, driven daughter would have to postpone her dreams because some guy he'd met a few days ago had knocked her up.

At least I have one thing working in my favor.

"I've been honest with you," she said. "But I haven't told you everything. And I guess now I feel like you deserve to know, because while where I go to school and what I do with my life is ultimately my decision, I owe a lot of my success to you." She looked at her stepmother. "You too, Rita. It was always tough not having my mom around all the time, but you were always there for me when I needed you." It made Rita smile, and I thought her eyes looked a little teary, though none fell. "Even when I didn't want you there," Taylor added apologetically.

"That's nice of you to say," Mr. Peterson said, "but get to the part where you tell us whatever you intentionally left out before."

"Okay," she said with a deep breath. "You remember what I told you about that guy Brad, right? The one who was"—she glanced at Sawyer and Lila—"bothering me."

"Of course." Mr. Peterson's expression changed then, shifting to something that fell somewhere between anger and fear.

I recognized it on him because I'd felt it myself so many times.

"Well, things with him were worse than I told you. I didn't want you to worry any more than you needed to. We thought we had it handled."

Our server approached the table from behind then, right as Taylor said, "But he attacked me, and we thought Ransom murdered him."

"I'll come back," the server said, already turning around to leave.

"He attacked you?" Mr. Peterson gritted out, his voice harsh and protective. "I'll kill that motherfucker myself."

"Dennis," Rita said, glancing at the kids and then at Taylor. "Maybe we should continue this conversation back at the house."

"No. She's explaining this now. The kids can go play in the game room."

They sat up straighter at the suggestion of getting to play the few arcade games available in the lobby. Mr. Peterson had already begun removing his wallet, and as soon as he handed Lila a twenty, they were gone.

Once Sawyer and Lila were out of sight and Taylor seemed sure they couldn't hear her, she began at the beginning: how Brad had been more of a threat than any of us had realized and how someone else's murder had led us to believe that we'd left Brad for dead.

Taylor's dad and Rita asked a few questions as Taylor spoke, including the obvious one: "Where is Brad now?" Her dad looked at me when he said it, and I wondered if he wished I'd finished what I'd started. Even if I went to jail for it, I was no one to this man. The only thing that mattered was that his daughter would be safe.

"I'm not sure," I told him. It was the truth. I *didn't* know where Brad was. Not at that moment anyway.

I'd hoped Taylor would leave out the threats Brad made to me and to Hudson, and I was relieved when it seemed like she didn't have any plans to share that part. Because while there was always a chance Brad would come after Taylor again—a truth I'd avoided thinking about unless I had to—right now he seemed more concerned with getting his stupid car and using Hudson as some sort of collateral.

"It's why I'd like to stay close to my friends. The idea of going someplace new, starting a whole new life without anyone I know . . . it honestly scares me."

"You're right," Mr. Peterson told Taylor. "You shouldn't go far away to school. You should move back home immediately."

"So you can do what? Keep me locked in a house you're barely in yourself because you're working all the time? Or so you can involve Lila and Sawyer in something that could potentially be dangerous? No way. It's not happening.

"That's why I'm telling you this," she added. "Not only do you deserve to know, but I need you to understand why I'm choosing to stay close to where I'm most comfortable. Where I'm safest. There are plenty of great schools I could easily commute to from where I am now. And I have Ransom and Sophia and Brody and a bunch of other friends who are part of our little Scooby Gang, and they won't let anything happen to me."

"Jesus," Rita said softly, dropping her face into her hands. I didn't know her well enough to guess whether it was out of frustration or fear. Once she looked up again, she turned to her husband. "And you didn't think it was important to share any of this with me when you knew some of it?"

"I didn't think you needed to know. Not that you don't deserve to or that I wanted to keep anything from you, but I didn't know the extent of it, and Taylor assured me she'd handle it."

"She's a twenty-one-year-old college girl, not a Green Beret." Rita sounded more rattled than I thought she would be considering we'd kept his current involvement in our lives from them. But I guess I'd underestimated her motherly concern for Taylor.

I was afraid for my sister, who was an adult. I couldn't imagine being a parent and hearing all this.

"I *know* that," Mr. Peterson replied, his tone just as full of stress as Rita's had been a moment ago. "But again, I had no idea things had gotten that serious."

"It'll be okay," Taylor said, her words sounding meaningless and empty. I assumed that Mr. and Mrs. Peterson wouldn't be convinced by the platitude either.

Mr. Peterson stared at her like he was appraising her sanity. "You said that last time, and then he attacked you in an alley." He paused a moment before looking at me. "If you hadn't been there . . ." He let his gaze fall to the table and didn't finish his sentence. He didn't need to.

None of us wanted to think about the what-ifs, but they existed anyway. What if Taylor had told her dad the full truth that time when she'd talked to him about Brad? What if I hadn't followed her out of the bar that night and heard her scream? What if Brad had finished what he'd started before I was able to find them?

But the reality was that Taylor was safe now. And really, that was all that mattered.

"I'll always do everything I can to protect her," I said. "I did before and I always will."

Taylor smiled, though it was so faint I wasn't sure if anyone else noticed.

"I promise," I added, more to her than to anyone else.

I hoped they knew how sincerely I'd meant that. If there was another way to get Brad out of the picture for good, I'd take it. But if he went after Taylor again—or Hudson, for that matter—I'd made up my mind about what I'd do. Regardless of the consequence on my own life, nothing would stop me from protecting the people I loved.

"You goddamn better," Mr. Peterson said.

Chapter Fourteen

TAYLOR

"I can't believe we're leaving here in a few hours," Ransom said. "The idea of going back to someplace freezing definitely isn't on my list of priorities." He put a hand around my shoulder and pulled me in close to him as we watched the sunrise.

We'd gotten up early to watch it rise and have coffee on the deck one last time before exchanging presents and driving back to the airport for our noon flight, when we'd finally be forced to trade paradise and orange sunrises for possible jail time and orange jumpsuits.

"I'm glad you had a good time," I said, snuggling into him a bit more. The last thing I wanted to do was ruin the beautiful morning by clouding it with negative words. Besides, I doubted Ransom had forgotten that we were heading home to worse things than the cold. "I guess the kids will be up pretty soon, so we can give everyone their gifts. I know Sawyer and Lila will be excited."

"What did you get them?"

"We," I corrected him. Naturally, Ransom hadn't gotten

them any of his own gifts because one, he didn't know them, and two, I'd volunteered to put his name on the gift so they'd be from both of us. There was no point in the two of us spending more money. And though I got my dad and Rita each something, I knew they weren't planning to open it until Christmas Day, which was still two days from now. "I got Sawyer a hoverboard and Lila some clothes and a manicure set that has the same files and buffers they use at nail salons."

Ransom seemed to be processing the last bit of information before deciding it wouldn't get him anywhere. "Hoverboard sounds cool. And now I know why you looked like you'd packed for a trip around the world and not for a long weekend."

Ransom pulled me closer and took a sip of his coffee. We were quiet as we watched the sun come up the rest of the way and listened to the small waves gently pulling up onto the sand. We enjoyed about twenty minutes of peace before I heard footsteps running inside the house.

"Sawyer, hang on a minute," I heard Rita call from inside. "I don't know where they are. They didn't leave yet, though, so calm down."

A few seconds later, I heard the French door to the deck open, and I turned to see Lila standing barefoot in her pajamas.

To break what was left of the silence, she turned toward the inside of the house and yelled, "I found them!" Then she ran outside toward us and wrapped her arms around my neck from behind. "We thought we'd be up before you."

Sawyer then rushed out, begging to unwrap whatever it was we brought him.

Rita and my dad followed shortly after, bringing out a carafe of coffee and some bagels and cream cheese.

"Anyone hungry yet?" Rita placed the food on the table and took a seat nearby.

My dad topped off Ransom's coffee and took a look at mine, but I declined.

"Please," Sawyer whined. "Can't we do presents first and then eat?" Without waiting for an answer, he ran back inside, yelling, "I'll get their presents!"

"Guess that's a no to eating first," Rita said.

As soon as he was gone, Lila stole his seat and, sounding more like a preteen than a ten-year-old, muttered, "He's so embarrassing."

My dad was buttering a bagel for himself. "Well, I'm going to eat my breakfast."

Sawyer came running back a minute or so later, his arms full of presents that looked like they'd been wrapped by him with possibly a little help from Lila. I doubted Rita had a hand in it because they were still a little rough around the edges, and I knew my dad hated to wrap anything at all, which was why when he bought Rita any gifts, he always shopped at stores that would gift wrap for him.

"Those aren't all for us, are they, Sawyer?" I asked.

He held two big boxes in one arm and was attempting to balance at least three in his other arm. I wasn't sure how he even ended up opening the door without dropping any of them, but the kid would be damn good at waiting tables one day.

"Yeah, but some Mom and Dad bought. Me and Lila don't have much money."

"Lila and I," Rita corrected him.

"You didn't have to spend anything on us," I told him. "Just being able to see everyone has been more than enough. You guys are the kids. People should be getting you presents, not the other way around. What was on your Christmas list for Santa this year?"

"He knows," Lila said.

"Knows what?" I had no idea what she was talking about, and I looked at Ransom.

He just shrugged like he didn't have a clue either.

It was my dad who supplied the answer, his mouth somewhat full with an everything bagel. "Secret's out. No more pretending a guy in a big red suit is the one getting these kids all the fancy gifts. It's about time we can take full credit."

"Don't be such a Scrooge, Dennis."

"I'm not being a Scrooge. But we may have had a gap of a couple of years in there right around when Lila was born when we didn't have to worry about accidentally using the same paper to wrap the presents from us as we did from Santa. It's too much anxiety."

Rita shook her head and laughed, pouring herself some more orange juice from the pitcher. "Well, since I can't remember the last time *you* wrapped any of the kids' gifts, I'm keeping the rest of the Xanax for me."

My dad let out an exaggerated laugh. "Like there's any left in the first place."

"Okay," I said, hoping to emphasize my annoyance by drawing out the word. "Can we save the prescription painkiller conversation for later?"

"Xanax isn't a painkiller," my dad grumbled.

"That distinction isn't as important as you think it is," I told him.

"Here," Lila said, thankfully pulling our attention to the festivities again. She grabbed the medium-sized gift off the pile that Sawyer had placed down on the table. "Open this one first!"

The box was heavier than I expected it to be when she set it on my lap. She was smiling at me, and I could sense the excitement buzzing from her.

"Is it something you made at school?" I asked.

"Not at school, but I did make it. Kind of. I designed it online. Open it."

I smiled back at her before tearing at the snowflake paper and trying to mirror the same excitement she exhibited.

Ransom leaned forward next to me, seemingly in anticipation of what was in the box.

I opened the lid, and from the top it looked like some sort of statue or something. I lifted it out of the box and, on closer inspection, recognized it was a bobblehead of me. Long blond hair, rosy cheeks, tight jeans, and a cropped cream shirt.

It had a heavy solid base like a trophy that displayed a plaque that said, "Best Big Sister." I was between laughing out loud at how ridiculous it was—because the damn thing looked just like me with a large head and small body in a cartoonish sort of way—and pulling Lila into a hug because the idea was so incredibly sweet. I opted for the latter.

"Li, this is adorable! And so funny! I'll display it proudly in my apartment where everyone can see it."

Ransom looked closer, and I handed it to him so he could see it better. "Aww, a tiny Taylor. This really does look like you," he said with a laugh.

"I'm glad you like it," Lila said. "I wasn't really sure what to get you, but I figured it was kind of like an Oscar or something."

Lila had always been pretty athletic, but I, on the other hand, hadn't played many sports growing up. And while my dad and Rita's house held several of Lila's trophies and awards from various sporting events, I couldn't remember a time when I'd ever done anything to deserve one.

And that included this time. Because the more I thought about it, the more I realized that I wasn't the best big sister. I hadn't been for a long time. Yes, it was normal at my age to go away to college and pursue my dreams, but I'd been so wrapped up in my own drama, I'd forgotten that I had a younger sister who looked up to me. And a brother too. And that made me feel like shit.

"Mine next!" Sawyer said. "The rest are from me."

I caught Lila rolling her eyes. "Quality over quantity."

"Whatever," Sawyer said, thrusting a gift my way.

"Jeez, Sawyer, you didn't have to get me all this."

My dad laughed before saying, "Well, wait until you open it up before you decide how much to thank him."

The first gift was a pair of socks covered in images of the face of our bulldog, Ace. They were actually really cute and warm, so though I'd definitely wear them, I couldn't promise I'd wear them out of the house.

The second gift was an Xbox controller that he told me would be mine when I came to visit so that we could play together. Though he quickly amended that to include Ransom also.

"You guys can take turns," he said.

"Nice, man. Thanks." Ransom seemed genuinely touched by the gesture, as if the offer had been symbolic of his acceptance into our family. At least by Sawyer.

My guess, since he took the controller from me and said he'd keep it at the house so we didn't forget it next time we visited, was that it was really a gift to himself. But it was the thought that counted.

Then there were two other gifts he made in school.

One was sweet—painted handprints of his in the shape of a Christmas tree, with fingerprints in different colors for ornaments. It was cute and my first official holiday decoration for my own apartment.

The last one was a piece of costume jewelry he'd no doubt bought at the Secret Santa shop at school. It was a silver necklace with a cherry charm that was made out of some kind of red stone or plastic made to look like rubies.

"Do you like it?" Sawyer asked.

I could hear his uncertainty in his voice, so I did my best to set his mind at ease by telling him how much I loved it and how pretty it was. I even had Ransom put it around my neck in front of everyone.

"I'll treasure it always," I told him. And I meant it.

I probably just won't wear it always.

RANSOM

Taylor and I had spent the remainder of the morning with her family, exchanging presents and eating breakfast, before we all headed out to take one last walk together on the beach.

I'd half expected Mr. Peterson to pull me aside at some point during the morning. I couldn't imagine he'd have nothing he wanted to say to me privately, so I'd been surprised when he hadn't approached me. But just as we were getting ready to leave and I was packing up the car to head out, he caught me under the guise of asking if I needed any help with our bags or anything.

"I think I'm just about done, actually," I said, placing the last few bags into the trunk of our rental. "Thanks, though."

Mr. Peterson nodded thoughtfully and then placed a hand on the roof of the car and faced me. I waited a moment for him to speak, but he didn't. He just kind of stood there, his eyes fixed on mine like an animal deciding whether another might be a threat to him.

"Thank you for coming," he said. The words sounded almost difficult to utter, and I could see why. I was sure the idea of inviting your daughter's boyfriend along on a family vacation didn't sound especially appealing.

"Yeah," I said. "Of course. Thank you and Rita so much for inviting me." I laughed nervously, reminding myself of my severe case of parental phobia that had obviously returned after being in remission for the majority of the weekend. "It was extremely generous of you to let me come along."

"Well, I missed my little girl. Her brother and sister missed her. Whatever would get her down here, I was willing to do."

That pretty much summed up why I'd been invited, and I knew that before he said it. But hearing the words... I wondered if he thought that I wouldn't have *let* Taylor leave to come down here for Christmas or if I'd have made her feel guilty about going. I hoped he knew me better than that by now, especially since Taylor had gotten out of a controlling relationship.

"I wouldn't have asked her to stay up there with me... if you hadn't invited me," I told him. "I would've encouraged her to see you guys." Despite the reunion with my bio family being a dumpster fire—or maybe *because* of that—I knew the importance of hanging on to a strong family unit when someone was lucky enough to have it. It's why I was working so hard to build that with Hudson.

I couldn't be sure because I didn't know him well, but the way Mr. Peterson scrunched up his eyebrows a little at my comment made me think he almost felt bad that he'd made me think that.

"I know," he said simply. "Whether I like it or not, my little girl isn't so little anymore. She makes her own decisions." He shook his head and laughed like the idea of it amused him. "Moving in with Sophia and finishing out the last year of her undergrad off-campus, not telling me the full story about Brad..." His expression grew sadder at that. "Then changing her plans for law school."

It sounded almost like an afterthought. "Taylor isn't someone who is easily influenced by other people's opinions," he continued. "Especially mine. The truth is it makes me proud that she's becoming independent and following the path of what she sees for herself. Taylor's smart in a way that I probably never gave her credit for, at least out loud. Deep down, I know I should trust her to make the right decision."

I was quiet for a moment before I couldn't help but say, "She'd probably like to hear all that."

Mr. Peterson laughed again, and this time a little more lightheartedly, before he said, "I'm not ready to put my tail between my legs just yet."

That made me laugh too.

"Plus, it's almost time for you to leave, and I can't let my daughter's new boyfriend fly thousands of miles away before we've had time to talk seriously."

I breathed in deeply, preparing for whatever might come out of his mouth next. He was a tough man to read, and even if he liked me just a little bit, I wasn't sure he'd ever let it show.

"I'm not one to mince words, so I'll be frank."

Oh, God.

"From what I can tell, you seem like a good guy. You risked your life and your future to keep my daughter safe, and you told me you're willing to do it again."

"I am, sir. I promised Sawyer and Lila I wouldn't let anyone hurt Taylor, and I'm making the same promise to you."

His soft exhale made me think that my promise provided him a bit of relief, which caused me to feel both happy because it meant he trusted me—even if he didn't have much of a choice not to—and scared as hell when I thought about what would happen if I broke that promise.

Not that I wasn't scared anyway.

"I appreciate that," Mr. Peterson said. "It's nice to have someone looking out for her." His normally hard features almost collapsed a little with his words. "I'm not sure if you're planning to have kids one day"—he looked at me but thankfully didn't wait for me to respond—"but I feel like I should warn you it's the hardest job there is out there."

I didn't doubt it.

"But it's also the most rewarding." There was a glimmer of light in his eyes I hadn't seen since I met him, as if he were reliving a memory he didn't frequently allow himself to revisit. "Which I guess is the only reason anyone would ever agree to take on such a demanding, exhausting job." He took his hand off the roof of the car and ran it through his graying hair. "God knows the pay's shit."

It was a good way to lighten the weight of the moment, and I think he knew it too. We laughed a little before he added, "And I meant what I said before. I appreciate you coming down. Not many guys would agree to stay a whole weekend with their girlfriend's family before ever meeting them."

"Clearly, I'm a special kind of stupid."

That made him laugh louder.

"Nah," he said. "Something tells me you're very self-deprecating, but stupid . . . ? Somehow I doubt that."

The moment didn't feel like it called for a response, so I simply smiled. Then Mr. Peterson put a hand on my shoulder and said, "It was nice meeting you, Ransom. I hope we'll see you again soon."

"Likewise."

I just hoped it wasn't at Taylor's trial for stealing something from her ex-douchefriend's parents' house.

Chapter Fifteen

TAYLOR

Once we were back at home, the next few days passed quickly. Filled with figuring out the logistics of how we would steal an item we hadn't even seen a picture of yet made the hours fly by, even though we were awake for most of them. By the time we were ready to head out to Brad's dad's house, we were as prepared as we could be, but the long car ride there had been filled mostly with silence and jitters.

At the start of the drive, Ransom and I tried to talk to each other, both of us probably thinking that attempting to make the drive as normal as possible would result in things actually *feeling* normal. But as we drove onto the highway, it seemed we silently agreed that no amount of small talk would make anything about the night seem small.

That feeling was confirmed when we pulled up to Brad's father's house—or rather, estate—and took a look around the grounds. Despite the cold weather, people seemed to be everywhere on the property. The yard held two large tents I assumed were heated, and there was a balcony above the entrance where a few men were smoking cigars.

The inside of the home was lit up throughout, making it easy to see all the people moving about—talking, drinking. The valet opened my door and took my hand to help me exit the Audi we'd rented for the night. It didn't seem wise to show up in Ransom's truck, both because it would stand out like a Sesame Street game of "One of These Things is Not Like the Other" and also because we didn't want to be seen leaving in a vehicle that was actually registered to one of us, should someone notice.

There were a million variables we couldn't plan for, but it seemed that we'd thought of everything. Or almost everything.

"How the hell are we going to conceal a two-foot-long model car when we leave? What if people are around?"

I sure as hell hoped Ransom had a plan for that, because my criminal brain cells had been consumed as quickly as beer at a frat party.

"I don't have that part sorted out just yet."

Surprisingly, he didn't seem too concerned about it, which either meant he was confident he'd come up with something once we got the lay of the land or he was damn good at pretending.

Once we were both out of the car, Ransom came around to my side and handed the valet the keys.

As Ransom took my arm in his, he leaned over and said, "Don't leave my side."

RANSOM

Getting into Palace Lacey had been easier than I'd expected.

It wouldn't have made sense for Brad to give us invitations that didn't get us into the party, but I couldn't shake the feeling that he might've done just that. Maybe he'd staged the whole theft to get us—or more specifically me—out of the picture.

Maybe tonight was a setup, and Brad and his dad would have police waiting to arrest us once the car was in our possession. It was a possibility I'd considered many times, and though I wasn't quite ready to dismiss it completely just yet, the chances were better that Brad's dad just wasn't too fond of him—which wasn't difficult to imagine—and that he had no plans to give him the car before he absolutely had to.

I also couldn't shake the feeling that it was obvious we didn't belong here. Though I dressed the part, I didn't feel it. Taking champagne flutes from trays of black-tied catering staff had never been part of my social life, and I wondered if the people around me could sniff out the interloper among them like a dog following the scent of another animal that'd come into its yard.

Taylor and I walked through the main hall, which looked like something that should've been in a museum instead of a home: marble floors, elegant wallpaper, and various sculptures made the entrance even more grand than I'd expected it to be. And the rest of the downstairs had the same vibe with paintings and chandeliers that I guessed were worth more than my truck.

I took two more glasses of champagne when one of the servers passed us and then handed one to Taylor before taking a sip of my own. I quickly downed the rest, hoping the extra alcohol would calm my nerves.

"Has he texted yet?" Taylor asked.

I looked at my phone for what felt like the hundredth time since we'd arrived. Brad was supposed to text a picture of the die-cast car and its exact location in the third-floor trophy room, but so far nothing. I hated even having to give him my number, but the last thing I wanted was for him to contact Taylor again for any reason.

We made another circle of the downstairs before my phone dinged. Taylor heard it too, and after quickly checking to see that it was from Brad, I searched for a place that would be a bit more inconspicuous than where we were currently standing. Neither of us wanted to risk someone seeing the picture over my shoulder.

Despite the palatial home, people seemed to be in all corners of it. The safest place to open the picture and study it with as much attention as I needed to give it would be the bathroom, so that was where I headed, grabbing hold of Taylor's hand and leading her with me. There were two downstairs— one off the kitchen and one in the main hall, but unfortunately I found them both occupied.

"Let's just look at it," Taylor said. "No one's paying attention. They're all too drunk or too busy with their own conversations to care what we're doing."

I wasn't so sure, and it wasn't a chance I was willing to take. If even one person recognized the picture and told Brad's dad about it once he discovered it missing . . .

"Excuse me, sir. If you're looking for a bathroom, there's one upstairs you can use if you'd like."

What the . . .

Taylor's eyes were already wide, and I spun around to see where the voice had come from.

"Brody?"

Brody pointed to the metallic name tag clipped to his crisp white shirt. "My name is Javier, sir. You must have me mistaken for another good-looking young gentleman."

The fuck I was.

What the hell was Brody doing here, and why was he dressed like one of the caterers?

He gestured toward the broad stairs, and I thought I detected an English accent as he said, "Allow me to show you where the upstairs lavatory is."

"Thank you, Javier." My eyes went wide as I said his name, hoping my expression would convey everything I couldn't say out loud.

Taylor and I followed Brody up the steps and down the hall until we reached a grand bathroom. "I'll be out in a minute," I said to Taylor. And then to Brody, "Don't let her out of your sight."

"I won't because we're coming in with you."

"Don't you think that's a little suspicious? There are people up here who might see you go in."

"Then the two of you go in, and I'll wait here. They'll just think you're heading in for a quickie or something."

"Oh, okay," I said, my voice heavy with sarcasm. "That won't draw any attention either—some random person on the waitstaff keeping a lookout for two kids who can't keep it in their pants."

We were interrupted by a woman who I guessed knew her way around the Lacey's home because she'd just exited what, according to Xander's map, should be the upstairs library.

"Excuse me," she said to Brody, and I hoped she hadn't heard me talking about keeping it in my pants. "Do you have any of the beef spiedini left? I was just telling my husband how delicious it was."

"I do think we have some downstairs still. Anyone from

the catering company would be happy to help you. I'm waiting for the little boys' room or I'd get them myself."

Brody flashed her one of his signature smiles. Then the woman thanked him and headed to the first floor with a man I assumed was her husband.

Once she was out of earshot, I asked Brody, "Do you even know if there is any beef spiedini left?"

"Of course not. I don't even know what beef spiedini *is*. But..." he said, emphasizing the importance of the word, "I do know what Brad's dad's trophy room looks like because I was just in there serving these little crab cake thingies that were fucking amazing. Are you hungry? I can go grab—"

"Jesus Christ, just get in there." I pushed him into the bathroom and then let Taylor enter before I did. Once we were all inside, I pulled out my phone so I could look at the picture again. No matter how much we tried to think things through and imagine how all this would play out, there was so much that couldn't be planned for. "It looks like a Lambo I think." It was a black car, but other than that, I wasn't sure I could pick it out if there were other cars similar to it.

"Yes!" Brody pointed at the phone. "I saw this one. I know exactly where it is. There's a table with this and one other car on it, but that one doesn't look like this."

"Well, that's helpful. Thanks." Even Brody should've been able to pick up on my sarcasm. "Can you possibly tell me where this table is located so I'm not wandering around looking suspicious? I have no reason to be in there."

We'd figured the best time to take it would be when the ball was about to drop because the other guests would be distracted—if there were even any in the room at that point—and Mr. Lacey would most likely be downstairs because Brad had said he's always front and center for the countdown to midnight.

"Oh. Sorry," Brody replied. "When you walk in, it's on the left, toward the back corner. You'll see a double window on the far wall. It's to the left of that next to a glass case on the wall adjacent to it."

This dude.

"Thank you."

A knock at the bathroom door startled us, and the three of us answered at once.

"It's occupied," I said.

"Be out in a minute," Taylor replied.

"Hang on," Brody said.

Then we all began arguing through tense jaws about how dumb that was.

"It's me" came the reply, but it was hard to identify the voice through the door.

Me who?

"Sophia?" Taylor said.

"Yeah, let me in."

What in the actual fuck...?

Chapter Sixteen

TAYLOR

I unlocked the door, pulled Sophia inside, closed it back up, and locked it again in a matter of seconds.

"What the hell are *you* doing here? Are you crazy?" I asked.

It hadn't surprised me *completely* that Brody had shown up. But Sophia? Also dressed as someone from the catering company?

Brody spoke before Sophia. "I just learned the other day that the term *crazy* is offensive and politically incorrect, so maybe we could try to be more sensitive and use another phrase like—"

"Are you out of your goddamn mind? This is dangerous!"

"And very illegal," Ransom whispered.

"And that's exactly why I'm here." Sophia's eyes had been on me, but now her hands were too, holding my arms just below my shoulders like the gesture was meant to make whatever she was about to say more meaningful. "You think I'm gonna let my best friend steal something from the home of the douchebag who attacked her and not be there for support?"

We both stared at each other in silence for a long moment that felt both sweet and mischievous. Then we pulled each other into a tight hug until one of the guys tapped me on the shoulder.

"Hey," Brody interrupted. "What about me? I wasn't gonna let my little sister's best friend go into this alone."

"She's not alone, asshole," Ransom was somehow able to joke, and I was thankful for it, even if I knew the feeling wouldn't last long.

I reached out and pulled Ransom into the hug too, and of course Brody followed. For as many friends as I'd made back at school, they were the kind that faded out when that time in my life was behind me. But the friends—and boyfriend—I'd made up here . . . they would be with me forever.

"I hate to ruin the moment, but it's after eleven thirty," Brody said. "We should probably come up with some sort of game plan."

"And I should probably find out if Annica remembered to tell the serving staff about a few of the guests' food allergies," said Sophia. "Cross contamination could be fatal for Diane Albertson."

Brody snapped and pointed at Sophia like he'd just remembered something. "Also, one of Brad's cousins has celiac disease. Not as serious, I know, but still super uncomfortable, not to mention embarrassing, if he has an attack here tonight. We thought *we* were in the bathroom for a long time . . ."

"I'm sorry," Ransom said. "Are you two *actually* helping cater?"

I'd wondered just how they'd managed to get inside without an invitation, and considering how they were dressed,

I assumed they'd walked in behind the caterers when they were unloading the food and supplies at the service entrance off the kitchen.

Brody and Sophia exchanged glances.

"Kind of," Sophia said.

Then Brody added, "It was a misunderstanding. I would never *volunteer* to work. Not when I'm not getting paid anyway."

Ransom stared blankly at him before saying, "You realize that's the dictionary definition of volunteering, right?"

Brody ignored him.

"We were trying to think of ways we could sneak in," Sophia said, "and Aamee suggested I call the catering company to get some info. She said her parents have had a million large events catered, and the turnover rate at those companies probably meant we could show up as new holiday hires and the staff wouldn't be the wiser."

"That's . . . pretty smart actually," I told her.

"Don't tell Aamee that," Sophia said. "So I called the company, posing as someone interested in having a wedding catered by them. I asked about their attire for formal events, how many people were employed on their wait staff, and how long most of them had been working there. That kind of stuff."

All were typical questions from any bridezilla, but those answers had provided them with enough information to fit into the scene.

"We showed up dressed like the other caterers and had our hands full of last-minute supplies: extra napkins and wineglasses, some trays, and other essentials that the company would likely need more of."

Brody eyed himself in one of the oval mirrors, fixing his

hair while he spoke. "We introduced ourselves to some of the other employees. Javier," he said, pointing to his name tag. "And Maxine."

Sophia tugged on her own name tag. "Turns out you can get anything on Vistaprint."

"Everyone was so happy they had more help for the night because they'd just learned about the allergy and one of the other workers had called out last-minute. They were overwhelmed," Brody said, sounding almost sorry for them. Maybe he was. "Just seemed like the right thing to do to lend a hand."

"So you did volunteer?" Ransom asked.

"Call it whatever you want."

"That's literally what it's called," Ransom said, his voice beginning to rise, but I guessed it was more because of the stress of the situation than Brody's stupidity.

I wondered if he realized that doing the right thing when it came to helping the caterers didn't exactly make up for the felony he'd come to help us commit.

"Plus," he added, "it made us look a little less sus if we worked while we were here."

Sophia raised an eyebrow at her brother. "Sus?"

"Yeah ... suspicious. God, don't you know any slang?"

"I know what it means, but who says that?"

"Obviously people say it or you wouldn't know what it means, now would you?"

Their voices faded into the background with the muffled din of the party as I lost myself in my own thoughts. If these three weren't going to be helpful, I'd need to come up with a plan myself before we ran out of time. I felt like Cinderella at the ball, but instead of dancing with Prince Charming, I was hiding in a bathroom while I listened to two idiots argue about Urban Dictionary.

"Take off your clothes," I blurted out.

Brody already had his shirt off by the time Ransom and Sophia spoke.

"What? Why?" Sophia asked just as Ransom said, "Taylor, this isn't the time or the place to—"

"Take off your clothes," I said again. "We're switching."

"You and me?" Ransom asked.

I tried not to be impressed by how quickly Brody had undressed. He was already in his boxers and was waiting for the rest of us to follow. If I didn't know better, I would've thought *he'd* been the professional stripper.

"No, dummy," Brody said. "You trade with me, and Taylor and Sophia switch. That way you guys will look like caterers when you enter the trophy room. Jesus, aren't you supposed to be the smart one between the two of us?"

Jesus, even Brody gets it. Ransom really needed to get with the program.

Ransom didn't speak but quickly seemed on board with the idea because he was taking his clothes off and handing them to Brody.

"Turn around, perv. The girls need to take their stuff off too," Ransom told him when Brody was staring at us. Though it was obviously just because he was waiting for us to do our part, I still appreciated the privacy.

"That's my sister," Brody told him, sounding completely disgusted.

"Who you pretended to date."

"*I* didn't pretend to date her. *She* pretended to date *me*."

Sophia handed me her white shirt and black jacket, and

I helped her zip up my dress. Luckily, we were only a half size different in shoes, so hopefully she wouldn't fall and kill herself in my heels.

"I did not pretend to date *you*," Sophia gritted out. "I dated Drew, who was pretending to *be* you."

"No offense," I said. "I appreciate the gesture of support, but I can't wait to get the hell out of this bathroom and away from all of you."

"Now, now," Brody said. "We're all friends here."

Once we finished switching clothes, we turned around to face each other again. Brody was by no means a small guy, but in Ransom's suit, he looked like a kid who'd gotten his older brother's hand-me-downs and been forced to wear them long before they fit. And Ransom looked like the Incredible Hulk right before his rapidly expanding muscles rip all his clothes to shreds and leave him wearing only a tattered pair of capris.

"Maxine," Ransom said, giving me a nod as he tried to button his jacket but failed. "You ready for this?"

"Not even a little bit."

Though if I had to commit a felony to avoid any further harassment from my stalker who'd risen from the grave like a zombie on *The Walking Dead*, there was no one I'd rather have by my side than Ransom Holt.

"But let's go, Javier."

RANSOM

Mr. Lacey's trophy room held all kinds of memorabilia: everything from autographed baseballs and jerseys to vintage comic books to a few of these die-cast cars. After seeing them in person, I didn't see what the big deal even was. I'd much rather have a Lamborghini I could drive than one I could only look at. But understanding rich people had never been one of my superpowers, and I was happy we'd been tasked with stealing a model car and not one I'd have to drive away in.

Taylor circulated the room, offering the guests in the room a fresh glass of champagne before the ball dropped. There were only about six people in the room—several men and women I assumed were their wives. Probably all business associates or close friends of Mr. Lacey, who I was happy wasn't in the room at the moment. I guessed he was downstairs near the big screen TV by the bar off the kitchen, waiting for the ball to drop. I hoped these people would head down there soon too, but I felt like they might need some encouragement.

"Excuse me, everyone," I said, "but I wanted to make you aware of the time in case you'd like to join the festivities downstairs. It's five minutes until midnight."

The two men standing closest to the Lambo looked up from whatever discussion they'd been involved in and thanked me.

"I didn't even realize how long we've been in here," one of them said. "I swear every year Thomas adds more to his collection."

"It *is* impressive. I could spend hours in here looking at his comic book collection alone," said the other.

One of the women approached him, her delicate frame moving elegantly in a way that it seemed only people of a certain social status were capable of. She put a hand on his shoulder and laughed in a way I thought sounded a little forced.

"You *have* been in here for hours," she said.

"I don't think it's been hours, plural. Maybe just over one."

"Why do you disagree with everything I say?"

"I don't," he answered, and I almost laughed thinking that the banter could've easily been coming from Taylor and me.

The woman rolled her eyes, and then she and the other wives gathered their husbands so they could all head downstairs.

I'd been cleaning up, tossing some discarded napkins and scraps of food left on plates into the trash bag I'd taken from the bathroom. It was large enough to fit the car, which I planned to put in there once the room was clear. But I didn't want either of us to be seen in the room by ourselves, so as the guests exited, we left also, following them down the first flight of stairs but heading back up again once they were on their way to the lower level.

I was sure no one saw us going back up since the majority of the guests seemed to be downstairs already, but still, my heart raced as we reentered the trophy room and shut the door behind us.

"Put it in here," I said to Taylor, holding open the trash bag.

Taylor's hands were shaking as she lifted the car and slipped it into the white plastic bag. We examined it after it was inside and tried to situate it in a way that disguised its shape. But our other issue was that when the car pressed against the bag, its black color showed through enough that, when combined with the shape, would surely draw attention to it.

"Fuck," I said, looking frantically around the room for something we could use to cover it and mumbling about how screwed we were if someone came up again.

"Here!"

I turned in time to catch the thin blanket that had been on

the leather couch. "So we're stealing two things now?"

"We don't really have a choice, do we?"

And because I knew she was right, I'd already been shoving the thing into the bag and around the car. The adrenaline releasing inside me was a sudden cold rush that seemed to freeze my veins as it made its way through my bloodstream.

We wasted no time getting out of the room, and we closed the door softly behind us. The cheers of the guests told me it was after midnight. I hoped by the time I made it out there, our car would be waiting and no one would notice me putting a bag that appeared to be filled with trash into it.

I shot Brody a quick text to meet us there. My plan was to have Taylor ride with him and Sophia. Somehow that made me feel like she was less involved in the theft.

I was heading through the foyer when—

"Excuse me. You with the bag."

My muscles ceased to move at that moment, certain that my fate as an inmate was all but confirmed. And once my eyes locked with Mr. Lacey's, I found myself incapable of all logical thought.

"Yes?" I managed to speak. I imagined how pale I might look, how strange in Brody's pants that were a few inches too short for me.

"There room in that bag for this stuff?"

Jesus Christ.

I felt like someone had tied me to train tracks and I'd managed to escape just in time to roll away from the oncoming train. This was some Houdini shit right here.

He pointed to some dessert plates on a nearby table next to the man who'd been in the trophy room with us earlier. Which, I hoped, helped because he'd seen us leave the room when he had and would probably assume I'd been down here since.

"Um, yes, sir. I'll get it," I croaked.

Then I gathered the trash he'd wanted cleaned, as well as some more that was sprinkled around nearby to hopefully cement my place on the catering staff. Not that a caterer was incapable of theft, but the more I looked like I belonged here, the better chance I had of getting away with this.

Brad caught my eye from the other side of the room. He was sitting on a couch, his jaw ticking from time to time. He held a beer in one hand and rested it on his thigh, which shook a little. He was nervous too. It looked like he was making an effort to seem unaffected, though. The rest of his body stood still, his arm draped around a blonde who looked frighteningly like Taylor.

I hated that he sat only feet from me and I couldn't do anything to him. It seemed to be a trend lately, and I planned on breaking it first chance I got. Even if it was just to smack that arrogant, pretty-boy grin off him.

I hadn't been paying attention to Mr. Lacey since I'd spotted Brad, which was probably an amateur mistake. But I was an amateur, so ...

"Here, son," the man with Mr. Lacey said as he handed me his plate as well.

I startled a bit and then tried to smile warmly as I took it and carefully added it to the bag.

The man turned back to Brad's dad and said, "Where do you even find all that stuff? Seems it'd be a full-time job just collecting it all."

"Some things I come across in my travels, and others I seek out. I find most of it at auctions."

The other man laughed. "I don't think I've ever been to an auction. Naomi dragged me to a charity one once, but I spent most of my time at the bar."

Mr. Lacey chuckled and said, "That would've been my father's attitude. Man was utilitarian to the end. Never saw the value in collecting objects."

Wait... what?

I knew I should've been getting the hell out of here, and I'd been slowly inching toward the exit since I'd encountered them, but Mr. Lacey's comment stopped me in my tracks.

Brad had said the car had been something his grandfather had collected. And while I knew it shouldn't have surprised me that the guy had lied—and I'd always expected we were being played in some way—for some reason, I hadn't thought of this.

I looked over at Brad, who nodded toward the kitchen when our eyes met, a clear nonverbal sign that I should get going. And I agreed with him, except...

The man asked Mr. Lacey if he ever planned to sell any of his collection, and Brad's dad replied, "I don't think so. There are things that museums have contacted me about over the years, so I'll probably donate a lot of it. I don't really have a need for it after I'm gone."

"What about the boys?"

"Jonathan's expressed interest in some of the Hollywood memorabilia, and I'll probably leave the model cars to my two grandsons, in Jon's custody of course until they're old enough to have them. And Brad?" Mr. Lacey laughed again, but this time it sounded full of disgust. "Well, Brad's always been more focused on money than sentimentality. I want my treasures to stay in the family or go where they'll be appreciated."

My focus was so fixed on Brad, I didn't hear if Mr. Lacey

said anything else about his son, but it seemed clear that Mr. Lacey had at least some inkling as to the kind of man his son was. I wished I could round out his assessment with a few more choice descriptors but knew that wasn't in my best interest.

I narrowed my eyes at that fucker and cranked up my glare to a scorching five thousand degrees. That selfish asshole could roast like a pig on a spit. He had no right to that Lambo. As far as I could tell, he had no right to anything because Mr. Lacey would rather give his prized possessions to strangers before he'd give any of them to his younger son.

And Brad would rather steal from his own nephews than accept his father's wishes.

Finally, I turned toward the kitchen with the bag and headed out to meet Taylor. I had an important decision to make, and I didn't like the idea of making it alone.

When I got outside, the car was waiting with Taylor behind the wheel. I slid into the passenger seat but put an arm out to stop her when she moved to put the car into gear.

"What?" she asked me.

"We can't do this," I whispered, more from disbelief at what I was about to suggest than from a concern about privacy. "We can't steal this car."

"Um, in case you haven't noticed, we've already stolen it."

I shook my head. "No. We can ... I can put it back. Or not back because I'm not insane, but we can leave it somewhere they'll find it."

"Why would we do that?"

I looked at her and took in her face, a frown of confusion marring her beautiful features.

"Because we're not these people. Because Brad's a fucking

liar and that car is meant for his nephews. Because I'll risk a lot of things for you, but I won't actually risk *you*."

She looked lost for a second before setting her shoulders and looking at me with firmer resolve.

"What do we do?"

I gestured down at myself. "I'm already in the outfit. I'll just go back into the kitchen, find a place to set it down, and walk away. If I'm not back in five minutes, just ... leave without me."

We sat quietly for a moment, simply looking at each other, letting the import of the moment sink in.

Then she ruined it by snorting and saying, "Whatever, Hero Complex. If you're not back in five minutes, I'm coming in after you."

"Sounds like you have a hero complex of your own. And way to ruin the moment," I griped as I got out of the car.

"It's all part of my charm," she replied as I let my door slam shut.

Going back into the house and finding a place to leave the car where it was likely to be found by Mr. or Mrs. Lacey instead of someone who'd try to take off with it—like their son—only caused a momentary panic.

I looked around the kitchen, spotted the refrigerator, and thought it was as good a place as any. The caterers were using coolers, so they'd be unlikely to go inside, and even if the Laceys weren't big chefs, everyone had to eat, right?

So I cast a quick look around, and when no one was watching, I slipped the car—which I'd already removed from the bag on my way inside—onto the top shelf of the fridge. In the end, leaving the car was almost anticlimactic in how easy it was.

I was back outside in under four minutes, and Taylor and I were speeding away from the Lacey residence, hoping this would be the last time we'd see any of them.

Too bad we knew how unlikely that was.

Chapter Seventeen

TAYLOR

Ransom and I got back to my apartment on autopilot. We hadn't spoken much on the ride there, and truth be told, I hadn't let myself feel much either.

We'd failed. Or maybe succeeded, depending on how one looked at it. We didn't steal the stupid little Lambo that would keep Hudson safe, but we also didn't become criminals. So there was that.

When I unlocked the door and stumbled through it into our apartment, our friends looked up in surprise, including Sophia and Brody, who were still dressed in our clothes.

"What the hell happened?" Sophia asked as she hurried over and enveloped me in a hug. "You were supposed to call when you left."

"How'd it go?" Brody asked.

When I pulled back from Sophia, I could see that all our friends had gathered around, and they were looking at us eagerly.

"We didn't take it," Ransom said, his voice low. "Well, we

did, but then we left it at the house."

"I'm confused," Brody said.

"Shocker," Sophia muttered.

But Brody forged on despite the interruption. "How did you steal something you left there?"

"We took it from the room, but before we left, I heard Brad's dad talking about how he'd collected everything in the trophy room himself and how the cars were supposed to go to his grandsons. Brad had no claim to the car, and we . . . we just couldn't take it. So I left it in the refrigerator and got the hell out of there."

"The refrigerator?" Xander asked.

Ransom held up his hands in a shrug. "It seemed like a good idea at the time."

"How do you know his dad was telling the truth?" Drew asked.

I shrugged. "We don't. But honestly, it doesn't even matter. Everything with Brad is shady, and taking something that's worth millions of dollars is just—"

Xander whistled as Aamee exclaimed, "Whoa, wait, what? Millions of dollars?"

"That got her attention," Sophia muttered again.

"Listen, Lassie, go fall in a well."

"Didn't Lassie *save* people from wells?" Toby asked.

Aamee glared at him. "This really isn't the time to take me literally." She turned back to us. "Except in regard to the millions of dollars. I *literally* want to know about that right this second."

"Brad sent us a picture of it at the party so we would know what we were looking for and exactly where it was," Ransom explained. "We always figured it was expensive because why would he want it anyway? But when we searched for it afterward, we found out it's a die-cast car worth six million dollars. Some kind of model Lamborghini that had gold fibers woven into the carbon and had diamonds on the tires or something."

"Diamonds?" Aamee perked up again.

"I'm sure that's why he waited to send us a picture," I said. "He didn't want to give us time to research the damn thing and back out."

"But you backed out anyway," Drew said, hurriedly adding, "Not that that's a bad thing. Six million... Who knows how far Brad's dad would go to find who stole that? You made the right decision."

"Yeah," I agreed, though even I could hear the doubt in my voice.

It wasn't that I thought we'd done the wrong thing. It's always better to *not* rob someone. But there'd be heavy consequences for what we'd done. I had no idea what Brad was capable of, and I was afraid to find out. He hadn't tried to call us yet, and I'd purposely not checked my email.

"What do we do from here?" Aniyah asked.

"I can set up some booby traps," Carter offered.

Aamee gave him an incredulous look. "Why would we do that?"

He looked at her like she was ridiculous. "Because it would be fun. And because he's probably going to show up here at some point. That dude's capable of anything."

"Thanks for that," I said dryly.

"You're welcome," he said with a smile.

Xander caught my attention because he kept shifting his weight and rubbing his hands on his jeans.

"Xander? You okay?"

His head jerked when my words got his attention. "Huh? Oh, uh, yeah. Yeah. Fine."

Ransom stepped closer to him. "What's up?"

Xander was quiet for a moment before raising his head and looking squarely in Ransom's eyes. "I can have him taken care of. If you need me to."

The silence in the room was thick as Ransom asked, "What do you mean?"

"Listen, my dad isn't great for a lot of things, but... I could go to him... for this. If I said Brad was blackmailing me or extorting me or whatever, he wouldn't ask questions. It would just get done."

Carter exhaled a heavy breath. "That's... intense."

"My dad's an intense guy. And he doesn't really give much of a shit about me, but he's not gonna let anyone take advantage either. So if it needed to happen... I could make it happen."

Xander looked like he was going to be sick, faint, or both. I didn't know anything about his dad beyond his having made his fortune in cybersecurity and being a shit father. But I did know Xander. And while his exterior said *fuck off*, his heart was too vulnerable to handle carrying something like that around for the rest of his life.

I walked over and drew him into a hug. "Thank you," I whispered, "but we'll find another way."

When I pulled back, he searched my face, and whatever he saw made him give a shaky nod and step back.

"It's late," I said to everyone. "Let's see if Brad reaches out, and then we can make a plan from there."

"Guess that's our cue, guys," Drew said.

"We don't mean to kick you out," I said, though it sounded

halfhearted since that was exactly what I meant to do.

"It's fine," Sophia said as she reached out and gently stroked my arm. "We're all tired anyway. Talk tomorrow?"

"Definitely. I'll call you."

Everyone filed out after giving hugs and back pats to both of us.

Once Ransom closed the door, he sagged back against it. When his eyes met mine, I gave him a smile.

"Well. You can't ever say our lives are boring."

He laughed softly. "I actually kinda wish I *could* say that."

I walked over and leaned against the door beside him. "Yeah, me too. Funny, I always used to feel like my life was so dull. Who knew I only had to date a sociopath named Brad to spice things up?"

"Lesson learned."

"Yup." We stood there quietly for another moment before I asked, "You wanna go to bed?"

"With you? Always."

I smiled as I laced my fingers with his and we made our way slowly into my room, turning off lights as we went.

We undressed quietly, both of us taking in the sight of the other with silent appreciation. But we were too exhausted—mentally and physically—to do anything more than hold each other tightly. I relished having these quiet, supportive moments with him.

And I swore to do anything to protect it.

RANSOM

Safe Haven was madness. Even though I was on break from

school, the kids were all back and hyped up on leftover Christmas cheer.

"Malcolm, if I see the phone again, I'm taking it until your mom gets here," I yelled from my seat, where two girls were giving me a pretend makeover. Though the elastic ties they'd somehow knotted in my hair didn't make it feel very pretend. I needed to get a haircut as a means of survival.

Malcolm grumbled but slid his new phone back into his pocket.

"Oh," a voice said from beside me.

I looked over to see Taylor smirking at me.

"I think you've found your new look. It's very . . . flattering."

The girls beamed as they grabbed more hair ties, causing me to glare at Taylor.

She snorted. "I'm going to put some snacks out."

"I'll help," I quickly offered, starting to stand.

"No, no," she hurried, holding a hand out to me. "You keep enjoying yourself over here. I can manage it."

"You know what happened to Benedict Arnold?" I asked.

She tilted her head for a second before saying, "Actually, I don't."

"Hmm. Me neither." I'd have to look that up later. "But I'm sure it was something horrible."

She looked at me pityingly. "Your threats need some work."

I shrugged. "Guess it's good I have a great personality, then."

She nodded—doubtfully, I might add—before walking away toward the snacks.

The girls went back to work beautifying me as I watched over the rest of the kids as they played. It was freezing out, so we were stuck inside. It was usually chaotic, but as the first day back from break, it made the place feel like a portal to hell.

The kids were loud and boisterous, but they weren't breaking anything or trying to fight each other, so I was content to give them space. Roddie had a few kids playing on the PlayStation he'd brought in to hook up to the TV he'd convinced someone to donate to us, and Inez had corralled a few kids into playing board games.

The other kids kicked back like they were killing time on a street corner, exchanging glimpses of whatever new gear they'd gotten for Christmas while surreptitiously making sure the counselors weren't watching them.

News flash: we were. I seriously hoped none of these kids turned to a life of crime, because they'd all be shit at it. They couldn't have been more obvious if they were holding signs that read *I've got the new iPad I wasn't supposed to take to school in my bookbag.* Or *Hey, come see my pet hamster I've got in my pocket.*

Wait…

"Kyle!" I yelled, shooting to a stand and striding toward the boy. "Tell me that's not real."

He looked sheepish. "It's not real?" The statement sounded like a question laced with a kind of hope only a twelve-year-old could muster.

"Bro, have you had that thing in your pocket all day?" He was wearing a shirt with a breast pocket that had a noticeable bulge and a wet stain. How had no one noticed at school? Was his teacher blind or intentionally obtuse?

"I had him in my pencil case for a little bit," Kyle said as he reached in and pulled out the hamster.

I rolled my eyes heavenward and prayed for strength.

"Listen, Dr. Doolittle, this never happens again, you hear me? What if you'd fallen and crushed him to death?"

Kyle looked horrified by that prospect.

Good.

"I didn't think of that," he said.

"Come on," I said as I put a hand on his shoulder. "Let's go find something to keep him in."

Finally, we got the hamster settled in a plastic container from the play kitchen, and then the kids went over to get the snacks Taylor set out. I was about to grab some apple slices for myself when I heard my boss, Harry, call my name.

"Can you come here for a second?" he asked when I looked over at him.

I walked over to where Harry was standing just out of sight of the kids in the room we used as a pickup point. It was managed by Harry's assistant, Edith, who was seventy if she was a day, and she ran the office like she was a warden. But she was currently missing from her post, a fact that she would probably regret since I was pretty sure she had a thing for Bill, who was standing across from Harry. He also happened to be my Safe Haven nemesis.

Bill was the community center's maintenance man, and for some reason, he despised me. Since I wasn't accustomed to not being liked on sight, I'd decided Bill was probably a serial killer.

"What's up?" I asked.

"Bill needs a little help upstairs, and I thought you might be willing to give him a hand?" Harry said, his face giving away that he knew I'd rather be hung from the rafters by my balls than spend one-on-one time with Bill but also knowing I'd never say no.

"Sure," I replied with false enthusiasm. "What did you need help with?"

"Gotta install a toilet," Bill replied gruffly.

Of course. Why wouldn't it be a toilet?

"Need a hand moving the old one out and setting the new one in place," he explained.

"Okay, no problem."

Bill looked me over gravely before turning to Harry. "You sure there's no one else in there who could help? Maybe someone a little more...rugged?"

What the fuck?

"What does that mean?" I asked, putting my hands on my hips in a way that accentuated the size of my traps.

"Doesn't that girl still work here?" Bill continued, as if I hadn't spoken. "Taylor? She's a tough cookie."

"Are you saying my girlfriend is stronger than I am?" Not to be sexist or anything, but what the fuck? I was a former collegiate football player for Christ's sake.

His face screwed up in disgust. "She's dating *you*? Pickings must be really slim around here."

"Now listen, you belligerent troll—"

My tirade was cut off by Harry. "Okay, I think we're getting off track here. Bill, I assure you, Ransom is the most capable person I have to help you."

Bill looked like he wanted to argue more but instead uttered a stern, "Fine," and turned around, mumbling about being seen with new-age millennial hippies.

I wanted to argue that *I* was the one who shouldn't want to be seen with *him* and that I wasn't a millennial, but I trudged after him instead.

And then, in the main hall of the community center,

as people pointed at me and snickered, I realized what the problem was. My hands flew to my hair, where I found what seemed to be a thousand little ponytails all over my head.

I groaned, causing Bill to turn around. "Why didn't you tell me I had these stupid things in?" I accused as I pulled them out—painfully, I might add, since the girls clearly weren't versed in ponytailing quite yet.

"How am I supposed to know what you kids are into these days? Thought it was some new *fad.*" The amount of disdain that dripped from the last word was impressive.

I continued to remove the hair ties as we walked up the stairs to the second floor. When I was done, I attempted to pat my hair down as best I could. God only knew what I looked like. I wished I had a mirror.

"You done coiffing your hair, Nancy?" Bill asked.

"Who's Nancy, Karen?" I asked just to be annoying. If the way he huffed was any indication, I succeeded.

He communicated mostly in grunts from there. Despite his doubts regarding my manhood, I was able to lift the toilet out of the way easily and hold the new one in place while he secured it. As I looked down at my shirt, which was dingy from having lifted the old toilet out of the way, I understood why Bill had requested my help for something that was really a one-person job.

Jerk.

"Anything else?" I asked when we were done.

"Nope."

"Hmm. I think there should be something else."

He looked at me with narrowed eyes and a curled lip. "What?"

"It starts with a *T* and ends with a hank you."

He snorted. "It's the board who should be thanking ya. Saved them money by you helping me rather than hiring someone to install it."

I looked around the bathroom that was empty save for us. "I don't see them here."

"Maybe put your head in the toilet and see if they're down there."

I shook my head as if disappointed. "That was a very lame response."

"Want me to use it first?"

"Now you're just being disgusting."

At that, the man honest-to-God growled. "Don't you have a job to be doing?"

"Well, yes. But I was taken away from that job so I could do yours."

As he approached me wielding a wrench, I decided I'd maybe gone a step too far. "Okay, okay, that was a shitty thing to say." I looked down at the toilet. "Ha. Shitty. Get it?"

He closed his eyes for a long second before refocusing on me. "Please go away."

"Sure thing. Don't hesitate to come to me with all your bathroom needs. Wait . . . no . . . that came out wrong. I—"

"Would you get out of here already?"

I hurried from the room as I laughed. Just before the door swung shut behind me, I heard a "And thank you . . . I guess," from Bill, and if that wasn't like winning a jackpot, I didn't know what was.

When I stepped back into Safe Haven, my gaze fell on Edith.

"You missed your boyfriend," I said.

"Which one?"

That response gave me a second of pause. "Bill."

"Oh yeah? How'd he look?"

"Like Bill."

She rolled her eyes. "Did he look happy or sad?"

"I don't think Bill is capable of looking anything other than annoyed."

She hummed in response.

"Why should he look happy or sad?"

"No reason," she said flippantly.

Against every grain of better judgment in my body, I didn't let her casual dismissal go.

"There has to be a reason. Come on, Edith. Tell Dr. Ransom all about it."

She sighed. "He may have come to my place for a cup of coffee after work last week."

"Last week? Why would he still be feeling one way or another from something that happened a week ago?"

She gave me a flat look. "I give very memorable . . . coffee."

I scooped up her hand and kissed the back of it. "Thank you, Edith. I didn't think I could experience anything worse than changing a communal toilet today, but you have proven me wrong."

She smiled. "You're welcome."

I took a step back from her desk and shook my entire body in an effort to rid the mental images that were assaulting me. Then I made my way back into the room where the kids were.

As soon as I stepped inside, Taylor hurried over.

"You're not going to believe this," she said.

"I'll actually believe pretty much anything at this point. Except in God. Because there's no way He'd have let me endure the last hour if He existed."

Her face was a mixture of confusion and worry, but she must have ultimately decided to ignore it as she showed me her phone.

"What's this?" I asked.

As she opened her mouth to reply, Malcolm appeared. "I thought we weren't supposed to have our phones?" he asked in a petulant, patronizing tone that said he knew he was being annoying and reveled in it.

I leveled a look at him. "I just helped a cranky old man change a toilet. Be careful what you say next."

"Jeez, were you helping yourself?" he muttered as he walked away.

I focused back on the phone and began reading the email that was on it. "What is this?"

"It's an email from Petey's mom. She wanted to check in and see if we heard anything about Petey's death."

"Okay," I replied, drawing the word out.

She took a deep breath, making me feel like I was unlikely to enjoy what came out of her mouth next. "I think I should go meet with her."

Jesus. When it rained bad ideas, it really freaking poured.

Chapter Eighteen

TAYLOR

I had a shift at the Treehouse after Safe Haven. Ransom joined me there after the last kid had been picked up because he said he was too tired to cook for himself, but I thought it likely had more to do with him being worried Brad would show up.

He sat at a high-top near the bar, which normally would've gone to the bartender for food and drinks, but everyone knew him by that point, so I went over and dropped a menu in front of him.

"Brody's meeting me here in a bit," he said.

"Okay."

"He's going to help me talk you out of getting involved with Petey's mom."

"Pretty sure she's already involved with her husband."

He shot me a look that said how *not* funny he found me. "You know what I mean."

I shrugged. "I just think there's something there."

"There is. Trouble."

"Well, that only makes it more appealing."

He shook his head forlornly. "Can I have a beer?"

I leaned in and smacked a kiss to his cheek. "Sure thing, babycakes."

"That's a horrible nickname."

"Then I shall use it forever."

He laughed as I walked to the bar and ordered him a lager on draft. As I waited, I let my mind percolate a little on meeting Petey's mom. I honestly couldn't see much harm in it. We'd already told her we didn't know Petey well, so she couldn't have had high expectations. And if Brad *did* have something to do with it, I might be the only one who could make that connection. Sounded like a win-win to me.

When the bartender gave me Ransom's beer, I walked it back to him. He groaned as I got closer.

"What?" I asked. "Is this not what you wanted?"

"I know that look."

"What look?"

"The one on your face. You already decided, didn't you?"

I set the beer down in front of him. "How could you have gotten that from my face?"

"Your eyebrows get into this, like, hard line when you're gearing up to be stubborn about something. It's like you have an overdeveloped muscle underneath you can flex or something."

"That sounds really attractive," I said dryly.

He ignored that and took a long pull of his lager.

"Seriously," I said. "What could go wrong?"

He drank more.

I finally reached out and grabbed the glass, lowering it to the table.

"There's more going on here. And maybe if we figure out

what that is, we can finally get rid of Brad. Because there's no way he's going to let the car thing go. And he's never going to go away unless we find a way to *make* him go away."

He sighed and looked at his almost-empty glass for a second before meeting my eyes. "I just don't know if involving more people is the answer. And while I know Brad is an issue, he's not even our most imminent one. We still have to figure out what we're going to do about Hudson's loans. And talking to Petey's parents doesn't help us solve that."

"I get that. I really do," I argued back. "But honestly, I don't think we're going to be able to get ourselves out of that one. We're either going to need to let our friends help or we're going to need to go to a bank and see if we can get some kind of loan."

He opened his mouth to reply, but I cut him off.

"Please, can we just... table that? For a few more days. The Brad situation is one we can solve. I *feel* it. So can we just try to get this one thing off our plates, and then we can turn our full attention to the other?"

"I think we're working in the wrong order. The issues with Hudson are time sensitive, and time is what we're running out of right now."

"But the Brad problem has spilled into the Hudson situation. And Brad is going to use whatever he has in his arsenal to mess with us."

I sighed. I knew Hudson was a priority for Ransom. And that was the way it should be. But this shit with Brad had been plaguing me for more than a year at this point. I needed to end it.

"While I'm seeing what we can find out from Petey's parents, you stay here and brainstorm a solution to Hudson's loans," I added. "And then when I get back, we'll turn our attention fully to getting her out of that mess. Because I do care about her, Ransom. Please don't think I don't. I just..." I paused for a second before continuing. "I can't wait around for Brad to strike anymore. We overlooked the whole Petey situation because...we were scared. And it was easier to not push and just hope things would magically get better. But we can't keep doing that. We have to face the situation for what it is and actively try to make it better."

Ransom opened his mouth to reply, but a voice behind me interrupted.

"Well, if you're involved, there's no way anything can get better."

I whirled around to see Aamee standing there. "What are you doing here?" I more so accused than asked.

"Brody said I should meet him here for dinner."

"He's not here," I said.

She rolled her eyes. "Obviously." Aamee took the seat across from Ransom and settled in. "So what bad idea were you two discussing now? Perhaps becoming drug mules? Kickstarting a human-trafficking ring? Running a puppy mill?"

I gave her a sour look, but Ransom—the traitor—answered her honestly.

"Taylor wants to meet up with Petey's parents to see if there's a link to Brad."

She looked confused. "Who's Petey again?"

"The guy who died in the alley," he replied casually, as if he were relaying his dinner order.

"Oh, that's right. How could I forget a name like Petey? Poor guy. What were his parents thinking?"

The fact that Aamee seemed to feel more sympathy over his name than the fact he was dead was the best demonstration of her character I'd ever witnessed.

"So why do you want to go talk to them?" she asked and then took a look around. "Shouldn't you be working?"

"Yes," I gritted out.

"Well, don't let us keep you. I'm sure Ransom can fill me in on all the ways you're an idiot." She turned her body slightly so she was effectively giving me the literal cold shoulder and faced Ransom more fully. "You know, I always used to think Sophia was the worst decision-maker, but then I met Taylor. Whew. What a disaster."

I opened my mouth to argue but realized there was no point and walked away instead. Business picked up a little then, and by the time I got back to Ransom's table, he'd been joined by Carter, Toby, and, oddly, Owen.

"Hey," I said to everyone before looking at Owen. "What brings you in with this motley crew?"

"I was teaching Carter some yoga poses to help him stretch after workouts when he got a call to come here. He said I could tag along."

"That's cool. How long have you been doing yoga?" I asked.

"My grandma wanted to start a baby goat yoga class at my parents' place last summer and asked me to be her partner. She said if I handled the yoga, she'd get the goats, but..." He shrugged instead of finishing his sentence, and I let it go because, ultimately, I didn't want to know.

"So when are you planning on going to make the lives of Petey's grieving family worse?" Aamee asked without looking up from her menu.

"I won't make their lives worse," I argued, indignant.

She gave me a cursory glance. "Well, you're certainly not going to make them better."

"How do you know?"

"Have you met you? When have you ever made anything better?"

I rolled my eyes. "Why do we even hang out with you?"

"Lack of other options, I imagine." Then she suddenly thrust her menu at me. "I'll have the chef's salad with a side of fries."

"Who gets fries with a salad?" Carter asked.

"Me. It's called balance."

"Aren't we waiting for Brody?" Ransom asked.

Aamee screwed up her face. "Why?"

"Because it's the nice thing to do," he said slowly.

"That's why it never occurred to her," I supplied.

"Ugh," she groaned as she picked up her phone from where it had been lying on the table. "I'll FaceTime him."

He answered on the second ring. "Where you at, yo?"

She shot the rest of us a look that said she also wondered how she ended up with a weirdo like Brody. "I'm at the Treehouse."

He paused a second before saying, "Why?"

"Um, maybe because you told me to meet you here."

"No, I didn't."

"Yes. You did. You said you were meeting Ransom here and I should join you."

"I thought we were meeting at Rafferty's."

Aamee sighed and turned the camera around to point at Ransom. "Does it look like he's at Rafferty's?"

"Hi, Ransom," Brody said.

Ransom laughed as he gave a small wave. "Hey."

"Scale of one to skewering my testicles, how mad is she?" Brody asked.

Ransom observed Aamee thoughtfully. "Probably somewhere around putting bug spray in your drink."

"Just once or repeatedly?"

"I think just once."

"Cool. I've survived worse."

Aamee turned the camera back toward her. "Are you coming here or meeting me at home later?"

"Why don't you come here?" he asked.

"Because I have to coordinate a road trip with Taylor."

"You have to do what with who?" I asked.

"A road trip? With Taylor?" Brody asked.

Aamee sighed as if she'd been charged with caring for a colony of lepers. "Yes, someone with some sense has to go to keep her out of trouble."

"And she asked you?" Brody replied.

"Why do you sound so surprised?" Aamee asked, her voice threateningly level.

"I just...uh...figured she'd ask...Sophia. Or someone else."

"You guys are all busy preparing for the new semester. It makes the most sense for me to go."

"And to clarify, I didn't ask," I yelled so Brody could hear. "Don't you have work?" I asked Aamee.

She smiled. "I should be able to arrange working remotely for a few days."

"That's...unfortunate for me," I muttered.

"When are you going?" Brody asked.

"They're not," Ransom loudly cut in.

Everyone at the table turned to gape at him.

"It's not safe," he added more softly. "We have no idea how Petey knew Brad or even if he knew Brad. Maybe they were mixed up in something dangerous together."

"Like bondage or . . . ?" Owen asked.

"That's, like, ropes and shit, right?" Carter asked.

Toby patted his arm. "I'll explain later."

I wanted to ask exactly how Toby planned to explain it, because the mental image of adorable Toby educating the behemoth Carter on anything regarding sex seemed really enthralling. Much more enthralling than arguing with Ransom and Aamee.

"I have a Taser. We'll be fine," Aamee said.

"Have you ever used it on yourself?" Owen asked.

"Why would I do that?"

Owen shrugged. "Police have to do it. I figured it was part of responsible Taser ownership."

"So if you buy a gun, you're gonna shoot yourself with it to show how responsible you are?" Aamee asked.

"Well, I'm a pacifist, so . . ."

She stared at Owen for a second before looking back at me. "When are we leaving?"

"You're not leaving," Ransom interjected.

"Sorry, but you're not my boyfriend, so you don't get to tell me what to do," Aamee taunted.

"You're not going," Brody said.

"Sorry, but you won't be my boyfriend anymore if you try to tell me what to do."

Brody's sigh was audible. "I can never win."

"I have to see what works for her. I'll text her later and let you know," I said, intentionally ignoring the glare of my boyfriend.

"Works for me." Aamee sat back in her chair, smiling widely.

"I'll remove your car battery before I let you two go on your own. See when she wants to meet, and I'll go with you," Ransom offered.

"First of all, joke's on you. I haven't driven my car in months, so the battery is probably dead anyway. Second of all, you start classes Monday. You can't miss time this soon into a new semester."

"So go on a weekend," he argued.

"I'm happy to do that, but I don't want to be under strict constraints to get back. If I find a lead worth following, I want to be able to follow it."

Ransom sat back in his seat and crossed his arms over his chest. "Listen, I don't mean for this to come across as some kind of chauvinist bullshit—"

"Ooh, it's never good when you have to preface a statement with that," Owen chimed in.

Ransom glared but otherwise ignored him. "But you need someone there who can help if things go south. I won't risk anything happening to you."

"I'm pretty sure I can outrun Aamee, so at worst, the bad guys would get her," I reasoned.

"I'll have you know, I registered for the Boston Marathon last year," Aamee said.

"Oh, cool. How was it?" Toby asked.

"How would I know? I didn't actually run in it. Gross."

Ransom gave me a look that spoke volumes about his faith in Aamee. Or lack thereof. But before he could voice it, Carter cut in.

"I'll go with Taylor and Aamee to see that Petey dude's

family. I have all the credits I need for graduation and have a super light semester. I can go."

I opened my mouth to object but shut it when I couldn't think of a good reason to do so. I pursed my lips and looked at Ransom.

He returned my gaze for a moment before sighing heavily in defeat.

I smiled. Looked like I was road tripping with the princess and the jock.

I wondered what that made me.

Chapter Nineteen

RANSOM

"I still think I should go," I told Taylor as we made our way into my bedroom after her shift. I'd felt safer with her staying with me while Brad was lurking out there, and she thankfully hadn't put up much of a fight about it.

We'd passed a sleeping Hudson on the couch. I knew she had been working as many shifts at her job as possible, and I hoped she wasn't pushing herself too hard. I'd done my best to be available to take her to and from work, and I checked in with her multiple times a day, but there were still times when our schedules didn't line up. I hated that I couldn't always be there to protect her almost as much as I hated the fact that she needed protection in the first place.

Taylor flopped back on my bed. "I already have two bodyguards. Though I'm not sure which is more menacing, Carter's muscles or Aamee's mouth."

I crawled into bed and quickly rearranged us so I was spooned behind her, holding her tightly. She sighed into the embrace, and I felt the tension leave her body.

"I don't trust anyone else to keep you safe," I murmured against her neck before pressing kisses there.

"That's why you're needed here. For all we know, Brad could go after Hudson if we disappear on him. Plus, maybe with you staying here, Brad will stay focused on that and it'll keep him from being too suspicious about where I've gone."

I pulled back from her a bit. "You have a point about Hudson. But I also think we're giving him too much credit."

"What do you mean? And keep doing that thing with your mouth," she demanded as she nestled back into me.

"It's hard to kiss you and talk." But I did resume my trek across all the smooth skin within my reach.

"Hmm, then no more talking."

"Nice try. And I meant that we're acting like Brad is some sort of CIA operative. He's just some spoiled rich kid who thinks he can order people to do his bidding."

She hesitated a moment before responding. "Maybe. But I don't think it'll do us any good to *underestimate* him either. He did manipulate Hudson into telling him all about her problems, successfully blackmailing us. He attacked me after stalking me for months. And . . . we have to face facts. There's a very real possibility that he's the one who killed Petey. Whether it was intentional or accidental, I don't know. But we can't pretend it didn't happen."

I knew she was right. As callous as it sounded, pushing the whole Petey thing from my mind hadn't been difficult. It was almost a means of survival. Or at least a means to retaining my sanity. Thinking about it meant accepting Brad was capable of murder, and that turned this into something far scarier.

"Maybe we should go to the police," I said.

"And say what? Here is our wild theory about the guy

whose house we broke into?"

"There's just . . . There's gotta be another way."

"Well, if you think of it while you're kissing me, I'm all ears. But until then"—she turned around so she was facing me and immediately lowered her hand to caress my dick—"I'd like to think about other things."

"Oh yeah? What kinds of other things?" Maybe I should've been ashamed of how quickly she could distract me with sex, but I wasn't. I hoped we always turned each other on as much.

"Some *hard* things. And long. And thick."

"This is starting to sound like a corny romance novel, but I'm still into it."

She laughed before I swallowed the sound with my mouth. Our tongues danced as we let our hands wander, slowly undressing each other until we were naked and wanting.

And as I watched her back arch off the bed, I knew I'd always want to be wherever she was. And maybe that was at the heart of my not wanting her to go to Petey's alone. Home was where she was. And whether she was on a well-intentioned but ill-planned trip or in law school, I wanted to be there too.

But I also wanted to make her happy.

So I'd stay behind. This time and next time—if there was one. Because as our breaths became pants and our whimpers became moans, I was confident that though we each *could* stand alone, we'd never do it for long.

As we came together in that moment, I was confident we'd always come back together in the future as well.

TAYLOR

After convincing Ransom, the hardest part of the trip was explaining everything to Hudson. We'd kept her in the dark about a lot, and we couldn't do it anymore. It wasn't fair when so much of this concerned her too.

"So, let me get this straight," she said over a bowl of Frosted Flakes. "You two broke into Brad's—"

"We didn't break in," Ransom corrected. "We were let in." The particulars had become very important to him when explaining this to Hudson.

I knew it was because he didn't want her to have a negative impression of him, but his attention to semantics was getting a tad irritating.

Hudson's eye roll showed me she agreed. "So you were let in to steal a toy car worth millions of dollars?"

Ransom grimaced. "It sounds really stupid when you say it."

Probably because it is *really stupid.*

"How does it sound when you say it?" she asked.

"Like *Ocean's Eleven* met *Fast and the Furious,*" he replied.

"Of course it does," she muttered. "So what did Brad say when he realized you didn't steal it?"

"Nothing," I answered.

"Nothing?" Her voice held disbelief.

"Well, we haven't heard from him since, so...yeah, nothing."

Hudson propped her elbows on the table on either side of her bowl and buried her face in her hands. "This is all my fault."

Ransom was beside her in seconds, squatting down to her level. "It is *not* your fault."

"It's definitely my fault. If I hadn't gotten involved with bookies and then run my mouth to the first person willing to listen, none of this would be happening."

"Yes, it would," I answered firmly, causing both of them to look up at me. "At least the Brad stuff, because it was already happening before you got here. If anything, it's my fault for getting involved with Brad in the first place."

Ransom opened his mouth with a scowl on his face, but I held up a hand to stop him.

"But I'm past that kind of thinking. All of this is only one person's fault. Brad's. He's the only reason any of this is happening, and we have to keep the blame there because otherwise he wins. He enjoys manipulating people's feelings and toying with them like a game. And if we start taking responsibility for the things *he* is responsible for, then he wins. I won't lose to him. Not anymore."

Hudson had dropped her hands and was gazing at me. She looked weary, but there was also a new type of resolve in the hard set of her eyes.

"So what's the plan?"

I took a deep breath. This was going to be the tough part.

Ransom sat in a chair next to hers and began to explain. "Taylor is going to visit Petey's parents. If there's a link between Brad and him that we can find, we may be able to end this thing so we can all get on with our lives. And I'm going to stay here and see if I can draw Brad out."

Ransom's theory was that an absent Brad was almost scarier than a present one. Xander hadn't been able to track him, so Ransom was going to bait Brad into making some kind of contact, though he hadn't expounded on how he planned to do that.

Hudson's eyes grew wide. "You want to *make* him come after you?"

"Well, not come after me, but show himself, yeah. It's been like running from a ghost for the past few weeks. I'm over it."

"And you're okay with that?" Hudson asked me.

The truth was, no, I wasn't. I'd never want Ransom to be in danger because of me. Well . . . any *more* danger because of me. But I also got what he was saying. And if I was going to insist on following up on the Petey angle, then I had to have faith in Ransom's plan as well.

Evidently, relationships were all about compromise. Who knew?

I gave her a simple nod because words were difficult in that moment as emotion lodged in my throat.

"Hudson," Ransom said softly to regain her attention. "If we're doing this, it means you're potentially not safe here. We can't trust Brad not to do something drastic. So we're going to need you to stay with a friend of ours for a few days."

She took a shuddering breath and looked like she wanted to argue, but she set her mouth in a firm line. "With Drew and Sophia?"

I cleared my throat. "We were worried that would be too obvious."

They'd been my first text this morning, but when Sophia had immediately called me back, we'd quickly deduced that Ransom might need Drew as backup if Brad showed up, and their place might be the next place Brad would look if he went after Hudson.

"So where?" she asked, her voice sounding small, reminding me of how young she was. Even though she'd gotten herself into very adult danger, she was still young. We all were.

That knowledge firmed up my resolve to end this. We all had a lot of life ahead of us to enjoy. I was tired of Brad delaying that.

"Drew called his brother, Cody, and he agreed to let you stay with him," Ransom answered. "He just moved into an apartment about twenty minutes from here. He also has a lot of flexibility in his job, so he'd be able to drop you off and pick you up from work most days. And the rest of the group said they could help out with that as well."

Hudson groaned. "I hate this. I'm such a burden on everyone, and I don't even know this Cody person."

"You did meet him once," I interjected. At her confused look, I added, "Briefly. He showed up to the Christmas party as we were leaving."

"The skinny blond guy?" she asked.

"That's him," Ransom said. "We've known him for a while. He's your age, but he's dependable."

"And he's a nice guy," I added. "Maybe a little rough around the edges, but he doesn't take any shit from anyone, which is a good thing in this situation."

"Hudson," Ransom said softly. "You're not a burden. *Brad* is the burden. It's not your fault you're tangled up in our issues with him."

He'd reassured her of this countless times, but I knew from experience that it was difficult not to take responsibility. It was hard not to wonder what I'd done to deserve all this bad shit that happened.

She sniffled, but no tears fell. "Maybe it would be better if I just called the bookies myself. Maybe I can work out a payment plan or something."

Ransom looked at me, alarmed, before returning his gaze to Hudson. "Let's deal with one thing at a time, okay? Once we have this Brad shit under control, we'll figure out how to take care of that."

She gave him a searching look for a minute before murmuring, "Okay." Then she looked at me. "You said Cody's job gives him a lot of flexibility. What does he do?"

I bit the inside of my cheek for a second as I pondered the best way to answer that.

To her credit, Hudson's eyes only widened slightly when I told her Cody was a nude model. Only a few months with us, and we'd already made her nearly unshockable.

I'd take my victories where I could get them.

Chapter Twenty

RANSOM

"There's no way he's gonna show," I said to Brody, who was shoveling spoonfuls of cereal into his mouth as he fixated on the back of a Frosted Flakes box like he was a kid stuck back in the nineties.

Brody picked up the box and looked at the side. "This has a shit ton of sugar in it." He didn't sound horrified by the revelation, but it sounded like a revelation nonetheless.

"They're called *Frosted* Flakes for a reason."

He nodded thoughtfully. "The bananas balance it out though, I guess."

"Not really."

"But it's fruit."

"Can you focus for a second?"

He glanced quickly at me before saying, "I am. But you keep interrupting me."

Jesus Christ. I tried hard to avoid rolling my eyes because I would need Brody's help soon. It was a request that sounded better in my head than it did out loud when I asked him, but there was no denying it. I couldn't risk an encounter with Brad by myself. There was no telling what he was capable of. Especially since it was a pretty safe bet that he'd be homicidal.

"I mean focus on what *I'm* saying, not Tony the Tiger."

Brody put the box down and looked over at me, clearly annoyed because I'd bothered him during his afternoon breakfast.

I'd called him over earlier in the day because last night Hudson had said she'd seen Brad walk by Bark Bar a couple of times while she was working. He hadn't gone in, but the sight of him had been enough to shake her.

So Brody'd agreed to come help me devise a plan for how we'd lure Brad out of whatever cave he'd been holed up in and then have my back when I met with Brad face-to-face. But now Brody seemed more focused on his—or my—cereal than figuring out what we should do once we met up with Brad. *If* we met up with him.

Threatening him wouldn't work. Promising him we would get the car wouldn't work. But we had to do *something*.

I shifted my attention from where I'd been staring out the vertical blinds of the sliding glass door that led to the balcony.

"I mean, he's arrogant, but he's not stupid."

After putting his bowl in my sink, he shrugged. "Douchebags like Brad are usually both."

He had a point there, and I hoped like hell he was right. After Taylor had left this morning, I'd emailed Brad from the account Taylor and I had set up to communicate with him before the heist. I'd done my best to pose as Taylor— composing a long-winded email about how I wanted to end this for everyone, including Brad. Then, I told him, we could go our separate ways once we all had what we wanted.

I said Ransom had gotten cold feet at the last minute but that there had to be a way we could get the car or something else of value from his dad's house. That I wanted to meet him one-on-one while Ransom was at class and figure all this shit out. I'd tried to sound desperate—desperate to be done with all this, desperate to get the money to pay off Hudson's bookies.

I'd edited the shit out of that email until I was certain I'd made it as good as it could get. But still, when I'd hit Send, I'd figured there was no way in hell Brad would believe a word of it.

So when his reply came—*Where and when?*—I figured Brad must've been pretty desperate too.

$$X_O$$

About an hour later, I opened my door to a disgruntled stalker. As I'd expected, he seemed surprised to see me, but more than that, he looked almost frightened. Brad's eyes grew wide at the sight of me and widened even more when he looked past me to Brody, where I guessed he thought Taylor might be.

"It's just us, fuckstick," Brody said. "Sorry to disappoint you."

Brad let out something that resembled a laugh that hadn't fully formed. "Well, I should be used to you disappointing me by now, right?" He didn't wait for a reply before he added, "So what is this, exactly? Because if you lured me here to kill me, you probably should've thought of a different location than your apartment."

"We didn't lure you here to kill you," I said, "but I can't make any promises that it won't happen."

Brad scrunched up his nose at me. "Better make sure I'm dead this time, then." He entered my apartment without any indication from me that he was welcome inside, but it was probably better that my eighty-two-year-old neighbor, Mrs. Davies, didn't hear us talking about murder and theft, so I didn't resist.

But I wasn't going to let him dictate how this meeting ran. "Sit down," I said after closing the door.

"I'm not your bitch."

"Oh, you're definitely *a* bitch," Brody told him.

He'd been a few feet behind me and made a move toward Brad, probably knowing I would stop him. Which I did. I put a hand on Brody's chest like I was preventing him from lunging at Brad, though it felt more like two of the kids at Safe Haven posturing without any real intent to fight.

"Fuck you," Brad spat. "I'm not the bitch here. That's you and your dumbass friends. You can't even steal a toy car from a rich guy who can go buy another. A fridge? Really? You practically had the thing out the door."

That made me smile. "I actually did have the thing out the door. Just decided to return it."

"You're such a fucking pussy. The car was as good as mine, and you returned it like a kid whose parents caught him stealing a pack of bubble gum from the corner store."

I shook my head, more disgusted than angry. "Stop with the lies already. It's over. You're not getting that car. It doesn't belong to you now, and it never will. Your dad's giving it to your nephews. And the rest of the stuff? He'd rather donate it to museums than see any of it go to you."

As I spoke, Brad's eyes narrowed a bit, and his expression shifted from arrogance to confusion.

He crossed his arms and took a step toward me. "What the fuck are you talking about?"

"Jesus, enough." I ran a hand through my hair in frustration. "We didn't do it, and we're not going to. Your little sob story about your grandfather? Bullshit. The car being rightfully yours? Bullshit too. Not only do you not have it now, you never will."

"Yeah," he said, his voice noticeably meeker than it'd been a moment before. "Go back to the thing about the museums."

It took me a few seconds to understand why he was asking, but once I did, I could feel the satisfaction spread through my body.

"You didn't know, did you?" I asked almost quietly.

He let his silence answer for him.

"I heard your father telling someone at the party. It's why I put the car back. Because not only are you not getting either of those"—I slowed my speech down a bit, hoping to emphasize my words—"you're not getting any of his prized possessions. Your own dad would rather see it go to strangers than to you. If that doesn't tell you what a worthless piece of shit you are, then I don't know what does."

Brad stayed quiet for a moment, and I could tell he was warring internally with himself—trying his best not to reveal the emotion I knew he probably felt. Even someone with a heart as cold as Brad's couldn't ignore the pain of his own father's lack of trust in him.

He obviously knew he and his dad weren't on good terms. Even Xander had picked up on the fact things were strained between them. But to not even get any of the things your father was most proud of? It had to be a blow Brad didn't see coming.

After a minute or so, he seemed to regain some of the composure he'd momentarily lost. "Whatever. I don't want any of that old shit anyway. I'm not a fucking antique shop. Only reason I wanted the car was so I could sell it for the money."

While I knew the part about wanting to sell the car was most likely true, I doubted he had no interest in inheriting any of his father's other possessions. Even if he didn't want the actual items, it must feel pretty shitty to realize he had no chance of getting them in the first place.

"Right," I said. "You keep telling yourself that because that's way easier to believe than the truth." I leaned in closer to him so the full effect of my words could be felt as I said them. "Your family doesn't trust you with their prized possessions because you're a selfish fucking snake."

With that, Brad pulled his arm back and swung, his fist connecting with the side of my face before I had the chance to react. I'd been hit harder plenty of times, so the contact didn't do much to faze me. But I wasn't going to let this fucker punch me in the jaw and not reciprocate. But before I got the chance to land a punch of my own, Brody's arm came from behind and rose up over Brad's head, and whatever he'd been holding in his hand connected with it.

Brad dropped to the floor instantly, and Brody stood over him like a kid who'd just taken down the schoolyard bully. Brad was out cold.

Then Brody looked down at his hand, which drew my attention to what he was holding.

When he raised it up toward his face to examine it closer, I almost laughed.

"This thing looks just like Taylor," he said, flicking the face of the bobblehead that Lila had given her for Christmas. He'd knocked Brad unconscious with the base of it.

Best Christmas gift ever!

Chapter Twenty-One

TAYLOR

The fact that Aamee had made it to her mid-twenties without ever being in a catastrophic car accident was astounding.

She'd insisted we take her car—a sporty, white BMW only she was allowed to drive—and drove the damn thing like an intoxicated Danica Patrick.

Her navigation warned her that our exit was a half mile away, but Aamee made no move to slow down or get into the right lane.

"You realize we have to turn off soon, right?" Carter asked worriedly from the back seat.

At first, I wondered why he'd elected to sit in the back. With as big as he was, I'd have thought he'd be uncomfortable in her small car.

As soon as Aamee's foot had made contact with the gas pedal, I understood. And for a moment, I wondered if I might actually be safer in a dark alley with Brad. Better to be cramped than hurtled out of the windshield. I'd made sure my seat belt was firmly fastened and was practically glued by hand to the *oh shit* bar.

"I know, I know," she said, clearly annoyed. "You guys are such back-seat drivers."

"I'm technically not in the back seat, so . . ."

The look she gave me, which she held for far too long considering she was careening down a highway at ninety miles an hour, was unimpressed.

"I can't believe I drop everything to do *you* a favor, even offering to *drive* you on this fool's errand, and you still have the nerve to give me shit."

"You're right. I do have lots of nerve." My body actually held zillions of nerves, and I hoped to arrive safely at our destination so I could prevent all of them from being severed by jagged glass as Aamee crashed us into a guardrail.

"That's not an apology," she said.

"I promise to apologize profusely if you manage to get us there in one piece."

She scoffed. "What do you mean, if I manage? I've gotten us this far. And I'll have you know, I have a perfect driving record. Well . . . I do now at least."

I wasn't brave enough to ask her what she meant by that last part.

"Uh, Aamee?" Carter said from the back.

"What?" she snapped.

"We're about to pass the exit."

"Shit! See what you almost made me do?" she said as she shot a glare in my direction.

I looked to the right to see we were alongside the off-ramp but still in the far-left lane.

What does she mean almost?

The disembodied voice of the navigation—who Carter had named Edgar because he sounded like a butler—had just alerted us that it was recalculating when Aamee gripped the wheel and jerked it to the right.

All I heard was the blare of a truck horn as Aamee took us on a route that sent us damn near perpendicular to the highway. Blood rushed through my ears as I grabbed the *oh shit* bar with both hands now and closed my eyes.

Once the car had been righted, I slowly opened my eyelids. We were—against all odds—safely traveling down the off-ramp. I took a deep breath, trying to calm my rapidly beating heart. When I accepted the fact that we had somehow survived, I turned in my seat so I could glare at Aamee.

"What. The. Fuck?"

She had the nerve to look perplexed. "What?"

"You almost killed us," Carter snapped from the back seat.

She rolled her eyes. "We were fine. I had it under control."

"Under control! Are you high?" Which, when I thought about it, would explain a lot.

"You guys are the worst. I had plenty of room to get over."

"Tell that to the semi who nearly jackknifed trying to avoid us," Carter griped.

"There was no knifejacking."

"Jack*knife*," he corrected.

"Whatever. At most it was a . . . a . . . butterknife-jack."

"What the hell is that?" I asked, flabbergasted at her nonplussed responses since I was very, very plussed.

"Like, a less serious jack . . . knife . . . jack . . . whatever that thing is you keep saying. Like how a butterknife can't actually hurt anyone. It was like that."

"I'd really like to test your theory that a butterknife can't hurt," I growled. The thought of stabbing Aamee repeatedly with a dull utensil sounded very appealing.

"Is anyone hurt or dead?" she asked. "No. See? Butterknife-jack."

Carter slumped back in his seat, drawing my attention. He looked ashen.

"You okay?" I asked.

He sighed. "Yeah. It's just... it's weird *not* being the dumbest one in a room."

"Well, we're not in a room, so maybe you should rethink that assessment," Aamee snapped. "Besides, you two are going to have to stop bitching because we're here."

I darted my attention out the window to look around. Sure enough, we were outside a two-story house that screamed upper-middle class, with its manicured lawn and perfectly painted shutters. I glanced at the navigation to confirm this was the place.

Staring at the house, I tried to focus on what we were there to do. Ransom and I had talked through how I should try to glean information without being too obvious, and Aamee, Carter, and I had discussed what each of our roles were in between bouts of fearing for our lives.

Initially I'd thought it might be better to meet with them alone. I was worried bringing two other people might muddy the conversation too much. But first of all, there was no way either of them were going to leave without getting to hear what Petey's parents had to say, because they were two of the biggest gossip hounds I'd ever met. And second of all, I couldn't deny they each brought something valuable to the table.

Carter was immensely likeable and could talk to a flagpole. So it was likely he'd be able to put Petey's parents at ease with small talk. Aamee was a shark, sniffing out shreds of information like it was blood in the water, but she lurked silently before going in for the kill. If anyone could manipulate information out of the Faulkners without them even realizing it, it was Aamee.

And I'd keep us on track. I knew what our general objective was, and I'd make sure we stayed on the best course to accomplish it. I hoped.

"Ready?" I asked the other two.

"Ready," they both said in unison, Carter following it up with a "jinx" that we both ignored.

We climbed out of the car and slowly made our way to the front door, all of us eyeing it as if it were covered in poison ivy. Finally, I stepped forward to knock, but it flew open before I could.

"You made it," Mrs. Faulkner said, her eyes bright with what looked to be relief. "We're so happy you came. Come on in."

We shuffled inside and gathered in the foyer.

"Let me take your coats. Pete is right through there," she said, pointing to a room to the left of the foyer.

I startled a little when she talked about Pete before realizing she was probably talking about her husband. I doubted Mrs. Faulkner had disinterred her son and staged him in the living room, but honestly, we'd been through enough weird shit that I probably shouldn't have ruled anything out.

I took in the room when we entered: cream carpeting, floral-patterned furniture, and white walls decorated with a variety of paintings, mostly of women and children holding parasols. There was also a large tin bucket in one corner that held an assortment of umbrellas.

Was there such a thing as an umbrella fetish? If so, I wondered which of the Faulkners suffered from it.

Mr. Faulkner stood when he saw us enter, extending a hand in greeting. "Thanks for coming," he said as he gestured for us to sit.

Carter, Aamee, and I squashed awkwardly on the couch as Mr. Faulkner fidgeted on the loveseat across from us. "How was your trip?" he asked after an awkward few seconds.

Saying we'd nearly been flattened by a semi was inappropriate, so I uttered an "It was fine" instead.

He nodded as if I'd just explained Fermat's Last Theorem to him, which, since it was one of the most complex equations ever, would've been impressive.

"Traffic has gotten so much worse around here the last few years," he said. "Industrialization at its finest."

I smiled and nodded while I internally prayed to whatever god helped blunt girls navigate sensitive conversations.

Thankfully, Mrs. Faulkner hurried in carrying a tray of snacks. "You must be hungry after driving all that way. Help yourselves." She set the tray on the coffee table in front of us. "Can I get anyone anything to drink?"

We all politely declined, and she sat down.

Carter leaned forward to put some ham and cheese cubes on a napkin and then sat back, munching away.

The air was thick with tension as we traded smiles and fidgeted.

"So," Mrs. Faulkner began. "You said you had news?" Her voice was so hopeful, it crushed me that I couldn't blurt out all my thoughts. But doing so would be reckless and potentially more harmful in the long run if I turned out to be wrong.

"More like... questions?" I said, my uncertainty coming out in the tone of my question. When her face fell, I rushed to continue. "There were some... coincidences that seemed suspicious, and I wanted to talk to you about them to see if we could make sense of it."

Her face perked up at that, and Mr. Faulkner leaned forward. "What kind of coincidences?"

"What do you know about Petey's friend Lacey?"

"Oh my God, do you think she had something to do with this?" Mrs. Faulkner asked.

"We can't make any assumptions about that right now," Aamee cut in. "We just want to know more so we can try to connect some dots."

We were being vague, and I was worried the Faulkners were going to call us on it, but they didn't. They had a right to know what we suspected in full detail, but they thankfully seemed, at least for now, willing to discuss things at our pace.

"We never met her," Mr. Faulkner said.

"But Petey mentioned her frequently," his wife rushed to add. "Anytime I asked what his plans were, he said he was meeting Lacey. I suspected they were dating, but Petey always denied it. I figured it was just him wanting his privacy."

It was odd to me that Petey never corrected his mother's assumption that Lacey was a female. Unless she was and it was simply a coincidence that was Brad's last name as well.

"Do you know her?" his mother asked, her voice bordering on frantic. "The police never were able to locate her."

I had to give them something, even though it was probably an error in judgment to do so this quickly. I'd wanted to build up to this after I'd asked more probing questions to see if I could figure out a connection between Brad and Petey. But ultimately, what was the point of drawing this out? It was probably better to get to the heart of it immediately.

"Had you ever considered that Lacey was a last name?

That maybe it wasn't a girlfriend but just a regular friend?"

His parents both looked shell-shocked for a moment. "No," his father said softly. "We never considered that."

"And the police never suggested it as a possibility. Maybe because I was so convinced it was a girl." She looked stricken, as if she thought her assumption had somehow hampered the investigation.

"We don't know that's the case. I just…after you mentioned a Lacey at the funeral, it occurred to me that it could be a last name."

"Do you know anyone with that last name?"

Here it was…the moment of truth. "There was a guy I knew at school. He was a year ahead of Petey and me. His name was Brad. Brad Lacey."

His parents looked contemplative for a second before his mother said, "No. He never mentioned a Brad."

"Was there a group he typically hung out with? Any other friends you know of?" Aamee asked.

Mrs. Faulkner suddenly looked uncomfortable, her hands toying with the edge of her loose, knee-length skirt. "Petey didn't have much of a social life," she said quietly. "He rarely mentioned friends or going out anywhere. That's why I was so excited when he started talking about this Lacey person." She looked over at her husband. "What if my nagging about being more social led him to someone who hurt him?"

She began crying, and Mr. Faulkner sat up taller so he could wrap his arm around her and pull her close.

"We just wanted what was best for him," Mr. Faulkner said. "None of this is our fault."

Sensing a need to redirect but floundering to figure out a way to do that, I looked helplessly at Aamee and then at Carter.

Carter winked at me and said through a mouthful of food, "What kinds of things was Petey into?"

Mrs. Faulkner sniffled a few times as she struggled to get herself under control. When she turned back to us, her head was held high and her jaw was set firmly. She might have been the strongest woman I'd ever been in the presence of.

"Computers. There was nothing that involved a computer that Petey couldn't figure out. Programming, developing, even hacking. Petey could do it all. He was already being recruited by firms across the US who wanted someone with his skill on their team."

That was... interesting. For as manipulative and scheming as Brad was, he wasn't great with... well, anything really. He'd been a business student and had gotten decent grades, but he wasn't exceptional at anything. As narcissistic as he was, everyone would've known if he had been.

My mind went back to how he'd known the route to take when he'd tried to kidnap me. How he'd seemed to know where there were cameras and where there weren't. Brad wouldn't have been able to access that type of information, but for a computer genius? It probably would've been simple. Xander was able to do incredible things with computers, and that wasn't even something he spent most of his time doing.

"Do you know if he was working on anything recently?" Carter asked, and I wondered if his mind had gone where mine did. Carter didn't always get the most credit for his brains, but the look on his face was assessing and astute.

Mrs. Faulkner shrugged. "He never told us much about the things he was working on." She looked saddened that she couldn't give us more information for a minute before her eyes lit up. "He did have a job, though."

"Doing what?" I asked.

She opened her mouth to answer, but Mr. Faulkner spoke first. "We don't know that. He never said he was working."

Mrs. Faulkner waved him off. "He had to have been. Where else would he have been getting money from?"

"Why did you suspect he was working?" Aamee asked.

"Because he stopped asking us for money. And when he came home last, he was wearing new clothes. And he'd gotten new glasses. Nice ones. Gucci or something."

"Is there a way to find out? Did he use a bank account that maybe you could ask for statements? Or maybe he had a computer he would've done work with or kept some kind of planner that might have notes on it? Anything like that?" I asked.

The more I listened, the more I convinced myself Brad and Petey were connected. The money, the secrecy, the name— there just had to be something to it.

"Not that we found. The police looked too, but nothing out of the ordinary popped up," Mr. Faulkner explained.

"Would you all want to have a look at his things?" Mrs. Faulkner asked.

I nearly leaped off the couch in agreement, but Mr. Faulkner's voice kept me still.

"Faye," he warned, his voice low and admonishing. "If the police didn't find anything, why would they? Besides, we don't really know them."

And damn it, but the man had a point.

"What more damage can be done?" Mrs. Faulkner asked, her voice sad and resigned. "We've already lost everything."

Do not cry, Taylor. Hold it together.

Watching Petey's parents—people who had obviously

adored their son—have a silent conversation about the things they had left to lose was nearly unbearable. I looked over to see Aamee surreptitiously wipe at her eyes and Carter's head tilt toward the floor.

I vowed, then and there, that if Brad were involved in the death of Petey, I'd uncover it. I had no idea *how* I would do such a thing, but I'd figure it out.

After a few more moments, Mr. Faulkner sighed heavily and stood up, cupping his wife's cheek and giving it a soft pat. "I'll be in the study if you need me." Then he left the room, Mrs. Faulkner watching him until he was out of sight.

Clearing her throat, she also stood. "I'll show you Petey's room."

I nodded, and we rose to follow her. She led us up a set of hardwood stairs and then down a short hallway to a closed door with a poster on it of Darth Vader and the words *Join us or Die.*

Not gonna lie . . . the message felt a bit foreboding.

Mrs. Faulkner paused only a moment before opening the door and gesturing for us to walk in before her.

I took in the room: sci-fi and anime posters covered the walls, computer parts were strewn across his workstation, and a few errant articles of clothing were on the bed and floor.

Mrs. Faulkner walked over to the bed and picked up a plush Yoda, clutching it close to her chest. "The police tore the place apart, but I put it back how he'd left it. I was tempted to straighten it up, but . . ."

Even though her words trailed off, I was still gutted by them. "We'll be careful not to move anything."

Once we were in the room, I felt lost as to where to begin. I was wholly unprepared to investigate what was going on or look for clues. I wasn't sure I'd ever been more out of my element, which was really saying something.

Aamee moved over to his desk, where a laptop sat. "May I?" she asked Mrs. Faulkner.

The woman nodded before saying, "But it's not the one he used at school. The police never found that one, which led them to think the whole thing was a robbery gone wrong."

None of us seemed to know what to say to that, so we went back to the task at hand. Aamee sat down at the computer and powered it on while Carter poked around the posters and pictures on the walls, moving them so he could look behind them. I guessed he was looking for some kind of hidey-hole.

"It's not password protected?" Aamee asked as she logged in to the laptop.

"Oh, uh, no. I used it sometimes, so he took the password off."

Which also meant we weren't likely to find anything on it. If Petey was as good with computers as his mom said, there's no way he'd leave anything important unprotected.

Aamee clicked around while Carter and I continued to search the room without disturbing anything.

After a while, Aamee shut the laptop lid with a sigh. "I didn't find anything."

"Me neither," Carter agreed.

I wanted to cry. We'd come all the way out here and given the Faulkners' false hope that we could help, and for what? Nothing. I stopped at a high dresser and rested my arm along the top with my back to everyone else as I tried to get my bearings.

There had to be a time when I'd make a situation better. I couldn't be a harbinger of pain and chaos forever, right?

I took a few deep breaths from my nose so my disappointment wouldn't show when I spun around. As I began to turn, my eyes caught on an object on top of the dresser. Picking it up, I studied it for a second before turning to face Mrs. Faulkner.

"Is this Petey's school ID?" I held up a lanyard that had his ID and a key on it.

She came closer. "Yes."

"Why's it here?" I asked, my voice sounding abrupt even to me. "I mean, he'd been on campus before he went to meet Lacey, right? He didn't come home first?"

The student IDs at my school were necessary to get into certain buildings, to eat in the cafeteria, all kinds of things. It didn't make sense that it would be at his house.

"The police recovered it from the . . . the scene. When they didn't pull any prints but Petey's off it, they gave it back to us." She came closer and ran her finger lightly over the picture of her son as I continued to hold it. "We weren't sure what the key was to, though. The police didn't seem to think it mattered."

My voice was rough when I replied. "I know what it's to."

"You do? What?"

I looked at my friends before focusing back on Mrs. Faulkner. "Our library has lockboxes that students can rent in the basement. They used to have a mailroom down there, and when it closed, they kept the boxes. The librarians keep track of it."

Mrs. Faulkner's eyes narrowed in confusion. "Why would Petey need something like that?"

I couldn't answer that question. Not yet. But I damn sure planned to find out.

Chapter Twenty-Two

TAYLOR

The campus was only an hour drive from Petey's parents' house, so it made sense to go straight there. The Faulkners had seemed a little hesitant to let us take the ID and key but had ultimately conceded.

Being back on campus was . . . surreal. I'd vowed to never come back after all the shit with Brad had gone down. I hadn't even walked in graduation. But it also seemed fitting that the place that had brought Brad into my life could potentially also be where I brought him down.

I led Carter and Aamee across the giant quad to where the library sat on the other side.

"Couldn't we have parked closer?" Aamee whined.

"The library is the center of campus, so . . . no."

"This place sucks," she muttered.

"I dunno. The football stadium looked pretty sweet," Carter chimed in.

Aamee didn't answer him as I continued to power-walk across campus.

"Are you worried they're somehow going to tear down the library if we don't get there in under five minutes? Jesus, slow down."

But I couldn't. It was like the entire past year had been building to this. If I opened this damn box and pulled out a bunch of porn mags, I was gonna be pissed.

As we walked into the library, I scanned my own ID at the turnstile that guarded the entrance and hoped it still worked. It did. "I'll grab two guest passes and be right back."

"Screw that," Aamee said. "We'll just scan Petey's twice."

That made me pause. What if his ID set off a red flag in the system and they refused to let us in? "I don't think that's a good idea."

"Of course you don't," Aamee muttered. "Whatever. Just go in and find the box. We'll wait for you out here."

"It'll only take a minute to—"

"It's fine. I'm hungry. Carter and I will go grab a snack, and you can do your little . . . *National Treasure* thing."

"Such a good movie," Carter mused. "Nick Cage is seriously underrated."

"Uh, no. He's definitely *over*rated," Aamee argued.

Carter looked at her pityingly. "Sweet, sweet summer child."

I was suddenly all too happy to carry on without these two idiots. "There's a coffee shop right over there," I said, pointing across the quad. "I'll meet you there as soon as I'm done."

They both waved me off as they wandered away arguing about the merits—or lack thereof—of *Con Air*.

I shook my head to remove the stupid before hurrying toward the back of the library, where the stairs leading to the basement were. As I descended the steps, I couldn't help but get caught up in the moment. I really did feel like Nicholas Cage in *National Treasure*, slowly creeping into a dimly lit basement that I wasn't supposed to be in. My brain convinced me that Brad was potentially hiding among the stacks of boxes and old library furniture that littered the room.

There wasn't really any danger. Logically I knew that. Even a place that time seemed to have forgotten had security cameras blinking down on me. But still...I was potentially unraveling a murder case. It was understandable if my imagination wanted to run away from me.

When I reached the wall of lockboxes, I withdrew Petey's key from my coat pocket. There was a number engraved on it that let me know which box it went to: *57.*

I scanned until I found it and then took a deep breath before sliding the key into its door.

I half expected to find a snake or tarantula guarding a satchel of papers detailing Petey and Brad's diabolical plans. So finding a simple flash drive in the shape of a turtle was a little anticlimactic.

After removing the drive, I swiped my hand over all sides of the box to be sure I hadn't missed anything. Confident that there was nothing else inside, I closed it up, pocketed the key, and hurried upstairs with the flash drive.

Even though pretty much everyone had a laptop nowadays, the library did have a bank of desktop computers pushed against one of the walls. They also served as a means to search the library database for books and online journals, so the area wasn't totally empty, but close.

I was able to get on a computer away from anyone else, logged in with my school ID number and password—which thankfully still worked; my school really needed to get better at purging their systems of graduates—and opened the flash drive.

At first, nothing on there made much sense. But as I continued to click, things came together like pieces of a really intricate puzzle. I'd need Xander to really make sense of it all, but it looked like...were they really...holy shit.

I carefully ejected the flash drive and hurried out of the library, heading toward the coffee shop where I'd sent Carter and Aamee. When I arrived, I went inside and found them sitting and talking at a small table.

"Guys, we gotta go," I said when I reached them.

"Why? What did you find?" Aamee asked, her eyes wide.

"I don't..." I looked around. "I don't want to talk about it here."

"Top-secret shit," Carter said. "I'm into it." He drained his cup and stood. "You want anything before we head back to the car?"

"Uh..." I eyed the muffin Aamee had in front of her and then the case along the front of the shop. "Yeah, I may grab a snack." All this private investigator work had made me hungry.

They both nodded at me, and I went and ordered myself a tea and muffin. When I made it back to them, they rose silently and we left. The walk back to the car felt agonizingly long.

As soon as we were safely inside, Aamee turned to me. "Well?"

"Let me call Ransom so I can tell you all at once." Pulling out my phone, I FaceTimed my boyfriend, who answered almost immediately.

"Uh, h-hey. How's it going?"

Well, this is awkward.

"You okay?" I asked him.

"Yeah, sure, definitely. You?"

He was being strange as hell, but I let it go, too excited to share my news with him.

"Are you with anyone?"

His eyes widened a fraction. "Um, no. Why do you ask?"

Okay, I couldn't ignore that one. "What's going on? You're being sketchy."

He looked panicked for a second before the phone left his face and Brody's filled the screen.

"Hey, Taylor. Sorry, Ransom hit his head, and now he's acting weird."

"He hit his head! Is he okay? Should you take him to the hospital?"

"Jesus Christ," I heard someone mutter before the phone changed hands again. This time, it was Drew who appeared. "Ransom didn't hit his head. We found Brad, and Ransom's reeling a little."

"Oh. Where is he?"

Drew hesitated. "Why don't you tell us your news first?"

That wasn't a reassuring request, but I acquiesced. "I found a flash drive in Petey's lockbox. I took a quick look at it in the library, and there's all this crazy stuff on it. Video diaries of Petey too, but I didn't want to watch those in the middle of the library. But the stuff I did look at . . . It looks like Petey was working for Brad's dad."

All three guys had somehow smooshed their faces on screen. They looked like some kind of confused Hydra.

"What's the issue with that?" Drew asked. "Brad could've just been doing his friend a solid by getting him an internship."

My face screwed up in response. "Does that sound like Brad?"

"Well ... no."

"I'm going to need Xander to take a closer look at it," I went on. "Some of the files are encrypted. But from what I could see ... it looked like Petey was helping Brad embezzle from his dad's company."

"Shit," Ransom said, rubbing a hand over his hair. "Any idea how much?"

"Not exactly, but I did find a spreadsheet on there. The last figure on it was over a half million dollars. But I didn't look long enough to see if that was what they'd already taken or a projection or what."

Brody whistled.

"So it's good you found Brad," I added. "Because there's no telling what he'd do to keep this from getting out. Where is he?"

The three of them shared a look that didn't make me feel better.

"Ransom?"

He looked down at the camera. "Are you sitting down?"

"Well, I'm in a car, so ..." My surroundings should've been pretty obvious from the way I was holding my phone.

"Oh, yeah, right. Well, the thing is ... Brad's here."

"Here? Like, in the city?"

He cleared his throat. "No. Like in my apartment."

Chapter Twenty-Three

RANSOM

I paced the living room, waiting for Taylor, Aamee, and Carter to get home. Taylor had said Aamee was breaking the laws of time and space on their way, so they should be back any minute.

"Dude, relax," Xander said. "It'll be okay."

"*Dude*, we have a guy tied to a chair in my bedroom who potentially murdered another guy to cover up an embezzlement scheme. What part of any of this is fine?"

Xander shrugged. "None of it. I was just trying to make you feel better."

I stared at him, flabbergasted.

"What?" he asked. "I'm not good at emotions and shit. So sue me."

"Understatement of the year," Aniyah muttered.

Xander glared at her. "Why are you even here?"

"FOMO," she replied casually.

"What does that mean?" Brody asked.

"Fear of missing out," Sophia answered.

Brody smiled widely. "Oh, yeah, I have that too." He

walked over and high-fived Aniyah, who looked amused by him.

The fact that these were the best people I could find to help me out of a crisis was not as comforting as I needed it to be.

Before anyone could say anything else stupid, Taylor pushed open the door, the others following close behind. She walked directly to me, and I enveloped her in a tight hug.

"It's going to be okay," I said quietly, offering the same empty reassurance Xander just had. Guess I sucked at emotions too.

She pulled back so she could look up at me. "So... kidnapping? That's an interesting add to your résumé."

I shrugged. "It seemed like the right thing to do at the time."

"And now?" she asked.

"I guess that depends on where we go from here."

She nodded once before lifting up on her tiptoes to press a kiss to my cheek and then pulling away completely. She reached into her pocket, pulled out a flash drive, and handed it to Xander.

"Hopefully you can make better sense of this."

Xander instantly pushed it into his laptop and began clicking. We all let him work, watching each keystroke intently.

"If I'd known I'd be putting on a show, I would've charged admission," he said.

We all ignored his comment. It was as if we were all holding our breath, anxiously waiting for evidence that we could breathe normally again.

"Shit," Xander said after a little bit of searching.

That was *not* a comment that encouraged normal breathing.

"What'd you find?" Drew asked.

"Pretty much exactly what Taylor thought she saw. It looks like Petey was working for Brad's dad. Once he was inside, he was able to hack into the company's mainframe and start moving money around. Never enough at a time from any one department, but he took enough overall to amass quite a sum. He even has information on the bank account he moved it to on here. Let me see if I can access it."

We watched avidly as he worked, pressing keys at a speed that seemed inhuman to me.

"That's weird," Xander eventually said.

"What?" I asked. Why did the guy keep saying cryptic shit without expanding on it?

"The account's empty. I'm looking through statements, and it seems like . . . it seems like Petey put all the money back."

Taylor and I locked eyes, and then she spoke. "So Brad gets Petey to help steal from his father. Petey does and funnels money into an account for . . . how long?"

"Looks like five months," Xander supplied.

"That's a shit ton of money to steal in only five months. How did no one notice?" Sophia asked.

"These are billion-dollar operations with departments that all work fairly independently of each other. He couldn't have gotten away with it forever, but a few months?" Xander shrugged. "Definitely possible for someone as talented at hacking as Petey. He wrote down all the ways he covered his tracks. Some of this is shit even *I* couldn't pull off."

"So they steal money for five months," Taylor continues. "And then . . . what? They just decide to give it all back? Why would they go to all that trouble and then return it?"

"I don't think *they* gave it back," Xander said. "I think that was all Petey. Watch this." Xander clicked on a thumbnail, and a video of Petey popped up.

"What is it with Gen-Zers always filming themselves?" Aamee asked.

"You do realize *you're* a Gen-Zer, right?" Sophia said. "And you have enough images of yourself on your phone to put any narcissist to shame."

"Shh," Taylor demanded.

Xander pushed Play, and the video started.

"Uh, okay, today is, um…" Petey looked down at his phone. "Today is October thirteenth, and I've…I've had enough. Lacey isn't… He hasn't been honest with me, and I can't keep doing this. It's wrong, and I don't think… This isn't the kind of person I want to be. So I wanted to record me giving the money back. So if I have to go to the police, well…here it'll be." Petey must have shared his screen because we were suddenly looking at what was on his screen instead of at him.

I couldn't even discern how I felt as I watched this young kid, with his unruly mop of blond hair and thick-framed glasses, make what amounted to an insurance policy in case the shitstorm Brad got him involved in went south.

It made me want to go into my bedroom and beat Brad within an inch of his life. Because this was what the asshole did. He took good people with bright futures, and he tainted them.

I looked over at Taylor and drank her in—not just her external beauty, but also her resilience. Her strength. Because Brad had impacted her too. He'd wounded her in ways she might always bear faint scars from.

But she'd persevered. And it looked like Petey had tried to persevere as well. He just hadn't had a two-hundred-plus-pound football player at his back when it had all gone down.

We watched as Petey clicked a few buttons, seemingly returning money from where he'd taken it. The whole process didn't take very long, and when it was done, Petey put the camera back on himself.

"I know Brad's not going to be happy when he realizes the account's empty. I'm not sure what he'll do, to be honest." Petey gave a small laugh at that, the kind that was full of nervous energy. Though I doubted even Petey would've guessed what Brad actually had in store for him.

"I have a few other things to set right," Petey continued. "A confrontation to have. And then hopefully, this will all be over. And if it doesn't end well . . . If the police find this first, and I go to jail . . . then . . . I guess . . ." Petey looked directly into the camera, his eyes intent and honest. "Please just tell my parents I'm sorry. And that I love them very much."

The video ended, but none of us moved. We all stood there and stared at the frozen image of a guy who thought the worst-case scenario was prison. Who hadn't even seemed to consider that it could be something so much worse.

"Whoa, okay," Carter said after a minute, rubbing a hand over his face. "So, yeah." He stood. "That bastard in there?" he asked as he took a step toward my bedroom.

I hurried to intercept him. "Carter—"

"No. No! You didn't . . . you didn't sit there, Ransom. You didn't sit there and have snacks with his family. You didn't hear the way they talked about him. Or how his mom put his room back together after the police trashed it so it would look just how he left it." Carter pointed over my shoulder. "That motherfucker in there is a monster. And we have to keep him from hurting anyone else."

"I know."

Carter struggled to get past me, and I gripped him tighter.

"Carter, I *know*. And we will. But not like this. Petey's family doesn't get closure if we do it like this."

Carter struggled against me for another moment before sagging against me, allowing me to embrace him fully.

He buried his head into my neck for a second as his body shuddered violently. "It's not fair, man. The guy... Petey... he looks kinda like Toby did when I first met him, ya know? A scrawny kid people think they can mess with. It's not... We can't let him get away with it."

I gripped him even tighter. "We won't," I said fiercely. "I promise."

After a second, he nodded against me, and then he pulled away. I let him go because it wasn't me he needed.

"Why don't you text Toby? I'm sure he'd leave class early to meet you here."

Carter sniffled. "He definitely would." That thought brought a small smile to his face. "But he thinks the professor has it out for him. I don't want to make things harder for him."

Sophia came up and rubbed Carter's back. "I think he'd care more about being here for you than what a professor thinks of him."

Carter was still for a second before saying, "Yeah, you're right. I'll call him." He pulled out his phone and began pressing buttons as he settled back on the couch.

"So what *do* we do now?" Sophia asked.

"We call the police and turn everything, including Brad, over to them," Aniyah said. "Right?"

"Yes," I said, drawing the word out in a way that probably denoted my hesitance.

"Why do you sound like that?" Taylor asked.

I rubbed a hand over my face. "I don't think any of you should be here when that happens."

"What?" Taylor practically screeched. "Why?"

"Because while we have pretty damning evidence against Brad, we also have him tied up in my room. And he can also implicate us in the attempted robbery. Maybe...maybe if you guys aren't here, the police will believe it was just me responsible for all of that."

I watched as Taylor's eyes hardened in a way that made me fear for my life, but I kept my face impassive.

She stepped into my space, her hands on her hips. "Let's ignore for a second that Brad's dad can easily look at the security cameras and see we were there and focus on the real issue. Have you *still* not gotten this martyr complex thing under control? Seriously?"

"I'm not—"

"You are. And the fact that you think I'd let you take the fall alone is really irritating, you jerk."

"I don't think there's a reason to name call."

"Trust me, jerk is the nicest thing running through my head right now."

"I'd forgotten how scary she can be sometimes," Brody whispered.

"Terrifying," Sophia agreed.

"Well, then what do you suggest we do?" I asked, my voice booming through the room. "There's no way Brad isn't going to turn on us the first chance he gets."

"He's going to do that no matter what," Taylor reasoned. "But he's also a murderer and a thief, which Petey admits on tape. We'll be okay."

"You don't know that. Ultimately all of this is Brad's word against some videos Petey left," I argued. "I can't . . . I can't risk you going to jail and having your entire future ruined." I looked around the room. "Any of you."

"There's nothing you can do about it, Ransom. Brad is going to sing like a canary as soon as they get him in an interrogation room. And he's going to take as many people down with him as he can. There's nothing you can do to stop him." Taylor looked at me as if she knew how hard being this helpless was. "And as for the rest, we can't really control any of that. We have to trust that the police will do their jobs and put the pieces together."

"Hey, guys," Brody said.

"There's gotta be a way," Sophia said.

"We just have to think on it a bit more," Drew added.

"Guys," Brody said again.

"Maybe Carter was on the right track," Xander said. "Maybe Brad just . . . disappears."

"We can't do that!" Aniyah snapped. "We can't even steal a toy. How do you expect us to murder someone?"

"Then what do you suggest?" Xander asked, his voice patronizing.

"Guys!" Brody yelled, effectively getting our attention. "I think I know someone who could help."

"I don't think involving more people is the answer," I said.

"Just . . ." He rubbed a hand through his hair. "I need you guys to trust me. Please."

Brody didn't have the best track record when it came to plans, and he knew we all knew it. But as he stood here imploring us with his eyes to consider him capable, I found myself unable to resist. After all, how much worse could things get?

"Okay," I finally acquiesced.

He smiled and pulled his cell out, touching a few buttons and putting it to his ear.

I heard someone answer, and then Brody shocked us.

"Hey, Vee. How ya been?"

TAYLOR

Aamee squawking was usually a sound I enjoyed hearing, but in this case, I was as gobsmacked as she was. Why the hell would Brody call his ex-fake-wife for help with this?

"Um, well, I've been better," Brody said with a sheepish grin at the rest of us. "I . . . I think I need your help. No, I don't need another pretend marriage," he said with a laugh. "It's a long story. Do you have time?"

Veronica must've said yes, because Brody launched into the story, leaving no detail out. I had to admit, the boy had a pretty impressive memory.

When he was done, he listened intently as she spoke.

"Yeah, we can do that," he told her. "Okay. Yes. We're at Ransom's place. Yeah, same place. Talk soon. Bye." He hung up and looked up at all of us. "She said to give her a few hours. She said to stay away from Brad until we hear back from her."

"Did she have any ideas?" Ransom asked.

Brody shrugged. "She didn't say. Only for us to wait to hear from her before doing anything."

"She's probably calling the cops on us as we speak," Xander grumbled.

Brody shook his head. "She wouldn't do that."

"I don't get how you think she can help," Aamee said.

Brody shrugged. "Maybe she can't. But it was worth a try."

There seemed to be a lot he wasn't saying, but we all left it for the moment.

Even though Ransom and I said we could hold down the fort if everyone wanted to leave, no one left, and I was thankful for it. Having my best friends around me was exactly what I needed. Toby appeared not long after Brody's phone call, and he rushed to Carter, speaking to him in low, soothing tones.

Carter visibly relaxed under Toby's attention, and that served to eke some of the tension out of the rest of us as well.

We puttered around, snacking and watching mindless TV for the next few hours, until a hard knock on the door startled us.

Ransom got up and slowly made his way to the door. He looked through the peephole before turning the lock and opening it.

And there stood Vee, smiling widely in a pair of jeans and a white cable-knit sweater. Did the girl ever *not* look gorgeous?

"Hi, guys. Long time no see."

"Hey, Vee," Ransom said as he gave her a brief hug before stepping back and letting her in. "How'd you get in?"

She moved inside but didn't close the door behind her. "I have some friends with me who . . . like to find their own way into buildings." She smiled as if this wasn't alarming news and continued. "They're going to take Brad, and in about two hours, you're going to take what you found to the police. Brad will turn himself in shortly after that."

My eyes widened. What the hell was even happening?

"I'm sorry, I'm confused. Why would Brad ever do that?" Ransom asked.

Vee sucked in her bottom lip for a second before

continuing. "The less you know, the better."

"That's ... so badass," Carter said on an exhale, hero worship clear in his voice.

Vee turned to Taylor. "You're going to tell the police you knew Petey and Brad. You're basically going to stick to the truth of why you went to Petey's parents' house and how you found the flash drive, since Petey's parents will be able to corroborate it. There's also no point in denying you dated Brad and that he was stalking you. Come clean about all of it. The only things you will not admit to were the plot to steal the car or beating up Brad in the alley. As far as they're concerned, you were never in either place. Got it?"

I nodded dumbly, still in shock at this shift in events.

"Okay. Go to the local precinct in two hours. I recommend you go alone, or at least without Ransom. We don't want to put him on the police's radar if we don't have to. Just in case Brad makes any accusations. Then, Brad will show up at the precinct an hour after that." She looked over her shoulder and said, "We're ready for you."

At her words, two huge men came in, followed by a slightly smaller man. The men in front wore jeans and long-sleeved T-shirts.

Vee pointed toward the bedroom and said, "He's in there."

They immediately went into the bedroom, and we heard Brad yell in protest, asking who they were.

A growled, "Shut the fuck up," silenced him.

The smaller man, though he wasn't small by ordinary standards, since he stood at probably just under six feet, wore black slacks and a red sweater. He had his hands pushed into his pockets and stayed next to Vee.

"So, these are the friends you made last summer?"

"Yup," she said.

"Interesting bunch."

She laughed. "You don't know the half of it."

"Well, any friends of my niece are friends of mine. We'll take care of this . . . *problem* for you."

"Oh, um, tha—thank you," Ransom said.

It was clear none of us knew what to say or think. Stuff like this didn't happen to normal people.

The men came out with a terrified-looking Brad a few minutes later.

"Whoever tied those knots did a real nice job," one of the men said.

"Thanks, man," Brody said with a smile filled with pride.

"Jesus," Aamee muttered.

Brad wasn't restrained, but the men were close beside him, forcing him along with their bodies.

When they reached the door, Vee's uncle stood in front of Brad. "They tell you what will happen if you try to run?"

Brad nodded vigorously. "Yes. Yes, sir."

He gave Brad a little slap on the cheek. "Good boy." And then he moved out of the way so the men and Brad could leave the apartment. He then turned to Vee. "We'll meet you downstairs."

When he left, Vee turned to us. "I know you probably have eight million questions. I won't be able to answer most of them, but I'm sure we'll stay in town for tonight. If you guys want to meet up later, I'll share what I can. Plus, it'd be nice to catch up with all of you."

"Wanna meet at Rafferty's? I can arrange for us to have one of the private rooms," Drew offered.

Vee smiled. "Sounds great." Then she looked at me. "Two hours."

I nodded.

"It'll all be fine. I promise."

Brody moved forward and hugged her. "Thanks for coming, Vee."

"For my ex-husband? Anytime."

Chapter Twenty-Four

RANSOM

The rest of the day was both the quickest and slowest of my life. We did what Vee said, and Taylor went to the precinct with Sophia instead of me. I wasn't comfortable with her going completely alone, thinking she'd at least need some level of support in recounting everything that had happened.

Not that I was able to stay home. I followed them in my car and parked across the street, just in case.

When they came back out, I could tell, even from where I'd parked, that Taylor was wrung out. I watched them get into Taylor's car—with Sophia driving—and head out. Taylor texted that they were heading back to my place, but I wasn't ready to leave yet.

I needed to make sure Brad showed up.

And sure enough, ten minutes after the girls left, a rumpled but still intact Brad showed up and walked—or maybe limped was a better word—into the precinct. I couldn't make out any marks on his face, but he looked like he'd been through hell.

Good.

A car slowly drove by as he made his way inside, and I recognized the driver as one of the men who'd taken Brad away. They'd definitely held up their end of things.

After that, I started off for home. I found a sleeping Taylor in my bed, and I quickly undressed and slid in beside her, pulling her close.

She snuggled into me, and we dozed for most of the afternoon. At some point, Taylor checked her phone and saw a text that said to meet at Rafferty's at seven. We stayed in bed until we absolutely had to get up to make it there on time.

$$X_O$$

By the time we arrived at Rafferty's, almost everyone else was already there. Appetizers and pitchers of water, soda, and beer were set out on the table, and my stomach grumbled at the sight of everything, reminding me I hadn't eaten all day.

We schmoozed and made inane conversation for a while until after a server took our dinner order. Then Drew closed the door and we all settled into seats.

Vee leaned forward and propped her arms on the table. "So, I guess you'd all like an explanation."

"Honestly," Taylor said, "I'm so thankful for everything you've done. So I don't want you to share anything you're uncomfortable with."

Vee smiled. "I'm glad to have been able to help. Men like Brad are predators. And they never stop until they become the prey. I'm proud to have had a hand in getting a guy like that off the streets."

She took a breath before continuing. "My family is involved in some . . . unconventional things. They don't always operate within the confines of the law."

"Must make wanting to be a lawyer a little awkward for you," Brody joked.

"You'd think so, but my family is very supportive. Whatever my brothers, my cousins, and I want, the family tries to provide. Besides, there are some uses for a lawyer in my family's businesses. Not that I'd ever be on their payroll," she hurried to add. "It was always very important to my mother that her children had jobs they could claim on a tax return. A desire my father made sure to enforce after she passed away."

In reading between the lines, I deduced that Vee came from some kind of . . . crime family? Maybe I could Google her last name.

Or maybe it was better if I didn't.

"My uncle's men let Brad know in no uncertain terms what would happen to him if he tried to implicate you in anything illegal," Vee continued. "He was also assured that our reach was far and wide. There is nowhere we couldn't touch him. Including prison. He seemed to get the message, but if he forgets, we'll issue him a reminder. My uncle will keep an eye on him for a while, but if you hear anything, make sure to call me immediately. Don't think you're bothering me. Now that we're involved, we have as much invested in Brad's silence as you do."

"I don't know how we'll ever be able to repay you," I said, my voice gravelly with sincerity.

Vee smiled. "There's a good chance I'll be moving back after I graduate. I've been accepted to a law school in town, and the firm I interned with last summer has expressed interest in having me join them when I finish. So your continued friendship is all the payment I'll need."

"You have it," Brody answered. "Always."

After that, topics moved onto more banal things, and I was thankful for a return to our less-thrilling lives.

"Owen texted," Carter announced to the room. "I told him to come hang out with us."

"Awesome," Brody said. "I love that dude."

"Who's Owen?" Vee asked.

"The weirdest guy ever," I answered.

"So he fits right in, then," Vee replied.

"Yup," I answered with a smile.

Owen arrived a bit later, looking as much the surfer dude as he always did, in baggy jeans and an O'Neill hoodie. When he caught sight of Vee, he stopped dead in his tracks.

"Whoa," he said.

Vee looked at him a bit oddly before approaching, hand outstretched. "Hi, I'm Veronica. You must be Owen."

He stared at her hand for a second before taking it gently in his and giving it a slight pump. "It's wow to meet you, great."

Vee laughed, and Carter went over and slung an arm around Owen's shoulders, causing him to let go of Vee's hand.

"What's up, buddy?" Carter asked.

"So much. So, so much."

Carter walked him away, but we all still heard Owen whisper, "Why didn't you tell me the most beautiful woman in existence was going to be here?"

"Smooth, man, smooth," Carter said.

The rest of the night was spent enjoying the company of good friends. And as it got late and we all visibly grew more tired, we settled up the bill and began gathering our stuff.

Vee came over to me as I was putting on my coat.

"You take care of yourselves, okay?" she said. "And if you ever need anything else, please don't hesitate to let me know."

I bit my lip, wondering if I could really ask something else of her. But this could be my one chance to get rid of all the shit that was holding us back from fully enjoying our lives. If I had a chance to make all that happen, I had to take it.

"There's maybe one more thing."

She smirked. "You name it."

TAYLOR

Ransom was having an animated discussion with Vee as she made some notes in her phone. I had a good idea of what they were talking about, but I didn't want to interrupt. Ransom would tell me later.

Our plan was to bring Hudson home the next day, which meant we had one more night in an empty apartment without Ransom feeling like he needed to be around for his sister. Not that I blamed him for those feelings, but it would be nice to reconnect without him having to worry he'd ditched her to hang at my place. I planned to make the most of it.

With a group as big as ours, it took us a little while to all say our goodbyes, but eventually Ransom and I were on our way back to his apartment.

We made the ride with small, inconsequential talk about our schedules for the week and how awkward Owen's fascination with Vee had been. A Casanova Owen was not.

It was so normal, I'd almost forgotten what a conversation that didn't revolve around our drama was like. Not that we were done discussing those things—not by a long shot. We still had a lot to work through and process, but it finally felt like we could exist without the shadow of past mistakes looming over us.

I was so desperate for that to be true, I was close to overflowing with hope. And desire.

As soon as Ransom let us into the dark apartment, I was on him, pressing my mouth to his in a dance we'd choreographed to perfection over the past months. We were all hands and hormones as we moved farther into the apartment.

My back hit a wall, and I used it to climb Ransom, wrapping my arms and legs around his waist like a sex-starved koala bear.

He rutted against me, not worrying about being careful with me, because if we'd learned one thing throughout all of this, it was that I wouldn't break. We were ravenous for each other, and I hoped it would always be like this between us.

He set me down only so we could rip each other's clothes off, and then I was quickly back in his arms, and just as quickly, he was buried deep inside me. We paused only for a brief exhale—the kind you uttered when you'd finally come home after a long time away.

We chased our pleasure until we caught it, riding the crest of euphoria together until we crashed back down to earth, panting and exhausted but very much alive.

I'd always been someone who felt a person shouldn't speak in finalities. No one ever knew what the future would bring. But as I slumped against Ransom, chest heaving, I allowed myself to believe he was it for me.

And that I was it for him.

Chapter Twenty-Five

TAYLOR

We promised Hudson we'd get her at ten the next morning, which I wouldn't normally have considered early if it weren't for having orchestrated the turning in of a murderer by the mob the previous day.

As it was, we were nearly late, pulling into Cody's complex with only five minutes to spare.

When we arrived at his apartment, the door flung open before we could even knock.

"Thank God you're here," Cody said, leaving the door open as he retreated inside.

"Uh, is something wrong?" Ransom asked warily as we came in and he shut the door behind us.

"How are you and that girl even related? You're so... chill. And she's, like, the opposite of chill. What's the opposite of chill?" He snapped his fingers. "Psychotic."

"I know you did not just call me psychotic, you anal-retentive drama queen." Hudson's voice blared down the hallway just ahead of her physical form. When she entered the room, she was glaring at Cody. "I swear, I've never met a bigger asshole than you. And that's really saying something because I'm wanted by bookies."

"You're lucky to be wanted by *anyone*," Cody retorted.

Hudson's mouth dropped open for a second before it hardened into a thin line. "You're one to talk. You have to pose naked for strangers because no one you know can stand the sight of you."

"Oh really? That's not how it seemed when you walked in on me in the bathroom after I'd gotten out of the shower."

Hudson gasped. "I was surprised." When Cody opened his mouth, she hurried to continue, "And *not* in a good way."

"Sure, sure, whatever you say, princess."

"*Stop* calling me that."

"Make me," Cody taunted like a five-year-old.

Hudson looked over at Ransom, clearly exasperated. "Ransom, make him stop."

It was the most juvenile argument I'd ever seen, and I worked at a kids' after-school program.

The place was also *oozing* sexual tension, which I would *not* point out to Ransom because Cody had done us a favor, and I didn't think Ransom killing him was a good way to show our appreciation.

"So I see you both got along well," Ransom said, fake happiness in his tone.

Two heads turned to glare at him before Hudson muttered, "I'll get my stuff." She retreated quickly toward the back of the apartment, where I guessed the room she'd been staying in was.

Ransom approached Cody. "Thanks for this, man."

Cody, who'd been watching Hudson as she walked away,

scrubbed a hand down his face before turning to Ransom. "No problem."

Ransom shot him a wry smile. "Kinda seemed like there were some problems."

"She's just...a little infuriating."

Which was funny because Hudson had been extremely accommodating since she'd arrived. With us at least. Something about Cody must've sent her normally affable nature haywire.

We made small talk until Hudson reappeared and declared she was ready.

Ransom thanked Cody again, and Hudson murmured a halfhearted, "Yeah, thanks," which made Cody grin.

"You're just so welcome, princess. It was a...well, not a *pleasure*, but, you know, it was...something."

"Yeah, great. Hope to see you never," Hudson called as she left the room, leaving Ransom and me to gape at each other before following her out.

We caught up to her at the elevator.

"That was tense," Ransom said.

"He's an ass," Hudson fumed.

And the girl kind of had a point. Cody was definitely a bit of a strong personality. I hadn't even spent much time with him, and even I could see how he could potentially be a little grating. But he *had* done us a huge favor, so I was a little put off by Hudson's reaction.

"He kept you safe," I said. "So at least he has that going for him."

"He kept me safe by circling me like a guard dog for the past few days. I couldn't go anywhere without him. If I tried, he followed me like a stalker." Realizing what she'd said, her eyes widened in apology. "Oh my God, that was a shitty thing to say. I'm so sorry."

I smiled. "It's fine. I know what you meant."

We stepped onto the elevator, and Hudson leaned back against the wall.

"He just got under my skin. But you're right. He did keep me safe, as promised. I'll stop being a baby about it."

"You're not being a baby," Ransom argued. "This has been a tough few weeks, and we're all navigating it the best we can. But things are definitely looking up."

She smiled. "Really? What happened?"

He smiled back. The doors to the elevator opened, and when we stepped off, Ransom slung an arm over both of us.

"Let me get my girls home, and then Taylor and I will tell you all about it."

I pressed tighter against him, loving the feel of being Ransom's girl.

RANSOM

Filling Hudson in on everything was both painful and cathartic. We'd kept some things from her that she was hurt we'd kept secret, but ultimately she'd understood. Reliving the past few months was hard, but it was also freeing. It was as if talking about it got it out of my body, and I was finally able to accept that we were truly going to be able to move past this nightmare.

But putting it all on the table for Hudson made a weird tension form between us. Like maybe we didn't know each other as well as we'd thought we did and were now strangers forced to cohabitate. Granted, we hadn't been in touch that long, so in some ways we *were* strangers. But still. Some of the closeness that had developed seemed to have evaporated.

I hoped like hell it was temporary.

Taylor must've sensed how down I was, because she was almost manic in her optimism. She was bouncing around the apartment like a Care Bear on meth, pulling us each into conversations about everything and nothing.

Finally, I cornered her in the kitchen and hugged her. "I appreciate what you're trying to do. But you're driving me a little insane."

She scowled up at me. "That's not very nice."

"Neither is your trying to get us to sing songs from *Dreamgirls*. I love you, but Jennifer Hudson you're not."

"Well, maybe if I had a stronger supporting cast like she did, I'd sound better," she groused.

I cupped her face with my hands and looked at her with all the adoration I felt for her. "No. You wouldn't."

She pulled away from me, flicking my chin as she went. "I don't even know what I see in you."

I laughed. "Me neither, but I'm glad you do."

"Maybe I've gotten nearsighted so I'm not seeing you clearly." She reached up and started feeling my face with her hands. "I bet you're not even that hot. It's all in my mind."

I laughed harder as I grabbed her hands and interlaced my fingers with hers. Moving closer to her, I brought my lips near hers. "I think you know just how hot I am."

"Hmm, do I?"

"You've had your hands all over my body for months. And I've had mine on yours. There's no denying it. We're so hot we're scorching. Especially together."

"Guess we have put the research hours in," she whispered.

"Yup. No more hypotheticals here. All scientific fact." And then I let my lips meld with hers. I'd intended to keep the kiss chaste, but I couldn't help myself. The two of us were too combustible.

But before we could get carried away, my cell phone began ringing. Though tempted to ignore it, I also knew Hudson was in the next room, so we needed to cool it anyway. I pulled away and dug my phone out of my pocket.

"It's Veronica," I said. Taylor looked at me anxiously as I took the call, not wanting to put it on speaker in case Vee said something I'd want to tell Hudson myself. "Hello?"

Taylor pushed in closer to me, and I dipped down so she could also hear.

"Hi, Ransom. How's it going?" Vee asked.

"Pretty well. Just trying to get back to normal. Whatever that even is for us."

She laughed a full, husky laugh that was unique to her. "I have a couple of updates."

"Okay."

"Brad's arraignment hearing is later today. Since he's in custody and they have the evidence you guys found, they're moving quickly. I thought you'd want to know."

"Yeah, I do. Thanks."

I glanced over at Taylor, who was biting her lower lip.

"Also, the situation with your sister has been resolved."

I shook my head a bit at her words, unsure I'd heard her correctly. "What do you mean 'resolved'?"

"My uncle made a phone call. They may have acted tough with your sister, but they don't want the kind of fight he could bring to their city. They've agreed to back off."

What even was my life? Had a crime boss really just

threatened another crime boss to solve my issues? "I didn't mean to cause your uncle any problems."

Vee laughed. "Don't worry about it. He loves getting to flex his muscles every now and then. And honestly, once I told him what was going on, he was happy to help. He doesn't stand for a bunch of wannabes taking advantage of young girls for kicks. Guys like my uncle . . . they live by a certain code. Those dipshits in Atlanta were behaving recklessly. Someone needed to . . . correct their course."

"I don't—" I cleared my throat, which had gotten thick all of the sudden. "I don't know how to thank you."

"I'm coming back down in a couple of weeks to look at apartments for when I start grad school. So maybe you and the Scooby Gang can take me to dinner while I'm there?"

"Absolutely. We'd love to see you. It's going to be great having you living here again."

I could hear the smile in her voice. "I agree. I've missed you crazy peeps."

We chatted for another minute or two, and she said she'd be in touch about when exactly she'd be down before we hung up.

Taylor and I gazed at each other for a second before leaping into a hug. The issue with Hudson had been the last thing hanging over us. With that gone, our entire futures opened up.

"Let's go tell your sister," she said into my neck.

I nodded and led her into the living room, where Hudson was sitting on the couch. She had her phone and her AirPods in, so I tapped her on the knee to get her attention.

She looked at me expectantly as she removed her earbud.

"It's done," I said, eloquent as ever.

"What's done?"

"The thing...with the bookies...the money you owe. It's done."

She stood slowly. "How?"

"A friend of mine took care of it."

She didn't look nearly as happy as I'd expected, but she squared her shoulders.

"Okay, that's great. I'll figure out a way to pay your friend back. Who is it?"

I stepped forward and wrapped my hands around her biceps. "No, you don't understand. It's done. You don't owe anyone anything. The whole ordeal is over. You can put it behind you and move on."

She began blinking fast, and I could see her eyes fill with tears.

"How's that possible?"

"We know people," Taylor said haughtily before breaking out into a smile.

"The same friend who helped us put Brad away. Her uncle talked to the guys you owed money to and sorted it all out. There's no more debt. You're free and clear."

With that, she pushed herself into my arms and hugged me tightly.

"I don't know how to thank you guys," she said against my chest.

"You don't have to thank us. I'm your brother. I'll always help you."

Somehow, she managed to hug me even tighter.

And I hugged her back just as fiercely.

Chapter Twenty-Six

TAYLOR

Once Vee had mentioned the arraignment, it was all I could think about. Even though he was locked up, Brad still felt like a loose end, and I was quickly unraveling at the prospect of not knowing how things went with his case.

I briefly entertained the idea of going back to my apartment so I could spiral in peace, but I didn't really want to be alone. So I focused all my manic energy on organizing Ransom's kitchen cabinets, which he told me wasn't necessary but dropped it when I glared at him.

When he saw me walking toward his hall closet with a trash bag, he clearly decided enough was enough.

"Let's go," he said, grabbing his keys.

"Where?"

"You know where."

I yipped for joy as I ran to get my purse.

"Can I know where is where?" Hudson asked.

"We're going to Brad's arraignment," Ransom told her. "You want to come?"

"And come face-to-face with yet another giant mistake I've made in my short life? No thanks," she replied.

And maybe I should've felt the same. Maybe I shouldn't have wanted to watch a man I'd once been intimate with be charged with murder, among other crimes. But I'd also been the one to bring the sucker down, and I couldn't help but want a front-row seat to that.

I texted Sophia to let her know what I was up to and that I'd check in with her after. Since gossip was our love language, I figured she'd want the scoop.

What I hadn't figured was that she'd show up with Drew, Aamee, and Brody.

Vee hadn't said a time, so we'd just shown up at the courthouse, content to wait until his turn. We'd already been waiting close to an hour in the hallway outside the courtroom when they arrived.

"Don't you people have jobs or classes?" I asked.

"As if stupid things like financial security and education can rival seeing Brad with handcuffs on," Sophia said as she plopped onto the bench beside me and tore off a piece of a pretzel Ransom had gotten me from a food vendor out front. Sophia popped it into her mouth and chewed obnoxiously.

"I wasn't sharing," I said.

She shrugged in response.

"We thought you'd want some moral support," Drew said.

"I never understood that," Brody chimed in.

"Understood what?" Aamee replied.

"Moral support. How do you support someone with morals? Or are you supporting their morals? And which of those would even apply in this context?"

"It means you're being a decent person by being supportive

of someone," Sophia explained like she was speaking to someone who was too dumb to have survived as long as Brody had. "Therefore, you're doing the right, moral thing."

"What if you're supporting someone who's doing the wrong thing?" he argued. "Are you immoral support?"

Sophia blinked a few times before looking at Drew. "Can you do something about him?"

"You're just saying that because you don't want to admit I have a point," Brody said.

"You haven't had a point since you played basketball when you were five and they let everyone score."

"They didn't *let* me score. I was talented."

"You scored in the wrong basket."

He pointed a finger at her. "That's hearsay. You weren't even old enough to remember."

"Guys," I hissed when I noticed a man walking down the hall in a pressed and tailored black suit.

Brad's dad.

If he recognized me, he didn't show it. He simply walked over to the doors that led to the courtroom and spoke to the officer who was stationed there. He must've been told to wait, because he took a couple of steps back and started tapping away on his cell phone.

Some other men in suits joined him a few minutes later, their briefcases making me think they were lawyers.

God, I hoped some high-powered lawyer didn't get Brad out of the mess he'd created. The evidence against him was damning.

I decided then and there that I'd never be a defense attorney. Defending people like Brad...no thanks. While I understood and respected that everyone had a right to competent counsel, I didn't have it in me to provide that counsel.

We were quiet as we waited—none of us wanting to attract the attention of Brad's father, who everyone else seemed to instinctively identify, since I didn't tell them.

Soon, the officer of the court announced Brad's case. We waited for his father and the lawyers to go inside before we followed and took seats near the back.

I wondered if Petey's parents would be there. It would probably have been a long drive for them to make on such short notice, but I knew they'd try if they could.

Things moved quickly after that. Brad was brought out, sadly wearing a shirt and tie instead of an orange jumpsuit. But he *was* handcuffed, so at least no one took that small piece of joy from us.

When Brad was taken to the table, his gaze locked on mine and hardened. Thankfully, the officer quickly spun him around, removed his handcuffs, and sat him down so his back was to us.

The arraignment proceeded quickly, with Brad reading over the charges and conferring quietly with his lawyers. When he was asked to enter a plea, he stood. His father and lawyers all looked at him expectantly, but Brad seemed unmoved. After a moment, he turned his head just enough to see me out of his periphery.

I straightened in my seat.

Then he turned back and said, "Guilty," in a raspy voice that sounded like he'd been gargling with sandpaper.

His voice, which had been used to manipulate and degrade and ruin, couldn't get him out of this.

After that, his hands were put behind his back, and the

handcuffs were put back on. His dad began arguing with the lawyers, obviously unhappy with Brad's plea.

Eventually, Mr. Lacey's voice rang out across the courtroom. "Why are you doing this, Brad? You're making a huge mistake."

But Brad didn't reply. He simply kept his head low and avoided looking at anyone as he was led away.

I leaned toward Ransom. "This is so much better than his funeral," I whispered.

Ransom's shoulders shook from silent laughter as Brad disappeared from sight.

RANSOM

After Brad's arraignment, we fell into a level of normal that felt so foreign it seemed *abnormal*. Ever since I'd met Taylor, our lives had been in some sort of flux, and now that the last barrier between us and the rest of our lives was gone—or at least on the way to being gone—we almost didn't know how to adjust.

But the next few weeks were a crash course in mundane. Despite my willingness to relocate, Taylor wanted to keep the gang together—at least for a little while longer—so she'd finally applied to all the law schools she was interested in within a fifty-mile radius. So Taylor worked and anxiously awaited her law school acceptance letters, and I went to school and work. And in the evenings, we came together for meals and movies and chats and sex.

Lots of sex.

We'd spent so much time together, Hudson finally sat us down and made us a proposition: Taylor should move in with me, and Hudson would take over Taylor's apartment.

My initial reaction had been a big, fat hell no because Taylor's apartment wasn't in the safest part of town. I'd recently waited in the car while Taylor ran up to grab some things she'd needed and watched a man walk into an alley, pick up a shoe box from the trash can, and pull a cell phone out of it.

I had *so* many questions, and none of them preceded good answers.

Taylor had gotten a little defensive at my reaction, and we'd bickered until Hudson had interrupted, explaining that she'd been hanging out with bookies for Christ's sake and that she wasn't a child anymore.

I'd wanted to remind her that she hadn't even realized they were bookies until they threatened to break her legs, but that seemed cruel.

In the end, we'd decided to give Hudson's arrangement a try. We'd moved her in the next day. Taylor didn't have much that she needed that hadn't migrated to my place already, so the transition was fairly seamless.

We'd been officially living together for about a week when Veronica called to say she was coming to town the next weekend and ask if we were we able to get the gang together. We said we'd make it happen.

Which was how we found ourselves hanging at the Yard, space heaters blasting, on a Saturday evening, surrounded by all our friends.

"Do you believe in ghosts?" Brody asked out of nowhere.

"Ghosts?" Veronica asked.

"Yeah. Like in *Beetlejuice.*"

She studied him for a second before saying, "No."

"Hmm, that's disappointing."

"Why?"

"Because I think a couple moved into my apartment. I wanna hold a séance, but I need people who believe."

"You're talking about ghosts, not Tinkerbell," Sophia said.

"What does Tinkerbell have to do with anything?" Brody asked.

"She said if you don't believe in fairies, they die."

Brody's brow scrunched up in confusion. "What the hell are you talking about?"

Sophia glared. "Listen, you're the stupid one here. Don't try to act like I'm the one who doesn't make sense."

"Why do you think you have ghosts?" Carter asked.

"Because stuff's been moving around my apartment."

"Aamee's probably moving it," Drew suggested.

Brody shook his head. "Aamee's one of the things that moves."

She whirled her head toward him, alarmed. "What?"

He nodded solemnly. "It's true. One night last week, you went to sleep next to me, but when I woke up later because I needed a snack, you were on the couch."

She rolled her eyes. "That was when you had a cold and were snoring like a chainsaw. I moved to get away from you."

Brody patted her hand. "It's okay to admit the truth. We can be scared together."

She opened her mouth to reply but closed it and rubbed her eyes instead.

"What about you, Owen? You seem like a guy who'd believe in ghosts," Carter said.

Owen didn't reply right away, too busy staring at Vee, who was sipping a drink from her straw.

"Owen," Carter said again.

"Huh?"

"Do you believe in ghosts?"

"Ghosts? Oh, uh, no. No, I don't believe in ghosts."

Carter looked surprised. "That . . . shocks me, actually."

"Most ghost sightings are strongly influenced by the power of suggestion, eliciting a psychological response that triggers fear that isn't based on logic and reality. Now, if you asked if I believed in poltergeists, that's a different story."

"Why is that different?" Xander asked.

"Oh, brother," Owen said as he clasped Xander on the shoulder. "That's an explanation for another party."

Taylor leaned toward me, her sweet scent filling my nostrils and making my cock twitch.

"Why are we friends with such weirdos?"

I smiled in response. I looked around at our friends, who really were fucking weirdos, but they were *our* weirdos, and I wouldn't trade them for anything.

"We should get a Ouija board," Toby suggested.

"I've already summoned a demon, thank you," Taylor said. "Thankfully, the criminal justice system is well on its way to exorcising him from my life."

And wasn't that the damn truth. Taylor had spoken to Petey's parents a few times, and they were thankful for all that Taylor had done for them. And for Petey. They could never get their son back, but the closure they gained from knowing Brad was behind bars was a good start to moving on with the rest of their lives.

"Yeah, we've had enough crazy shit happen over the past year and a half," Aniyah agreed. "We don't need to be messing around with anything like that."

"Wait," Xander interjected. "Are you saying that you,

Miss Nothing Is True If It Can't be Verified by at Least Eleven Sources, are afraid of the power of a Ouija board?"

She gave him a hard look. "You're verifiable proof that evil exists, so, yes, I'm afraid of Ouija boards."

"You guys are too funny," Vee said. "I'm going to get another drink."

Owen shot to his feet. "I'll get it for you."

Vee gave him the kind of smile someone gave a kindergartner who offered to cook dinner. "I got it."

"Oh, um, okay. I respect your words and desires. But, maybe, um, could I come get one *with* you?"

Vee's smile widened. "Sure."

"Cool. Totally cool. Cool beans."

They made their way over to the bar that was being manned by Reed, one of the new bartenders at Rafferty's.

As I tracked them to the bar, my gaze snagged on Hudson and Cody, who were standing at the bar together. Hudson looked frustrated, and Cody seemed to be relishing that fact.

"What's with those two?" I asked Taylor.

She followed my gaze and then sighed. "Young love."

"Wait . . . what? What do you mean *love*?"

"Don't be one of *those* big brothers."

"And what kind would *those* be?"

"The overbearing kind that doesn't let his sister have a little fun. Cody's a nice guy. He clearly drives her crazy, but I'd bet money she likes it."

"Who likes being driven crazy?"

She gave me a pointed look.

"Hey," I said, affronted. "I don't drive you crazy."

"You did at first."

I scoffed. "You just needed to get used to my charm."

"Whatever you say, love." She leaned in and kissed my cheek, and suddenly arguing didn't hold as much appeal.

I wrapped an arm around her and pulled her closer to me.

"Hey, where did Veronica and Owen go?" Brody asked as he looked around the deck.

We all looked around too, but they weren't out there anymore.

"Huh, that's weird," Sophia said.

"Maybe she wanted something we don't have out here," Drew reasoned.

We all shrugged it off, confident they'd turn up soon. She was with Owen. What could possibly happen?

We spent the next little while talking and busting on each other. Hudson and Cody joined us, and while they kept their distance from each other, they both kept sneaking glances. I'd have to keep my eye on that development.

We were in the middle of debating the best pizza joints in the area when Carter interrupted us.

"Uh, guys." He was looking down at his phone, a frown on his face. "Owen just sent me a text saying that Vee was moving in with him and was making him the happiest man in the world."

The words took a minute to sink in, and when they did, all I could do was laugh.

Taylor elbowed me. "What's so funny?"

"It's just so . . . us."

She stared at me for a second, a smile slowly blooming across her face. "I guess it is."

"What do you say? You ready for another crazy adventure?"

She leaned up and kissed me again. "With you? Always."

Also by
ELIZABETH HAYLEY

The Love Game:
Never Have You Ever
Truth or Dare You
Two Truths & a Lime
Ready or Not
Let's Not and Say We Did
Tag, We're It

Love Lessons:
Pieces of Perfect
Picking Up the Pieces
Perfectly Ever After

Sex Snob
(A Love Lessons Novel)

Misadventures:
Misadventures with My Roommate
Misadventures with a Country Boy
Misadventures in a Threesome
Misadventures with a Twin
Misadventures with a Sexpert

Other Titles:
The One-Night Stand

Acknowledgments

First and foremost, we have to thank Meredith Wild for allowing us to achieve our dream of writing a rom-com series. This has been a cathartic experience for us, and we'll always be grateful to you for this opportunity.

To our swolemate, Scott, these books wouldn't be what they are without you. Thanks for giving us room to push boundaries while reeling us in when it's necessary.

To Robyn, thank you for managing our writing lives—haha. We're honestly not sure how we made it this far without you.

To the rest of the Waterhouse Press team, you simply kick ass. Thank you for everything you do to help us be as successful as we can. You're an amazing group of people, and we're lucky to have the honor of working with you.

To our Padded Roomers, we don't even know where to begin to express how amazing you all are. You're funny and crazy and supportive and crazy and fierce and crazy, and... have we mentioned crazy? You make this process all the more enjoyable because we get to share every success and setback with you. Thank you for everything you've done for us, such as posting teasers, sharing links, reading ARCs, writing reviews, and making us laugh. We don't deserve you, but we're damn glad to have you.

To our readers, there's no way to accurately thank you for taking a chance on us and for your support. Thank you for letting us share our stories with you.

To Stephanie Lee, thank you for coming up with the name Ransom. It's perfect for him.

To Google, thank you for providing the means for us to research things including, but not limited to, fraternities, sororities, marketing degrees, alcoholic drinks, dean responsibilities, business class topics, college codes of conduct, Gen Z lingo, and popular clothing trends.

To our sons for inspiring the last names of our main characters. Our lack of originality strikes again.

To Elizabeth's daughter for being a spitfire and inspiring the way she writes female characters.

To our husbands, we know it's not easy. Thanks for hanging in there. We honestly don't deserve you.

To each other for pushing one another forward when we stall. The ride hasn't been easy, but it's sure as hell been a lot of fun. On to the next.

About

ELIZABETH HAYLEY

Elizabeth Hayley is actually "Elizabeth" and "Hayley," two friends who love reading romance novels to obsessive levels. This mutual love prompted them to put their English degrees to good use by penning their own. The product is *Pieces of Perfect*, their debut novel. They learned a ton about one another through the process, like how they clearly share a brain and have a persistent need to text each other constantly (much to their husbands' chagrin).

They live with their husbands and kids in a Philadelphia suburb. Thankfully, their children are still too young to read their books.

Visit them at AuthorElizabethHayley.com